As Good As Dead

Locomotion (stories)

The Blue Hour

Carter Clay

Rowing in Eden

Suicide's Girlfriend (stories)

As Good As Dead

A Novel

ELIZABETH EVANS

B L O O M S B U R Y

NEW YORK • LONDON • NEW DELHI • SYDNEY

Published by Bloomsbury USA, New York
Bloomsbury is a trademark of Bloomsbury Publishing Plc

All papers used by Bloomsbury USA are natural, recyclable products made
from wood grown in well-managed forests. The manufacturing processes
conform to the environmental regulations of the country of origin.

LIBRARY OF CONGRESS CATALOGING-IN-PUBLICATION DATA HAS BEEN APPLIED FOR.

ISBN: 978-1-62040-298-6

First U.S. Edition 2015

1 3 5 7 9 10 8 6 4 2

Typeset by Hewer Text UK Ltd, Edinburgh
Printed and bound in the U.S.A. by Thomson-Shore Inc., Dexter, Michigan

Bloomsbury books may be purchased for business or promotional use.
For information on bulk purchases please contact Macmillan Corporate
and Premium Sales Department at specialmarkets@macmillan.com

for Steve

Our doubt is our passion.

Henry James, "The Middle Years"

PART ONE

1

The fateful morning—no exaggeration, *fateful*—that my long-lost friend, Esmé Cole, showed up on our front steps, I was sitting at the desk in the room that I used for a home office. My chair, I remember, made an uneasy perch, all slippery and lopsided because I hadn't bothered to remove the items that I'd dumped on the seat the night before: a manila folder crammed with information about a job applicant being considered by the English Department; a puke-green envelope holding an entry for a book prize I'd reluctantly agreed to judge; and, then, a three-ring binder of my own writing that creaked whenever I shifted in the chair.

The sky in the window over my desk was a clear blue that morning. The temperature outside would climb into the high eighties as the day progressed, but the room faced north and its exterior wall still held the cold that settled in on desert nights—this was October in Tucson, Arizona—which meant that the ancient space heater at the level of my feet pinged away, giving off a metallic odor that might have been unpleasant to somebody else (I connected it with writing and comfort, and so I liked it).

Esmé Cole *Fletcher*, I should call my long-lost friend. Esmé Cole—betrayed by me twenty years before—did take the name of the man she married. Once upon a time, she and I had vowed to keep our own names forever, but this is a tale about nothing if not about changes of heart.

At the moment that Esmé rang the doorbell, I was not at work on either my own writing or that of my students. I was looking out that window over my desk. From there, I had a view of our backyard's Sonoran Desert natives (creosote bush, barrel cactus, cholla), the very tips of the highest of the Tucson Mountains, and—along the western edge of the yard—the fifteen-foot-high hedge of red-flowered oleanders that I had planted from one-gallon pots eleven years before to give our then-new yard some color and shade. Earlier in the morning, I'd set a plate of canned tuna beneath the oleanders in hope of feeding a black cat—a definite hitch in its step—that had skulked past the sliding glass doors of the dining room, where my husband and I sat, eating breakfast. "Could that be Bad Cat?" I had asked—speaking almost to myself, I suppose. At any rate, Will had not looked up from the *Times* to offer an opinion. The cat—whether it was the cat we called Bad Cat or not—looked pitiful, all skin and bones, its black fur matted and also covered with odd patches of pale fluff, as if somebody had poked it around under a bed to sweep up dust bunnies. When I got up from the table and walked toward the door to peek out, Will had set down his paper. In the deep and resonant voice that had mesmerized me from the start, he'd said, "Don't you start feeding that cat, Charlotte." As if the thought hadn't entered my mind, I'd rolled my eyes. Nevertheless, after he headed off to the university—a brilliant art historian, Will, really, so good his lectures could bring tears to my eyes—I had trotted out back in my bathrobe with a can opener and a can of tuna and a plate, just in case the scrawny cat came around again.

I remember this day, and the days that followed, in the precise manner that we remember those bolt-bright days after we've learned that someone we love has died or a national tragedy has occurred (*Where were you when the Twin Towers fell?*).

When Esmé rang our front doorbell that morning—an obnoxious thing, door*drill* was more like it—I jumped in my desk chair. Swore. Telephones ringing, doorbells drilling—I always preferred to let Will answer. He was better at handling that sort of thing, and who could be at the door at eleven-something in the morning, anyway? Our house sat in an older part of Tucson that, although encircled by neighborhoods with conventional sidewalks and lawns and paved streets, remained staunchly gravel roads, home to coyotes, Gambel's quail, and even the occasional long-tusked javelina. Apart from friends in a formal mood on nights when they brought flowers or wine for a dinner party, the only people who used our front door were UPS drivers, evangelists, and those poor teenage boys lugging around Styrofoam coolers of candy whose profits, each sweating kid swore, by rote, would keep him *off the streets and away from a life of drugs and crime.*

Still, I got up from my desk.

Will liked the living room drapes closed. I preferred them open but was less consistent about carrying out my wishes, which was a boon that morning, since it allowed me to peek out at the caller from a slit between the panels.

A stout, red-faced woman stood on our front steps. Boxy, olive pantsuit. Cropped hair the color of Vaseline. Partly turned away, she was just a profile with a single eye squinting against the Arizona sunshine. Impossible for me to have guessed that this was the Esmé Cole who had been a student with me back at the Iowa Writers'

Workshop in 1988, my roommate in a brick apartment house on Burlington Street. *That* Esmé Cole had been stylish and slim in retro capris, vintage cashmere cardigans; a lovely twenty-five-year-old with a bushel basket of red hair pinned up in a cloud of glorious dishevelment (brave, I'd thought, wearing your hair that way, like keeping a swan for a pet and walking the thing around town, an announcement that you knew you were fabulous).

Could the woman on the front steps be a Jehovah's Witness, panting to hand over a copy of the *Watchtower*? But didn't Witnesses travel in pairs, and didn't the women wear dresses?

I definitely did not want to open the door. But I worried over that Pepto-Bismol pink face. And those blocky hands, hanging so inert and glossy and red they could have been shrink-wrapped packs of hamburger. Suppose the woman was one of the poor souls discombobulated by our quiet neighborhood's gravel roads that looked like driveways and driveways that looked like roads; she'd hoped to get in a walk this morning but now, on the point of heatstroke, had resigned herself to asking for directions and a glass of water. Suppose she was looking for a lost pet or, worse, a lost child who'd wandered off into this semiwilderness of cacti, rattlesnakes, the occasional grandfathered-in swimming pool with no proper safety fence around it.

Two years before, I had been irked when a *Poets & Writers* profile described me as looking "like a Sunday school teacher." *A Sunday school teacher!* Since adolescence, I'd done war with the same fifteen pounds, but I'd been on the winning side at the time of the profile and aimed for an edgy, rock-and-roll aura (hair very blond and shaggy, eyes rimmed with black kohl à la Kim Gordon). When Will tried to cheer me by noting that the profile said I looked young for thirty-nine, I'd responded, "Whatever" (decidedly sour). For what it's worth, shortly after the *P & W* piece appeared, I rode several stories in a Manhattan elevator with Gordon and wouldn't have known it was she had my agent not told me so after we stepped out of the car.

The bulky Esmé Cole Fletcher who stood on Will's and my front steps—she looked so different from the Esmé whom I remembered that even after I had opened the inner door and she said her name through the screen, I needed her teasing reprimand, "Charlotte, c'est moi," before a current began to flow between us. Weak at first. Then that dull, chunky lady began to acquire a soft glow, and it was Esmé, and joy is what I felt, alongside a dread that must have made my face go white.

Yes, in the fall of 1988, there had been lovely times between my Workshop friend and myself, such as a fall morning when, side by side, we knelt on the linoleum of our Burlington Street kitchen and, dent by dent, using the nails of our little fingers, pressed our names—Charlotte, Esmé—into the many coats of built-up, yellowed enamel on the kitchen cupboards. Even better, once we finished, Esmé added a plus sign between our names. Esmé + Charlotte. As if we were sweethearts.

Also true: At the end of that year's Thanksgiving vacation, I had spent an idiotic, blotto evening sloshing around on the chilly water bed of Esmé's Workshop boyfriend, an Alabamian named Jeremy Fletcher, whom I'd generally regarded as a giant blowhard.

The worst thing I ever did in my entire life: betraying not only my friend but also Will, off in Italy at the time.

A thoroughly ridiculous person. That was what I'd been.

Amazingly enough, neither Will nor Esmé learned of that drunken mess, and, shortly afterwards, Esmé became pregnant, and Jeremy Fletcher declared he could not write "up North" and the two married and left for Mobile, Alabama. How lucky I felt in that period of reprieve—maybe eighteen months—in which Esmé wrote me long letters bewailing her inability to find a friendship "even close" to ours, but also reported pleasure in her new life as a Southern wife and then a mother! On behalf of her baby, I learned to knit and—a Madame Defarge of repentance—created an afghan of a turquoise so remarkably pale that it looked like something you could blow away with a sigh.

"Hated tearing open your 'brown paper package, tied up with string,'" Esmé wrote to me in her charming letter of thanks. "It looked like the greatest hot-cross bun of all time, but the contents were even finer, you dear girl!"

Then, her letters stopped. No explanation. I assumed that Jeremy Fletcher had confessed to his and my evening on his water bed. My guilt festered. I excoriated myself for not confessing. *If you had been braver, you rat, she would not have married the man, who, by now, she probably realizes is a rat, too.* I grieved, but, after a year or two, finally gave up writing letters that never received a response. They had started to feel bizarre—they never could include an apology, after all, since I did not know *what* she knew and I did not want to cause a marital disaster where one did not exist.

Yet, now, here stood my old friend, on my front steps, smiling what remained the most glorious of smiles, the big, white-toothed Esmé Cole smile that had told me—to my confusion, more than any other smile that I'd ever known—that I was better than okay, I was some-body special. That smile! Her familiar scent of cigarette smoke and L'Air du Temps! My throat constricted with emotion: inconceivable that I had betrayed my friend. Though I sensed that grabbing her in a remorseful hug might be too much, a husky "Esmé!" did escape me while I threw open the screen door.

Esmé herself, stepping over the threshold and into Will's and my front hall, appeared to be in a mood more jolly than nostalgic.

8

Imitating Billy Crystal's fulsome eighties parodies of Fernando Lamas, she said, "Charlotte, dah-ling, you look *mah*-velous! Ab-so-lute-ly *mah*-velous"—actually, I'd carried out only basic hygiene, wore a pair of sprung yoga pants and one of Will's flannel shirts—"while I, it must be said *immediately*, am a whale!" She raised an index finger to stop me from contradicting her. "But let us not tarry! Eliza, repeat after me: 'In Hartford, Hereford, and Hampshire, hurricanes hardly happen!'"

The perfect handling of that awkward moment. It was Esmé who had introduced me to the old Broadway musicals adored by her favorite aunt, one of them being *My Fair Lady*, and I was more than glad to take up the role of the *h*-dropping Eliza Doolittle:

"'In 'artford, 'ereford, and 'ampshire, 'urricanes 'ardly 'appen!'"

2

Some history:
   Eleven years before Esmé's arrival at our front door, the same semester that Will had finished a postdoc at the University of Minnesota, the two of us had the amazing good fortune to win tenure-track jobs at the University of Arizona (Will in art history, myself in creative writing). The week we packed for our move to Tucson, we took a break one night to attend a fund-raiser at Minneapolis's Walker Art Center. Will stepped off to get a glass of wine at the bar set up for the event and I—wisely, if gloomily abstaining—went to say my good-byes to Chuck Close's giant *Big Self-Portrait.*

Good-bye, bespectacled, drooping eyes, each as large as a head. Shockingly gorgeous black-and-white bits of ash on a colossal cigarette hanging so tipsily from pillow-size lips, good-bye.

While I stood there, so full of admiration for Close, and rubbing my arms to stay warm in the museum's air-conditioned tower of brick and glass, I sensed a body detaching itself from the cluster of attendees near the bar and sidling my way. A moment later, from behind me, abrupt and loud as a honk, a voice said, "Charlotte Price!"

A poet I'd known slightly during my Iowa Writers' Workshop days. Her height threw me initially (she had on six-inch heels) and I couldn't think of her real name, only the one that Esmé had given her—Queen Turd—in honor of her supercilious airs and the slippery-looking tawny braid that, back then, she'd worn coiled on top of her head.

"I'm a *reformed* poet now!" she declared with a great *haw-haw*. The woman always had impressed me as someone who viewed herself as a kind of celebrity, and I sensed that, like an interviewer, I was supposed to ask her to explain the "reformed poet" business. Of necessity, had she given up poetry the way that I'd given up alcohol? Or was Reformed Poetry perhaps a movement? From the retro hippie look that she'd favored in the eighties (Birkenstocks and Third World cottons), the poet had moved along to those towering high heels, sleek charcoal knits, tony earrings made up of alternating strips of gold and anchovy cans. Gone the turdish coil, replaced by a jet-black bowl cut above a swath of skull shaved to a high-maintenance smoke. She swigged the amber drink in her plastic cup, then squeezed my forearm and said, "I hear you've published, Charlotte!" Her squeeze—I admit, it stirred me. I was a sucker for a warm gesture—but before I could reply, up went her eyebrows like window shades set flying, and she added with another *haw-haw*, "Anything I should read?"

I was almost thirty years old by then, but my party skills remained on par with those of a cuckoo clock; I could count on coming up with a little something only once an hour or so. Defending another person—I'd lost a triangle of my two front teeth after jumping between two unmatched boys in my high school's cafeteria—I was good at that, but could be rendered perfectly dumb by a personal remark. With an arch smile, the poet swiftly shifted the conversation to gossip about Workshop people, some of whom I remembered, some of whom I didn't. Who'd won prizes, who hadn't. I am half deaf (nineteen, riding a bike with my blood alcohol at three times the legal limit, I went flying over the pickup truck of an unfortunate hog farmer and did serious damage to several parts of my body), and, in the hubbub raised by the art patrons, I missed a lot of what the poet said, but after I mentioned that I was about to start a job in Tucson, I *did* hear her exclaim:

"But that's where my Workshop friend Esmé Fletcher lives!"

Esmé lived in Tucson? Old guilt, grief, and fear swamped me—what would happen if we ran into each other?—and, then, a bit of jealousy showed up, too: When, and how, had Esmé and this woman been friends? It was Esmé and I who had sat up until all hours singing songs from *A Little Night Music* and creating Cindy Sherman-esque tableaus and discussing whether or not we had the right to call ourselves writers before we published our first books (Esmé declared a vehement *no*; I, an equally vehement *yes*). It was Esmé and I who could recite poems to each other—or even in tandem—because, before we met, both of us had memorized some of the very same works.

> To be born woman is to know—
> Although they do not speak of it at school—
> That we must labor to be beautiful.

And so I elbowed in. "Sad that Esmé and I lost touch, given that we were roommates and all."

A sharp look. The poet ran her index fingers to the stark beginnings of the black wings of her dramatic eyebrows, traced the fingers along the eyebrows to their ends, stopping at her temples. I had the queer sensation that she was preening, using me for her mirror. I should have excused myself, walked off, but I was flummoxed in the way that I—a hick, the only student actually *from* the state of Iowa during our years at the Workshop—regularly had been flummoxed by people there.

"Roommates?" she murmured, then demonstrated that she knew all kinds of up-to-date things about Esmé that I did not:

I knew that Esmé had the one child, of course, and that he'd been given a Southern-sounding name, Rob Roy, which I'd supposed was Jeremy Fletcher's choice; the poet knew not only that there was a second boy, Daniel, but what sports the boys played. Esmé, the poet said, had become a real estate broker after the boys started grade school. My surprise at the idea of Esmé as a businesswoman must have shown, because the poet laughed. "Oh, yes! Unlike some of you, Esmé and I have to work in the *real* world! She's doing well, though! Jeremy sells advertising, I think—and maybe does some journalism?—but Esmé brings home the real money."

So Esmé's life was good. The news gratified me. For a moment, I even thought, *Suppose that, in Tucson, she and I wind up friends again!* a notion quickly followed by a firm mental correction: *No!* While the reformed poet talked about the resort—La Paloma—at which she'd stayed on a visit to Tucson, I scoured the art center's crowded lobby for a sign of Will. There. The back of his dear, shaggy head. The band of skin exposed between the collar of his blue work shirt and fair hair suggested that he was talking to someone of a more average height (at six foot five, Will regularly had a sore neck after such events). Oh, he was patient, Will was. Even if a person happened to wax on about Will's specialty—Italian Futurism—Will listened, made a correction only if an error were truly egregious. I hoped the person he spoke to was a male. Often, Will did end up talking to the best-looking woman at a party. "She came up to me!"

13

he would say in his own defense, and, true, he was not flirtatious. In fact, I'd assumed he thoroughly disliked me the night we met, which had not prevented my being flattened by his loping, lanky Abe Lincoln good looks (blond, but his dreamy blue eyes had looked out from under a ledge of caveman's brow; his big and knobby wrists poked boyishly from the too-short sleeves of his flannel shirt).

Both from pride—I remained astonished that he'd chosen me— and to change the subject, I said to the reformed poet, "You remember Will Ludlow?"

"The art historian! Of course! Mystery Man!"

I had not heard the nickname in years. It was something dreamed up by certain female graduate students at the University of Iowa who had found Will's desire for privacy both annoying and tantalizing. I pointed across the crowded lobby. "Over there. He and I are married now."

"Charlotte! Congratulations!" The poet held up her free hand for a high five. Easier to go along than leave my hand hanging, looking like a party pooper. She rattled her plastic cup of ice cubes at me. "Trip to the bar? A toast?"

A familiar voice told me that running a fire-hose blast of vodka around inside my brain would scour away the edgy crap filling my head, but then the voices of people from the Alcoholics Anonymous meetings to which I too infrequently dragged myself reminded me: Girl, you and alcohol never, ever are going to get to hang out together again, be any sort of pals.

"I think I'll just wander around a bit," I told the poet. We started to move off in different directions; then I steeled myself and turned back and called, "Hey, you wouldn't happen to have Esmé's address with you, would you?"

Later, I would flush when I noticed that the address that the poet had copied onto her cocktail napkin was not for Esmé's home but for the brokerage firm where she worked. *Did* the poet know about Jeremy Fletcher and me? No matter. I felt certain of my next step, and, the very next day, dropping by the English Department at the University of Minnesota to deliver grades for a workshop I'd taught as adjunct, I nabbed a sheet of letterhead from the front desk and carried it with me to the lunch table in the faculty/staff break room. There, with a fountain pen—a fountain pen with blue-black ink can sometimes fortify me—I wrote, "Dear Esmé."

That was as far as I got.

The expanse of good ivory bond beneath "Dear Esmé" and the handsome university insignia had opened before me as vast and daunting as Death Valley. I did not see how I could survive crossing all that space. And suppose that Esmé took the stationery as showing off. Was it showing off? Or, paradoxically, trying, from insecurity, to let her know that I had value? Both? *Curiouser and curiouser,* as Alice said when she found herself telescoping, taller and taller, and worried that her feet, now far out of sight, might no longer be willing to carry her where she wanted to go.

I tore the sheet of letterhead in half, threw it in the office recycle bin, and headed back to Will's and my duplex, which was stuffed with the cardboard boxes we'd scavenged from behind liquor and grocery stores. I located and slit open an already taped-shut box labeled CHARLOTTE'S DESK. It had held bananas and released a sharp stink while, from its strata of smaller boxes and bins, I removed a pretty postcard of the Ponte Vecchio at sunset that I'd rejected repeatedly over the years as its message area was so crowded with historical information. In what now appeared a blessedly tiny space, I wrote, "Dear Esmé—Will and I are moving to Tucson. We'll be teaching at U of A." We had purchased a house on a chockablock three-day trip to Tucson in early June, and I included its address before I closed, "It would be great to see you after all these years! XO, Charlotte."

The exclamation point. Maybe it was simply the writer in me, but I worried about it at the time and later. Suppose she found it . . . *fulsome*? It made her want to vomit? Suppose I'd left it off, and she'd written back and everything had turned out differently?

After Will and I had been settled in Tucson for a month or so, and Esmé hadn't contacted me, I'd driven my car north, into the foothills of the Catalina Mountains. I had enough sense of the town by then to know that the brokerage firm she worked for must be upscale as it sat in Casas Adobes Plaza. In suave black script, the firm's name scrolled across a creamy canvas awning that wasn't doing much for the scorched tropicals out front but still conveyed a sense that the people within had class.

I drove by the office twice, but I could not make myself stop to say hello. Not too long after that, however, I did telephone—albeit very late on a Sunday, when I felt certain that no one would be in, and I'd be able simply to leave a voice mail. Even so, I was incredibly nervous. *Please, please,* I found myself praying as soon as the telephone started to ring, *please,* shoulders tight up around my ears, *let the next voice I hear be a recorded one.*

It was.

The reprieve allowed me to sound genuinely cheerful and enthusiastic when I left my name and new telephone number and a closing, "It would be wonderful to see you, Esmé!"

I must clarify: I *did* believe that it would have been wonderful—in the best of all possible worlds (as the optimists had sung on Esmé's CD of *Candide*). I would have stayed on the line if Esmé had picked up the telephone. I would have been happy as a clam if she wanted to see me. But those waiting prayers of mine made it painfully clear to me that my call and earlier postcard had been, above all, preemptive strikes. By putting myself out there, pretending that never in a million years would it occur to me that Esmé Cole Fletcher would be less than pleased to see her old pal, Charlotte Price, I meant to lay a path for civility. I aimed to create a world in which I would not feel obliged to jump, heart thumping, behind a telephone pole if I saw Esmé coming down a Tucson street; to duck into a restroom or an alcove at a literary event, bookstore, gallery opening.

Above all, I wanted to make it possible to act surprised if Esmé gave me the cold shoulder in front of Will. If she gave me the cold shoulder, Will would want to know why, and he never could know why.

This being the case, when Esmé didn't respond to my card or my call, I got nervous, and decided to pay Will a visit at his new Art Department office.

Will's office hours (1:00 P.M. to 4:00 P.M., Tuesday through Thursday) were neatly penned on an index card that he'd taped to the lower right hand corner of his door's privacy glass. It was Monday and not quite eleven when I arrived in the Art Building. No lights shone behind the glass, but I knew that, outside of office hours, Will worked in the dark so that the office would appear empty. Mornings were his writing time and precious (we both felt the weight of our new jobs; on top of our teaching and the pressure to publish in the right places, we now were experiencing the burden of university committee work, too). After a soft rap on the glass, I whispered, "It's Charlotte, I'll just be a second," then slipped inside.

"What's up?" he asked but kept his eyes on the computer screen in front of him—something to do with his application for a Guggenheim Fellowship, I saw as I went to stand behind him and massage his tensed shoulders. I'd temporarily been assigned the office of a notoriously randy medievalist, off on sabbatical, and, while I proceeded to rub Will's neck—I wanted to entertain him—I explained that, during my office hours that morning, I'd shoved a five-drawer file cabinet out of what I registered as an illogical spot and discovered that it hid three of those cheap full-length mirrors available at places like Wal-Mart.

"Crazy," Will said, "but what you're doing feels so great. Could you do my shoulders again?" and, rubbing away, I went on to tell him what I'd truly come to say:

"You know, something hit me today. Before we left Minneapolis, I sent our new address to Esmé Cole—because I'd found out she was living here?—and she's never responded."

Practicing these words as I'd walked across the sunlit, busy campus, I'd assumed that Will, distracted by his work, would pause only long enough to file my information in his prodigious memory, and that, friends, would be that. Instead, he swiveled in the squealing office chair and grabbed my hands. I still could view such gestures from Will as thrilling, but, on that particular morning, I'd envisioned a quick getaway and so I was startled by his attention. Also by the unexpected and rare expression of repugnance that crossed his face when he said, "That woman, though—I remember you being upset with her when I was in Italy, Charlotte. You called me, remember? And you haven't heard from her in *years*, right?"

I nodded, but without looking at him. I stared at his office window. It sat so high in the wall that all I could see was sky.

"I'm sorry you're disappointed," he said, "but remember that Thanksgiving dinner from hell we had with her and her creepy boyfriend? Whom she married, right?" He grinned, the impish expression also uncharacteristic. "Look at the bright side! If you and your friend had reconnected, we probably would have had to see him, too! Maybe it's not so awful!"

Such luck! I'd thought. Will viewed Jeremy and Esmé Fletcher as merely a couple of people I'd known while he was off studying in Italy, people he had met over a dud Thanksgiving dinner that had left all of us with food poisoning.

To Will, they were inconsequential.

3

Inconsequential.

Had he been in our front hall the morning that stout, pant-suited, forty-something Esmé suddenly stepped forward and wrapped her hefty arms around me, he would have seen my eyes fill with tears. Indeed, I was so affected—and startled, that was part of it—that I almost blurted, *I'm so sorry for what I did, Esmé!*

But, then, as fast as she had stepped toward me, Esmé stepped away and turned and began looking around herself. If she noticed that I had gone teary-eyed, she did not let on. With one of her characteristic great whoops of laughter, she declared, "But, Charlotte, your house is adorable!" The tip of her tongue held merrily between her front teeth, she made as if to rap my arm with her wagging index finger. "Now why on earth aren't you on Facebook, you?"

Confused, chagrined, I opened my eyes very wide to stop any tears from escaping. I worked to make my voice match hers, gave it a *droll* spin. "Oh, it's—not for me, Esmé."

"Not for you." She seemed to contemplate the taste of the words. She rolled her mouth a little, like someone testing a sip of wine. "But do you remember Ann Abbot, Charlotte? She's how I found out about you! You remember Ann?"

"Sure, sure. Pretty. Published a collection with Knopf when we first graduated. Boyfriend wore his hair in a mullet. I remember everybody from back then." Not all that smart, making claims about your memory to a woman whose now-husband you once screwed in the bad old days, so I added, "Which can be a curse!" followed by a laugh that came out punier than I would have liked, but it didn't seem to matter. Esmé was off, talking at a gallop, very emphatic, smiling, nodding. I felt dazed. Esmé in my front hall.

"Of course, I read your *P in Paris*, but I could have sworn the jacket copy said Charlotte Price lived in Minneapolis!" She jabbered something—briefly, her voice rose to a pitch I found hard to hear— something about the "reformed poet" whom I'd run into all those years before at the Walker Art Center: "I'm positive *she* told me you lived in Minneapolis, but maybe I got it wrong! Maybe she just said she'd *seen* you there. You and *Mystery Man*!" She zoomed her face toward me—I remembered Jeremy Fletcher doing that in the old days, an imitation of the Guy Caballero character from the popular *SCTV*—"Anyway!" She clapped three times in quick succession, like a grade school teacher getting the children's attention before moving them along to the next activity. "Anyway, last week, Ann saw a copy of *another* book by you—with glowing blurbs!—and it said you and Will lived *here* and taught at the U!" She shook her index finger at me again and said a playful, "Why didn't you let me know, you?"

Queasy and a little unsafe. That's how I felt. Also exhilarated. She'd made no reference at all to my postcard or telephone call of eleven years earlier, and I asked my dizzy self, *Is it possible that somebody at her office mistook the postcard for junk mail? That she never got the phone message?* These questions were high-flying, multicolored balloons whose dangling strings I happily grabbed. With daffy hope—I *had* treasured the friendship—I let them loft me right over her twenty years of silence. My voice small, I said, "I did, though—eleven years ago—I did write you, Esmé. With our address. Here." I raised my hands, indicating the house around me.

Well, her mouth fell open. "Are you serious?" Her voice was low, sorrowful. "My god. You're serious, Charlotte." When I nodded, she grabbed my hands with hers and she squeezed them and said, "Oh, honey! How can that be? For *years*, you mean, we could have been seeing each other?"

A rueful, smiling nod from me. Here was Esmé. Standing in my front hall. Not hating me. My old friend. The same lovely lips with a pretty petunia-petal crinkle to them. I didn't dare mention that I'd left a telephone message at her office, too. I wasn't sufficiently confident that she could have missed both. I decided to be satisfied that she wanted to see me again.

"But how fabulous is it," she asked, "that you're living out our dream, girlfriend? A famous writer! And tenured! Will, too, I suppose? Hey, and Jer and I can claim we know you both!"

Compliments always had come easily to Esmé, but I felt self-conscious at her calling me a famous writer; also uncomfortably obliged to contradict it (she had to know that I was strictly a midlist author). I crouched to tug flat the rug that I'd rumpled in opening the front door. "Tenured, yes," I mumbled. "Famous, no."

"Oh, well!" She laughed and stepped around me and into the living room. "Eventually you'll be famous, right? Make the old Workshop proud!" She rubbed a hand across the top of one of the pair of wingback chairs that flanked the fireplace, and, her back to me, she asked, "But did you ever write about hanging around the playground when you were little, hoping a teenage boy would think you were your playmate's babysitter and ask you out on a date?"

I warmed to the thought that she recalled our ancient conversations; then remembered what a terrible gut spiller I'd been in those days. Still could be. Beware. "No, I never did."

"You should!" She leaned over and picked up a pillow that sat on the wingback and, from my vantage point, appeared to plump it before she walked toward the floor-to-ceiling bookshelves at the back of the room. "Let's see what all you have hidden here, Charlotte!" she said.

I wondered if she might be giving our modest house a quick appraisal. She had worked in real estate; maybe she still did. Should I ask about her work? Or would the housing market's recent collapse make the subject awkward?

Hands behind her back, like a kid who has been told not to touch, she leaned forward and inspected the opalescent vase of purpled Venetian glass that Will had brought me when he'd returned from his studies in Italy back in 1989. It never had been to my taste, and I wished—stupid, I knew—that I could convey the fact to Esmé, to make certain that she didn't think less of me for owning the thing.

She moved along to looking at a photo of Will and me and the poet-professor who had introduced us. It might be that she expected me to ask if she and Jeremy Fletcher still wrote. Would be insulted if I didn't ask. Or—if the answer were no—would be uncomfortable if I did. Not long after she had stopped responding to my letters, a very good story of hers had appeared in a quarterly that everyone at the Workshop admired. I hadn't seen work from either her or Jeremy Fletcher since those days but that did not mean they weren't writing. Or publishing. Publishing had already started undergoing big changes when we were at the Workshop. Now there were so many literary magazines—print and online—that no one could read them all. I'd always found Jeremy Fletcher's work histrionic, pretentious—Southern Gothic mates with Synonym Finder—but, for all I knew, the man had an online fan base of a million members.

"Charlotte"—Esmé turned from the bookshelves and said, her voice low—"I don't see evidence of kids."

I shuddered inwardly but responded with what I hoped sounded like a preoccupied, "No kids," and proceeded to make a little theater piece of myself: The parlor maid in laced boots and white mob cap nimbly goes up on tiptoes to push open the drapes to the left of the fireplace (the drapes through which I had peeked out at my guest minutes before), then the drapes to the right. No denying that Esmé and I had "talked kids" in the old days. For the sake of our writing, we would limit ourselves to two apiece. *And if the sexes work out right*, Esmé had declared—I was incredibly flattered—*we'll force them to marry each other so you and I can be related!*

"Your books are your kids, though, right, Charlotte?"

Thank you, thank you for that. I turned to smile at Esmé and nod but was stopped by the dramatic way her lower lip stuck out, revealing its wet and pink inside. *Pity*, I thought, and a wave of anguish passed through me, followed close by a wave of confused tenderness for this old friend, for our history. When I was able to speak, I said—the words coming out in a croak—"You have two boys, right?"

She nodded, her face still grave. Then she sighed and said, "They're getting old, Charlotte. Rob Roy is already off at college, and Brannon will go next year."

But here we were, together! I wanted to shake off the gloom! Now it was my turn to clap my hands like a schoolteacher. "Come out in the kitchen! I'll make coffee!"

"Oh, no, no"—she looked toward the window—"I'd love to, sweetie, but Jer's waiting."

Sure enough: When I looked out to the gravel road beyond the screen of fine-leaved creosote bushes, I made out a beige SUV holding a gray figure behind its gray-tinted windows.

The idea of Jeremy Fletcher so nearby made me feel slightly ill, but Esmé was laughing. "He said, 'Tell Charlotte I apologize for not coming to the door, but I am in a foul, foul mood and would not want to expose another soul to it!'"

After twenty years, she could ape his Southern accent to a T. I made a friendly humming noise meant to signal, *You can tell me more or not; no problem, either way.*

"Oh, you know Jer, Charlotte!" She smiled the lovely smile. Gave her head a fond shake.

She always had taken pride in everything about the man. His moodiness, outré redneck views, overwrought Gothic fictions, the Confederate flag tattooed on the back of his hand. *Isn't he brilliant, Charlotte?* I never had understood. Now, however, it struck me as simply wonderful.

4

My first view of Esmé Cole, back in August 1988, had been from below and behind.

I'd just entered the dim hallway of a squat brick apartment building where I was to meet a rental agent. I heard swearing from the narrow staircase rising in front of me. There, a young woman, her legs coltish in cutoff blue jeans, was kicking at the corner of a fat, navy-blue futon that had gotten wedged into the landing.

"Can I help?" I called.

She turned. Very pretty, even while frowning and wearing her red hair in Pippi Longstocking braids that stuck out comically from either side of her head. Then the frown broke into a dazzling smile that seemed miraculously to confer immediate friendship. "Would you mind?" she called down to me. "I have to get this nasty thing up to the third floor!"

Better and better. A potential friend. I doubted that she was all that much older than I was—I'd turned twenty-one the week before—and the apartment that I'd come to view also was on the third floor.

The next time that I would see Esmé—perfectly made up, dressed in boutique capris, hair all retro Gibson Girl—I initially wouldn't recognize her, and, then, when I did, I'd feel almost . . . tricked (also entirely too *zaftig*). But I was so happy that first day, working my shoulder under her unwieldy, flabby futon.

"Hurray!" Esmé shouted as we got the thing moving upward. I liked the noise of her, though it did make me a little nervous. My parents tended to grimace at any display of self-assurance or enthusiasm on my part (I'd been a surprise the year my mother turned forty-one), and this young woman with the red braids was actually beginning to *sing*—pausing to add a question mark at the end of the first line: Want to join in?—a very boisterous version of "Erie Canal."

"Oh, I had a mule and her name was Sal?"—

It was strictly because my brainy, older boyfriend, Will Ludlow, had received a chance to spend the fall semester in Italy that I had undertaken the job of finding us an apartment on my own. " Though I felt a shock at this stranger's bravado, nothing could have charmed my lonely self more, at that moment, than the opportunity to join in on a song that my elementary school classes had regularly belted out on Music Fridays.

Low bridge, everybody down!
Low bridge, for we're coming to a town!

My rental agent hadn't shown up by the time we got back down-stairs, and this fun person needed help, so I joined her in carting stuff from the yellow U-Haul trailer parked on the street up to the third-floor apartment. There was a TV and a video player and a table-size trunk. An astonishing amount of stuff: suitcases, boxes, laundry baskets, and pillowcases crammed with clothes and dishes and books and photo albums and knickknacks. An hour must have passed before it hit me that my rental agent was not going to show, that the apartment I had come to view was the apartment into which this young woman and I almost had finished moving her possessions. I took the no-show personally (back then, I'm sorry to say, I took most everything personally). We were in the middle of singing "Johnny Verbeck"—a song I'd learned at Scout camp about a man who ground his neighbors' pets into sausages—and lugging upward the unwieldy wooden stand that would hold my companion's futon, when I just completely lost heart.

I broke off singing. The UPS man who'd had to flatten himself against the wall scowled as we trundled past. "Sorry," I told him.

My companion stopped singing, too. Her eyes went sober. Dark eyes with heavy lids slightly downturned at their outer corners. In a voice that was low and tender to my ears, she said, "You're shy, aren't you? I can tell because I am, too."

Although this seemed highly unlikely, I did love the *idea*, and I confided, "I'm nauseatingly shy, though."

She grinned. "I'm *ridiculously*!"

While we set up the futon stand in the apartment's little living room—grinning at each other—we developed a long list of adverbs to describe our condition.

Me: Morbidly!

Esmé: Ludicrously!

Me: Pathologically!

Esmé: Magnificently!

I felt giddy. Giddy! Because, honestly, didn't most of my shyness derive from fear that my encounters would not turn out right? Female friendships always had been so hard for me, fraught with relentless deconstructions of who liked whom better, but this person seemed utterly available! Utterly suited to me! She offered me a cigarette and it was a Kool! We both smoked Kools! I didn't know anyone else who smoked Kools!

While we sat smoking—she on the dusty futon, myself on the ratty orange sofa that came with the place—she told me her name: Esmé.

My mother had finished the eleventh grade; my dad had left school at thirteen to help support his family. He was a brakeman for the railroad; she was a part-time egg handler at the big hatchery in our tiny and shrinking Iowa hometown. The idea of being the offspring of parents familiar with the classic J. D. Salinger stories— surely that was too good to be true, but the name was unusual enough that I had to ask:

"As in 'For Esmé—With Love and Squalor'?"

She nodded and said, sounding wearily content, "The parents grew up as fans, although I think their tastes these days run more to Richard Ford. But, hey"—she grinned—"you're not, by chance, going to be at the Writers' Workshop, are you?"

Her response to my nod was a mixture of wail and laugh that I would come to know well. "And I bet you're here to see this apartment, too! What an idiot I am, Charlotte! But"—she grabbed my hands and pulled me up from the sofa and turned us around in a circle—"rent with me! Look at all this space." She started running around the little living room, doing a goofy crawl stroke with her arms to demonstrate how large it was. In reality, there had been just enough room for us to add the futon to the furnished pieces (the ugly sofa, one easy chair, a side table with a fake hurricane lamp). "You can have the bedroom and I'll sleep out here, on the futon, so it's no problem at all!" She hesitated. "Unless you need an apartment all to yourself?"

I'd already started consoling myself with the thought that I would have turned down the place for Will and myself, and not so much because of its decrepitude—the World War II—era wooden floors worn to the texture and gray of dirty suede, the hinges on some of the kitchen cupboards hanging cockeyed—but because it stunk; from where I stood in the middle of the living room, the kitchen's smell of mice was almost but not entirely overcome by a shriek of odor that I'd identified as most likely emanating from a yellow, buckled swath of plaster over the bathtub. But the prospect of having this terrific person by my side at the notoriously intimidating Iowa Writers' Workshop! A friendly pal with whom to attend the readings by famous authors and the parties afterward—a vague, but ideally dreamy, creamy future filled my head, something heartwarming and gloriously pink and orange and frame-filling as a sunset.

I sighed. "Actually, though, my boyfriend's in Italy for first semester. I'm looking for a place for the two of us—that will work for when he gets back."

Esmé Cole laughed. "So live with me just fall semester! We'll both save money! All kinds of places are bound to open up in January, and I can tell you and I would have such a good time!" She jiggled her shoulders and said a teasing, "Why should your boyfriend be the one off having all the fun, right?"

I laughed even though I did not like her evoking a picture of Will, off in Italy, having fun. That morning, during a telephone call to my parents in which I'd explained that I'd be looking for an apartment large enough for Will to share with me after he returned from Italy, my father had said—not for the first time, "Don't be a sap." Then my mother, echoing a fear of my own, had chimed in on the extension, "Would someone who genuinely loved you go off to Italy and leave you all alone, Charlotte?"

"Come on!" Grinning, Esmé Cole held her palms pressed together as if in prayer. I had to think. I was honored that I'd received a graduate teaching assistantship from the university, but the pay *was* low. And Will—surely he would be glad to be relieved of the obligation to pitch in four months' rent on a place in which he didn't live. As for Esmé: If I didn't move in with her, we might not be friends. I would be alone—

"Okay," I said.

"Hurray!" she shouted. "Hurray!" Like a cheerleader after the team scores a point, her red braids bouncing, she jumped up and down on the apartment's battered wooden floors. "Hurray, Charlotte!"

Despite my upbringing, her enthusiasm had overtaken me. I began to jump up and down, too. I shouted, too. "Hurray! Hurray, Esmé!"

5

The morning of her surprise visit to Will's and my house, I did not watch Esmé walk back to the beige SUV parked beyond the creosote bushes. As soon as she left, I collapsed against the front door. I was drained—elated and sick-nervous. I wanted to tell Will—the person I was closest to—but I checked that impulse: What could I say that Will would understand? Also, he would be irritated that I'd accepted an invitation to eat lasagna at the Fletchers' house without asking him (we always consulted each other over plans that involved both of us). Obviously, I could not speak to him about my happiness at a chance to redeem myself with my old friend. *Redeem yourself for what?* Also, I had no idea where my cell was, and if Will saw that I was calling on the land-line, he'd flip: *Shouldn't you have left for school by now, Charlotte?* Yada, yada, yada. Yes, I appreciated the way the man looked out for me (ran my car to the gas station if he saw that the tank was low, printed me Google Maps if I traveled anywhere without him, stopped by the store if we were low on this or that), but his generous—and so hard to resist—gestures could suggest that he saw me as incompetent. Irresponsible. A child.

How glad I was for the twice-a-day mantra that had made me half-way decent when Esmé rang the doorbell! *I always wash my face and brush and floss my teeth before bed, and first thing again in the morning.* I'd initiated that jingle at age thirty when, on a visit to my elderly parents, I got up in the night and found, at the back of their bathroom sink, two gleaming grins sunk in matching tumblers of Efferdent.

Eleven forty-five read the clock on the kitchen microwave. Was that possible? I checked the clock on the DVD player. Eleven forty-six. Christ! My undergraduate fiction workshop met at twelve thirty! I started slapping together papers and books, racing around the house. Will's flannel shirt was big enough that I could yank it over my head as I moved, blind, toward the bedroom closet, where my old standby, a gray Chinesey cotton jacket, hung on the left hook. No time for socks. Step into black Dansko clogs. Into the bathroom for lip gloss and powdered blush. Too much of the latter. I looked sunburnt. With one hand and a dry washcloth, I rubbed down the pink, with the other, stuck a charcoal eye pencil into my bra (I'd try to dab a bit along my lash line at a stoplight). Time to make a sandwich? Eleven fifty-four. No time.

Christ. Definitely *not* looking forward to leading the undergraduate workshop. On page four of the syllabus handed out at our first class I had written: "Please do not submit any story that features porn, torture, or weapons-wielding that might make your classmates and me afraid to point out your dangling modifiers," but I had not gotten around to reading one of the stories up for the workshop until last night, and so there had not been time for me to e-mail the class a veto of the tale of a happy-go-lucky psychopath who, for a finale, burns down the house in which he has duct-taped a pair of tots to one another in a bathtub of kerosene and experiences great happiness as he stands on the sidewalk, across the street, and takes in the aroma of the children's roasting flesh.

Christ.

I wheeled my rattling fat-tire bike off the ramada out back and started around the house toward the road. What—

—yes, a twitch of furry tail near the base of the oleanders. The scrawny black cat had found the plate of tuna. "Hey, there!" I called jubilantly.

The cat did not look up. Could it actually be Bad Cat, so named by Will and myself a year or so earlier, during a period in which, almost every morning, we witnessed its flying into view and, before we could spring from the breakfast table to object, racing off, mouth firmly clamped on a house finch or sparrow that had been drinking from the birdbath a split second before?

The contracted expression on the cat's face as it took its bites of canned tuna suggested some bitterness. Cats were supposed to be picky eaters. "Finicky," the ads said. Maybe it would have preferred salmon or chicken? I wished that I had time to stop and see if the poor thing would tolerate some petting. When it had stopped coming around, I'd worried that the coyotes had gotten it. "Nice to see you, kit-kit," I called. Still no response, so I whispered to the glittering gneiss boulder that Will and I had picked out for my fortieth birthday, "Thank you for your loveliness."

The gravel road hissed under my tires as I pedaled toward the Third Street bike route. Back in '98, Will and I had been looking for a solid neighborhood with a good grade school. In order to buy in this area, we'd had to take a fixer-upper. We'd felt good about all of our sweat equity during the housing run-up. In 2004, prices for the neighborhood shot up twenty-five percent in nine months. Now, four years later, the local newspaper reported that the collapse of the market had put us back to the levels of 2001.

For Sale signs stood in many of the front yards of the homes I was pedaling past, and I supposed that a number of them meant fore-closures. Supposedly, corporations were scooping up houses to rent to people who'd lost theirs in the crash. Here was one, I bet: sere oleanders, a citrus gone leafless and even losing its bark, several slumping cardboard boxes and a tire leaned up against the front door.

As I got closer to the university and rode through the old and historically desirable Sam Hughes neighborhood, I spotted classic adobes—always well-kept family homes—that investors now crammed with as many student renters as possible. Boys, mostly. Former front yards held multiple pickup trucks and SUVs. Riding home recently—dark coming earlier—I'd noticed several living rooms lit up with neon signs for Corona and Dos Equis.

During our house hunt, Will and I had looked at an adobe in this neighborhood—it had been far out of our reach. Maybe it still would have been, collapse or not, but now its arched window sported what had to be a student's Confederate flag.

That flag. One of the great and terrible features of being human is surely the way that—just trying to build a good warning system based on information about our past errors—the brain captures dreadful moments of our lives with the finest brushstrokes. So it was that a veritable Vermeer of Jeremy Fletcher's attic apartment in Iowa City came into my head as I passed that flag—just like the flag tacked to the wall above Jeremy Fletcher's stove.

The flag, the crusts of a peanut butter and jelly sandwich on a card table that also held several spiral notebooks, some new and still sleek, others fluffed up by use (the turning of pages, the addition of pencil lead or ink). Also on the card table: the cloudy emerald-green bong of which Jeremy Fletcher and I had made use the evening that I visited the attic apartment. Across the dun, unpainted drywall ceiling over his water bed, an initially confusing, gray ghost trail of boot prints had been left by some long-gone construction worker. *Red Wing, Red Wing.* And here was Jeremy Fletcher's attic bathroom: varnished car siding as shiny and brown as pretzel sticks, towels the dark green of pine needles—the towels gifts from Esmé, I knew, because I had been with her when she purchased them to replace "the regular horrors" she'd found when she first stayed over.

And now Jeremy Fletcher himself. A fleshy man, older than most of the Workshop students in '88, already well into his thirties. His fine hair had started to recede. Wrinkles radiated out from his rheumy blue eyes and formed a light necklace along the fold of a double chin not entirely concealed by a red sea-foam beard.

On a green light, I pedaled across Campbell Avenue and continued toward the Modern Languages Building. The sun was high, the sky almost white, as if the heat of the day had baked out the color, but I shivered at the memory of Jeremy Fletcher. In his bathroom, sitting next to the base of his toilet, there had been a can of Comet cleanser, and, before heading back to Esmé's and my apartment, I had sprinkled rills of that bleachy blue stuff on my index finger; scrubbed it into my teeth and my tongue before bending low over the tiny sink, there, and rinsing out my mouth with water that whined as it made its trip up to the attic. "Brontë!" Jeremy Fletcher had called from bed as I turned the doorknob to escape his apartment. *Brontë* was a joke that he had started a few days before, over the Thanksgiving dinner that he and Esmé and I had been ready to tuck into when— the most fantastic surprise, it seemed at the time—my beloved boyfriend, Will Ludlow, just flown in from Italy, had shown up at the door of Esmé's and my place on Burlington Street.

How about: *I was so young?*
How about: *I was raised by wolves?*
No, no good blaming the wolves for what I did back then. The wolves themselves had been raised by wolves, and, no doubt, the same holds true for our dour British Isles ancestors who picked away in coal and slate mines and survived on soda loaves and potatoes and are known to me strictly from sepia studio photographs (some of them in finery rented from studio photographers: the women with ruffs of fur around their necks, the men in top hats and long, heavy coats done up with glossy silk frogs instead of everyday buttons).

How about: *I was*—as folks sometimes described themselves at AA meetings—*an egomaniac with an inferiority complex?*

What I had done with Jeremy Fletcher—on top of my betrayal of Esmé and Will—the whole thing had been a crazed, nightmare collaboration against myself. And to think how lucky, lucky, lucky I'd felt those early September mornings in Iowa City when I walked down the apartment's twig of hallway and found my new best friend, Esmé Cole, bundled in her puffy, pink fumble of bathrobe at our Formica dinette! By the time that I got up, Esmé already would be smoking a cigarette, drinking a cup of the strong coffee that she brewed each morning, and undertaking—with the help of a makeup mirror surrounded by many small lightbulbs—those beauty routines whose results I envied but whose execution I could not have withstood (running a pin through her eyelashes to eliminate telltale clumps of mascara, plucking her brows as fine as a flapper's, trimming her cuticles with a metal device that left each moon of her perfect nails impeccably revealed). If it isn't *triceratops!* I would say, in honor of the jumbo-size pink plastic rollers that She used in order to establish the requisite volume for her grand Gibson Girl hair. *Miss Piggy*, she'd call me (she considered it scandalous that I sometimes went to class in the same clothes I wore for running and rarely folded what I brought home from the Laundromat).

We did not see each other as much as I had imagined we would since I usually studied and wrote at the library or the computer lab, both of which sat close to the English-Philosophy Building, where I taught and attended classes, but I cherished our friendship. Minus Will—and writing stories for the Workshop, studying nineteenth-century British novels, and teaching two classes of undergraduates—I sometimes felt untethered. I loved that Esmé always was at the apartment in the mornings. We had our little routines. "Pill time!" Esmé would say, and, together, we'd go into the kitchen and pull our respective birth control packages from the back of the silverware drawer and down our pills with orange juice. Then, as if we were a cozy married couple, we would carry cups of coffee into the living room. We'd arranged the furnished sofa and Esmé's futon to face each other and, from the futon, Esmé would read aloud to me the crime reports that, having grown up near Chicago and done her undergraduate degree at Columbia, she found hysterically innocent.

A red leather Coach bag containing a matching wallet, keys, and a DynaTAC cell telephone was reported stolen from a first-floor carrel at Main Library, approximately 1:30 P.M.

Officers were called to a disturbance near playground equipment at Mercer Park. Staunton Overby, 21, of Coralville, Iowa, was arrested and charged with procuring alcohol for a minor and resisting arrest. Two juvenile males were released to the custody of their parents.

Drug paraphernalia and several ounces of marijuana were reported found in a washing machine at Suds and Duds.

She loved to read "Dear Abby" aloud, her voice ringing with the old-fashioned advice columnist's displeasure, "Going to the man's wife and admitting to your affair might make *you* feel better but could end any chance of the couple's repairing their relationship!" Or, applying a soothing balm to a question of etiquette, "Though you should *not* wear a white wedding gown if you and your fiancé currently are living together, I'm sure that you would look lovely in a street-length costume in ecru."

We made each other fall into that breed of delicious laughter where we had to get down on our knees and *hoot-hoot-hoot* and snigger and plead, *Stop, please, I mean it, stop.* Helpless, we pounded the apartment's worn wooden floors with our fists. Then, after a period of panting and leaning up against her futon frame, Esmé would jump up and put a CD in her boom box, maybe the acid house music that was big in Chicago and also in London, where she and a person named Sarah had spent the summer—or it might be Shostakovich or Bach partitas or yowling Sinéad O'Connor or one of those work-your-heart-to-a-bloody-stump musicals that she had been raised on and that I already had learned to love. We'd sing—looking into each other's eyes, egging each other on, grinning like maniacs, unless the song was sad, in which case, we might get choked up—and that, too, could result in our laughing our heads off. "I'm Gonna Wash That Man Right Outa My Hair" from *South Pacific*—Esmé liked that one because of her recent breakup from a Dartmouth guy she'd met in London, and I, suffering a constant, low-grade, irritable fever over the absence of Will, liked being saucy about him in Esmé's company. "There's A Boat Dat's Leavin' Soon for New York." That was fun. Stephen Sondheim's "Every Day a Little Death" or "Not While I'm Around."

Each time that Esmé and I sang "Not While I'm Around," I had the notion—it made me proud—that the song, with its sweet and fierce declarations of loyalty, was *our* song. A sad irony, as things turned out, of course, but that September I did feel as if I would do anything for Esmé—even risk my life for her, it once occurred to me (with a little thrill). I never had had a friend like her. I felt . . . *blessed* by her friendship. The word sounds pious, but *blessed* was precisely what I felt the morning that we walked home from our first pancake breakfast at the Hamburg Inn and she, laughing, plucked a gorgeous handful of red and yellow maple leaves from a grassy lawn and showered them down over my head. *Blessed* the afternoon that she showed up at the student union's cafeteria—the River Room—where I sat eating my sack lunch near the floor-to-ceiling windows, and we wound up talking for four hours straight about the writers we adored (Edna O'Brien, Babel, Munro, Nabokov, Chekhov: swoon!). So very *blessed* the afternoon that I fell asleep on the sofa, grading student essays, and woke up to her carefully covering me with her very own afghan.

Her family, I'd quickly learned, was given to acts of thoughtfulness. That afghan had been knitted for her by her grandmother. In the short time we'd lived together, several packages from her mother had arrived (scented soaps, hoop earrings, funny cards, a vintage cashmere cardigan of a charming greenish-yellow with seed pearls stitched on in a pattern of ferns upwardly unfurling—"She knows I'm crazy about citrine," Esmé had confided). Even her little brother—Toffer, short for Christopher—mailed her letters and goofy gifts (one of the "bloody smiley face" T-shirts that people bought at raves and a plastic penis on wheels that Esmé kept on the kitchen windowsill). The petit point pillow on the futon was a gift from her beloved aunt and featured a blooming morning glory twisting its vines around dark blue letters that spelled ESMÉ. Her dad telephoned the apartment. "Just to gab," Esmé would say afterward. She did not seem aware that there might be anything special about such attentions.

I had a sister, but she had graduated from high school the year before I was born. We hardly knew each other. There had been a rupture in my mother's relationship with her family when she married my dad (he was not a Baptist-Methodist or a Methodist-Baptist or something along those lines) and both of his parents were long gone. The only relative from outside our immediate family that I ever had met was my dad's sister Patty, whom—until she died at the age of fifty, liver shot from working overtime on gallons of Gilbey's gin—Dad could not prevent from showing up at our house, now and then, drunk and rabid with apologies and recriminations.

To me, Esmé's gesture with the afghan felt practically exotic. I was so afraid to break the spell of it that I pretended to go on sleeping. I didn't even know in what *key* to respond, and so I had stayed on the sofa for a good half hour after she moved off before I finally allowed myself to sit up and produce a lot of noisy yawning and say a casual "Hey, thanks for the blanket!"

6

From the front of Room 201 in the University of Arizona's Modern Languages Building, I addressed the sixteen undergraduate members of Advanced Fiction Workshop in their tablet desks. Told the students of the importance of regularly reminding readers that their characters exist in a physical world.

I wiggled my fingers in the air to suggest just how fast the world of the story could dissipate. "And if there's no world, there's no possibility of consequences, guys!"

Inspired by all this, I gave a kick to the leg of the table where my grade book and the students' stories sat—a hard enough kick that I registered it in my big toe, and the grade book and papers slid across the table. I winced for my audience. "If your character can't even stub his toe," I said, "how can anything significant happen to him?"

A few students smiled, as if they took the point; a few frowned in what looked like disapproval of my theatrics. No response from the girl checking her cell phone. Nor from the boy using an index finger to work from behind one of his molars a white lump of what the crinkly wrapper on his desk indicated was a Subway sandwich. Nor from the girl with the platinum locks who had told me—how to respond?—during office hours that her life's ambition was to *be* the heiress Paris Hilton, and who now looked up at ML 201's ceiling and blinked and blinked again as she distilled Visine drops into her party-boiled eyes.

Really, I was too shy a person to ever be entirely comfortable in the role of professor.

I rapped together the papers that my kick had disturbed. Glanced at the clock. Each clock in Modern Languages displayed a slightly different time and I could not remember if this one was fast or slow. Was it time for our break? I was ready. For fear that their own stories might be critiqued harshly, most of the students in that bunch made tepid remarks about one another's stories ("Good read, man!" "Held my interest despite a few typos!" "LOL!"), which meant that I'd had to do the heavy lifting for the psycho kid-killer story (when I'd finished, the author—a guy with hair shaved down and dyed the green of pool table felt—had muttered, "I guess you didn't get that it was supposed to be *funny*").

Bang! At the rear of the room, the door swung open. *Esmé,* I thought, in the fraction of a second before a male voice from the hallway said, "Sorry! Wrong room!"

Nervous laughter filled the room as the door swung shut. "So, okay," I said, "this is probably a good time to take a break. Fifteen minutes, please."

I'd known that Esmé was on my mind even before that door to-do. Twice, I'd caught myself wondering what she would think of my classroom presence. Maybe my flamboyant kick at the table had been for her benefit. Once, at Iowa, she'd shown up while I was in the middle of teaching one of my undergraduate classes. She'd looked about the room with her usual sunny curiosity while she unwound a gigantic pink scarf from her neck and then removed her creaking leather motorcycle jacket. Fortunately, I'd planned that day's class carefully and been able to recover from the surprise of her visit. Afterward, radiant Esmé had run up to the front of the room and thrown her arms around me and declared, "You were magnificent!"

And here I was, a score of years later, walking through the halls of Modern Languages, on my way to check my mail, Esmé's "You were magnificent!" still ringing absurdly bright around me—though I also recalled wishing that she had delivered her praise in a softer voice because, as two students turned our way, Esmé stuck out her tongue at them and said, "Brats! You had no right to act bored!"

Had they been bored? I could not say. I always had tried to teach a good class, but after years at it, I knew that certain undergraduates thought I was great and others wanted to string me up by my thumbs, and often for the same reason: I gave their stories very thorough edits and required that they read and analyze the work of published authors, and—this was the main sticking point—thoroughly revise their own stories.

Sometimes I doubted my decision to support my life as a writer through teaching. Maybe I should have been an editor? All that time and energy Will and I had spent getting tenure, our lives on hold! Now promotion to full professor lay ahead—ever more publishing in the right places and getting good teaching evaluations and serving on the right committees, all of it stuff to list on the performance review that each faculty member had to turn in each year (and try to fashion in such a way that, while sounding humble, we also proved ourselves figures with a "national presence").

Ah, cigarettes! In the breezeway that linked the two halves of Modern Languages, a cluster of the Advanced Fiction students were lighting up their break-time cigarettes. Another vice of mine that long ago had bitten the dust. Maybe seeing my old cigarette-smoking pal Esmé was stirring up that longing in me. A yip of laughter. That would be my student Jaime. Jaime stood no more than five feet tall, and his cheeks were flamingo pink beneath what I took for a veil of ointment (he'd mentioned a character's skin condition in one of his stories), and he wrote work as interesting as anything that I'd read in recent *New Yorker*s or the top quarterlies. Every year, Creative Writing selected its incoming class of graduate students from a big applicant pool, so the people in our graduate workshops were generally pretty terrific; I found it uncanny, though, how often—at least once a year—a truly gifted writer turned up in my undergraduate workshop. It was like finding the Hope Diamond in a jewelry box that, otherwise, held a few nice sterling silver bangles, a sweet rhinestone costume piece or two, then a bunch of those plastic bead necklaces people throw all over New Orleans during Mardi Gras. Always, I'd been a cheerleader on behalf of the gifted undergraduates when they came in during office hours: *Apply to our graduate program—any graduate program—and I'll write you recommendations! Be persistent! Start sending out work now so that editors get to know your voice! Guard your time!* Very few had stuck with writing, though, and, thinking of this, I felt a pang of sadness.

I supposed the sadness was related to Esmé's visit, too. Esmé and Jeremy Fletcher—true, I'd never liked his work, but, back in 1988, both were deemed talented enough to be admitted to Iowa. Had fiction simply not sunk its claws deep enough into them? Demanded that they stay the course? Getting a story right could drive me crazy, but writing remained—along with Will—my greatest treasure. You could see the proof on my right shin: a large, still-pink scar from a day when—high on a story I was in the midst of composing—I gleefully ran from my desk to the kitchen for a fresh pen; crashed, full force, into the open door of the dishwasher; and then—rather than stop for the stitches that a scolding doctor later swore I should have had—with a fresh pen in hand, I'd hustled back to my desk and let my sock and running shoe go soggy with blood while I resumed writing.

7

In the murk of the fourth-floor hallway—due to the anti-education legislature's hacking away at our budget, each ceiling fixture now held a single fluorescent bulb instead of four—I determined that the angular, towheaded figure coming my way was my colleague Jenny Ambrose. Jenny's adorable twin daughters—four-year-olds adopted from China—had stopped to mess with the spout of water that I knew for certain had overshot the drinking fountain's basin for at least ten years.

Jenny waved to me while she called over her shoulder, "Come on, girls!" then she twirled her raised arm and fist overhead, as if she worked a lasso up there that she soon would turn and drop over the dawdling twins. When they continued to ignore her, she called in my direction, "Is anybody witnessing this? Can I get a witness here?"

I laughed and wagged my hand in the air as Jenny abandoned her cowpoke bit and proceeded to transform herself into a dull-eyed bull (head below her shoulders, one foot pawing at the linoleum).

She adored the twins but liked to act beleaguered. "Look at me, girls!" she called. "I'm turning into the serious mother!"

Bobbed, silky black hair flying straight out from their heads, the girls came running. Poppy and Dolly. Darlings in lace-trimmed anklets and overalls decorated with pink and purple hearts and flowers. Once they reached Jenny, they stood behind her floor-length black skirt and made a game of peeking out at me. "You remember Charlotte," Jenny said. Poppy gave me a thrill by smiling at me with her tiny, perfect white teeth, but Dolly, who had cuddled in my lap at the English Department's picnic just a month before, declared a fierce, "No, we don't!"

As the four or us made our way into the much more highly lit office of the Department of English, Jenny muttered to me, "We call Dolly the Drama Queen"; then she added in a louder voice, "Of course you do, silly. Charlotte's the friend who gave you your Tickle Me Elmo dolls last Christmas."

Oh, Christmas. And birthday parties. A chance to tuck somebody into bed at night. Buy little socks and, later, bigger socks. Stick glow-in-the-dark stars on the ceiling. From where I stood, the lives of people with children looked like a fairyland, a sugar-encrusted delight. "I'd invite you guys to my office"—a student recently had brought me a piggy bank that doffed its hat when you dropped a coin in the slot on its back; the twins would like that—"but I'm on break. I'm just here to check my mailbox."

The twins ran to the break room to see if anyone had left "treats" behind. Jenny raised her arms in a big stretch, the very loose sleeves of her linen top falling all the way to her shoulders, exposing the tender skin of the undersides of her arms, a milky crease of deodorant. She yawned extravagantly. A woman at ease. "Look at me, Charlotte!" she demanded. "I'm growing addlepated from lack of sleep! Some twin or other always needs a glass of water or for me to

drive off the monsters under her bed or else Gregor's elderly prostate has him up, peeing for the umpteen millionth time!"

Gregor was Gregor Poulos, a paper products mogul who'd been
newly retired and widowed a few years ago, very much at loose ends,
hence, overjoyed at taking on the much younger Jenny and rein-
venting himself as a papa—also the patron of the novel prize for
which I was to be the judge (I pictured that puke-green envelope on
the chair of my home office, the novel within as yet unread).

"Don't look smug, Charlotte!" Jenny said. "Give Will fifteen
years; it'll happen to him, too!"

Impossible for me to imagine that I had looked smug at the
thought of Gregor Poulos's poor prostate. I did not feel smug. "It's
just my face," I said, which would have impressed me if I hadn't
been fairly certain that it was a line I'd picked up from some saucier
soul in a movie or a book.

Briefly, Jenny looked puzzled; then she laughed. While I pulled a
wad of mostly junk mail from my box (notices; book catalogs; a
menu from the latest ethnic restaurant; yet another of those envelopes that Creative Writing's Goth-girl assistant, Pema Barkley,
was using as she passed along the Poulos Prize finalists to me),
Jenny said, "I've been meaning to call you, Charlotte, but Will
always sounds so fierce when he picks up and—well, you know, *eek!*"
She lifted her shoulders and clasped her hands: the frightened
maiden.

I laughed (actually, Will's brusque way of answering the telephone could mortify me).

"Anyway, I wanted to ask—Gregor's curious—how's your reading
going, Char? For the book prize?"

I was tempted to explain that Pema Barkley had held up things.
Pema Barkley was pissed—understandably—at having the adminis-
tration of the Poulos Prize dumped on top of her other duties. In

addition, Pema Barkley and a boy with heavily "gauged" ears were starting an Internet company (sports accessories, I gathered), and it had been a real challenge to get Pema to swerve her heavily outlined baby blues from her monitor's hectic displays of bike helmets, water bottles, and workout gloves so that I could remind her to create a log for the contest entries; and, later, to circulate the entrants' fifty-page samples and synopses to the screening panel; and, then—once the screeners had selected their top ten—to send the finalists the good news and request the complete copies of their books.

So far, Pema had given me just three of the ten finalists' books. Still, I sympathized with her. I understood why she wanted out of a job that required that she spend most of her time dealing with the complaints of tetchy professors and students. And how could I honestly suggest to Jenny that I was concerned that I'd received just three of the novels when I'd read only two of them?

"Oh, Jen," I said, "we—the fiction faculty—we just finished reading and evaluating the thirty pages that each grad student turns in for fall ranking, and, honestly, with all that stuff connected to Melody Murphy's campus visit"—both Jenny and I had attended job applicant Murphy's very fine lecture on Erasmus Darwin, plus her demo class and a lunch at the union and a dinner at El Charro in her honor—"I've just gotten a start, but I'm going to plunge in over the weekend."

Jenny's "Oh?" carried a touch of censure, but here came a fine distraction: her twins, laughing, the heels of their little patent leather shoes clicking on the linoleum floor as they ran out of the break room and straight toward their smiling mom. The twins brought themselves to a stop by grabbing hold of Jenny's legs, tugging at the fabric of her long, black skirt. Jenny laughed and smoothed her hands down the girls' silky heads. An automatic, enviable gesture. The twins must have calmed her because when she spoke again she sounded warm and friendly. "Of course, Gregor's so grateful that you agreed to do it!"

"It's an honor," I said, which wasn't exactly how I'd felt about taking on the job—the chairman of the department clearly had expected me to say yes—but I liked Gregor Poulos, his riddles, baggy eyes, and tomato-soup-colored pants, his sweet ways with the twins. Also, the state of Arizona needed every art patron and prize that it possibly could get.

Jenny smiled. "You and Will and Gregor and the girls and I—we have to get together!"

"I'd love that." I crouched to the twins' height. "If you come over, we can make cookies or something. I have a stuffed lion big enough that *both* of you could sit on it—and lots of kids' books and toys, too."

Dolly disappeared behind Jenny's skirt again, but Poppy tipped her head back to ask, "Can we, Mama?"

"Well, Daddy and Mommy are kind of overwhelmed right now, sweetie." Jenny widened her eyes at me: Help! "And so's Charlotte. Right, Charlotte? Maybe over Christmas break?"

Poppy looked to me for confirmation. I smiled and nodded. "Sure. Over break would be great." I doubted that those cookies ever would get baked. It had been a good two years since Jenny and I had managed even to meet for a cup of coffee.

After I said good-bye and started toward the door to the hall, Dolly peeked out at me from behind Jenny's skirt one last time. Her face was blank. Pointedly blank? As if she wanted to unnerve me? Was that possible? "Feel my hair!" she had commanded while she snuggled in my lap at the fall picnic, and after I happily complied and said an admiring, "Oh, it's so smooth, Dolly!" she had nodded and closed her eyes and murmured a satisfied, "I know. It feels just like satin."

8

It had been Will's contention that we ought to wait to have kids until one of us found a tenure-track line. I had gone along. A year into our Arizona jobs, though, with the service work and publishing pressures piled on, Will had said that we better revise upward. He looked swampy that second fall, poor guy, his skin skim-milk blue, despite having spent the school year in a state lacquered in sunshine. His was the pallor of days spent in libraries and museums; many academics are that same hue.

"We need to wait until we get tenure," he said.

"*Six* years?"

He had sounded serious, but now he laughed. "You're young, Charlotte! Your writing's going great! And don't you want to finish what you're working on first? It's the best thing you've ever done . . . and we're happy the way we are, aren't we?"

The expression on his face—a combination of a smile and a frown—convinced me that our marriage needed for me to say, *Yes, of course*. And maybe we were happy, to the degree that people obsessively bound up in their work could be. On his second try, Will did win a Guggenheim Fellowship to work at Yale on the Marinetti archives. After a lot of nail biting and neurotic, perfectionistic revision, in my fourth year at the university, I sold a third book. This meant that the chairman of the English Department encouraged me to "go up" for tenure early. Maybe, I decided, it *would* be a good idea—get it out of the way before I had a baby—and I plunged into the paperwork necessary for initiating the tenure process.

Before I had finished, however, my sister was diagnosed with stage 4 breast cancer.

Martie was seventeen years older than my accidental self, a middle school teacher back in our Iowa hometown. Divorced. Her three kids were grown and had lives (and jobs) in California and Oregon and Washington State. Our parents, in their mid-seventies, remained in the hometown—Webster City—but they were not much help (after telling me about Martie's diagnosis, my mother had said, "Well, your dad and I never had cancer so it can't be our fault!"). Matters were complicated because, as was the case with a lot of small towns, Webster City had lost its hospital years before, and most everything that Martie was going to need—surgery, radiation, chemo, follow-up appointments—would require driving to the town of Fort Dodge, half an hour away.

Martie was a self-reliant person and uncomfortable with the idea of my taking a leave of absence from my job in order to help her. I myself was nervous—I hardly knew my sister; I was nervous about falling behind in my writing and stopping "the tenure clock"—but I acted as if it were not a big deal. "Let's just see how it goes," I told her, and I moved into the spare room of her duplex and wound up staying for a year and a half.

I did fall behind in my writing, and the university was not happy with me, but that was an important time. It allowed Martie and me to become sisters. We went on drives—to a nice place called Briggs Woods or just through the countryside (we'd grown up with cornfield vistas, so we were fairly easy to please). We found a Dairy Queen in Fort Dodge that made good hot fudge malts, for when she had an appetite. Sometimes, we carried peanut butter and honey sandwiches to the same stone picnic shelter in the downtown park where a ponytailed boyfriend and I had smoked cigarettes as teenagers. I bought a blow-up kiddie pool decorated with dinosaurs and set it in a shady spot behind the duplex; it was comforting, lying hip to hip, in the tepid water, talking or not. I learned that, like myself, my sister loved the old Kendall Young Library, and we regularly hung out in that enchanted place: stained-glass windows, mosaic-tiled floors suggesting ancient worlds, dark paneling, columns carved from marble that appeared perpetually lit by a sunrise—and you were invited inside! You were welcome to the books, shelf after shelf of books, which had released a sweet, baked odor when opened to pictures of Babar the elephant in his Crayola green suit and, later, to Laura Ingalls Wilder's stories of life on the banks of Plum Creek and, then, the poetry of Emily Dickinson. Books had been Martie's childhood friends, too (the land to the west of our house had been fields when she was little, and she told me how she would flatten a square of alfalfa plants into a bed and, hidden, with the bees feeding at the purple flowers on all sides of her, lie there reading for hours).

Nights, on Martie's DVD player, the two of us watched movies from the 1930s and '40s, things like *Now, Voyager* and *Stella Dallas* that centered on the lives of women played by classy actresses. When her grown-up daughter, Jessie, came for a visit, while we watched Joan Crawford in *Mildred Pierce*, Martie filled in Jessie's and my eyebrows à la Crawford and had us walk around her little living room with books on our heads—mostly she was being funny, but she did say emulating Joan Crawford's posture would help us to project more self-confidence. She demonstrated that she could channel Bette Davis in fraught situations; turning down the corners of her mouth, tipping up her chin. "My de-ah," she said—the imitation was very good—"when the man grew vi-o-lent, I loffed in his face!"

Apparently, her husband had hit her. That was why she had left him. I never had known. We talked about marriage and female friendships and AA and having children. Martie told me, "Don't put off getting pregnant any longer, Charlotte. It may be later than you think!"

Sometimes our parents dropped by Martie's duplex to visit her. They usually brought Martie a pint of ice cream or some other treat that they hoped would "put some meat on her bones." The two of them looked good (far better than that dwindling, bald daughter with the bowl of melting rocky road in her lap). Age actually had emphasized our mother's great cheekbones. Our dad still had his full head of curly hair. He was as prickly as ever, though, and our mother, as always, was eager to go along with his moods. After sitting with us in Martie's living room for half an hour or so, Dad invariably would declare that Martie and I were too damned *loud.* He would wince and put his hands over his ears and glare at Mom until she winced and covered her ears, too.

Once, toward the end, after Dad had made one of these complaints, Martie said, "For Christsakes, Dad, I'll be quiet soon enough!" He acted as if he hadn't heard, but Mother—I'll never know what went on inside her head—said a scolding, "That was cruel, Martha Marie!" Martie had blinked at that while I laced my fingers through hers (little twigs) and said, "We will not be squashed, you guys!"

When she died, Will flew to Iowa to join me for the funeral. The night that we arrived back in Tucson—it was June, and the sweet odor of the excelsior in the swamp cooler made me feel truly at home again—I fished my package of birth control pills from my suitcase and held it over the kitchen garbage pail.

"Ready?" I asked Will.

"Are you? You don't want to get settled in for a while?"

"Will!" I wanted to prevent him from saying another word. I was thirty-six. Ever since our move to Tucson, I had been preparing myself for a pregnancy. I had bicycled to the Himmel Park pool every day during open season; during colder months, I'd bicycled to the university rec center for weight lifting and running on the treadmill. Back in Iowa, while Martie stayed in bed, sleeping, I'd gotten up every morning to do squats and lunges and abs-strengthening exercises and Pilates DVDs. I'd cooked Martie and myself righteous meals crammed with greens and sweet potatoes and kidney beans. I'd taken vitamin pills that included folic acid, because I knew a folate deficiency could cause a developing fetus to develop spina bifida.

"Well, if you're sure," Will said.

As it hit the bottom of the metal garbage pail, the hard plastic birth control pill package had given out a satisfying *gong*.

However, I did not get pregnant.

In the back of my mind, I always had worried that something like this could happen. For years, in fact, I had taken care of my birth control and Pap smears in the relative anonymity of Planned Parenthood. Now I made an appointment with an ob-gyn listed in "Tucson's Best Doctors."

I liked that the office was located in a deep-eaved, old Craftsman-style bungalow painted a benevolent olive green. The examination room itself would have been a bedroom, once upon a time. I liked that the wallpaper (pale blue hydrangeas) looked a bit scuffed. Across the tops of big reference books on a wooden desk, there lounged various pink plastic parts of a female reproductive system that put me in mind, in a friendly way, of the pink lawn furniture and sports car that had been part of a grade school classmate's Barbie doll collection. The doctor herself turned out to be all warmth and goodwill; also admirably without vanity (sensible sandals exposing bare feet, no makeup, graying curls a bit mashed on one side of her head). During the pelvic examination, she and her assistant and I carried on—making an allowance for the lamp and speculum and goo—an amazingly normal chat regarding which shops in Tucson carried the best secondhand furniture.

After I got back into my street clothes, the doctor returned to the room. She was tall enough to easily settle herself on a corner of her wooden desk. Wooden shutters covered the bottom half of the room's double-hung windows and, nervous, I looked out over the shutters at the blue-blue desert sky and a tendril of cat's claw vine that, now and then, waved into view.

The doctor cleared her throat. The frown on her face signaled concern, not disapproval. Still, my heart seized even before she said, "Has anyone ever told you that you have endometriosis?"

I shook my head.

She wiggled a finger in her ear, as if an itch, there, prevented her from continuing. "You do understand your records are confidential? I ask because your endometriosis looks like it's a result of Asherman's syndrome, but you didn't indicate any previous intrauterine surgery in your history."

Up until that moment, I'd told exactly two people in the world that I'd had an abortion: Esmé—I'd had no choice in her case—and Jacqueline C., a bighearted Tucsonan with whom I'd once shared what Alcoholics Anonymous called a *personal inventory*.

"Thank you," the doctor said after I'd tearfully made her the third person. She pulled a paper towel from the dispenser over her sink and handed it to me. "It's very important for me to know your history." After she removed a few of the pink plastic reproductive organs from the top of her reference books, she pulled one of the books toward herself and flipped through the pages until she located a black-and-white photograph of what, when she turned the book my way, looked like a heap of crepe paper streamers. "Asherman's," she said, "is the result of surgical scarring. At present, your uterus isn't competent to support a pregnancy. I'd recommend a hysteroscopy—it's outpatient and usually takes about thirty minutes. We'd use microscissors to snip the adhesions in the uterus, then insert a Foley catheter of saline solution. That keeps the adhesions from re-forming. You would take a course of hormones—also antibiotics to reduce the risk of infection."

She rested a hand on my arm. Her teeth when she smiled were crooked, but very white. "We can't guarantee that the procedure will enable you to have children—*biologically*, that is—but it's your best shot."

Endometriosis was common enough in women who waited until they were older to have children that I did not need to excuse or explain the condition to Will. We'd known two women—one of them his sister—diagnosed with it. Both had had surgery and gone on to have successful pregnancies.

The Asherman's syndrome—I did not tell Will about that.

Two weeks after my meeting with the doctor, Will drove me to the university medical center for the outpatient procedure. He brought along his briefcase and a heap of student essays to read; and, after the procedure, when an orderly—hospital protocol—wheeled me to the hospital entrance, he was waiting with the car

already running. I felt pretty lousy—both aching from the procedure and upset. On our drive to the pharmacy where we were to pick
up the necessary prescriptions, I said—as if the idea never would
have occurred to me on my own, or been valid if it had—"The
doctor's mentioned adoption as an option a couple of times—if
things don't work out. Because I'm over thirty-five. When you're
over thirty-five, the success rate for this isn't great. One place I
looked at online said just twenty-three percent."

Will frowned. An exemplar of the frown. I was not intended to
miss it. Now that he was getting older, I saw his father in his frown.
His father, John Ludlow—with a good wife by his side—had been
pastor of a Lutheran church in little Brainerd, Minnesota (putative
home of Paul Bunyan) for almost forty years. Negativity was not
countenanced in the Ludlow home (my husband had grown up
peeing at a toilet over which hung a sampler stitched by his mother
that read, "Christians: Not perfect, just forgiven").

The pharmacy came into view and Will switched on his turn
signal and slowed. "You're incredibly healthy," he said, "you'll do
fine." Then, a moment later, he was out of the car, loping across the
parking lot toward the store's entrance. His combination of confidence and what I took for disapproval set me chewing at my nails,
something that I did only in moments of extreme anxiety. Suppose
I wasn't *fine*! The doctor wouldn't have mentioned adoption to me
twice if she assumed that I would be fine. Twenty-three percent was
not great. Shit. I bent forward with a cramp and rued the fact that we
had not worked on a pregnancy sooner.

Will returned from the pharmacy very quickly. I remember, as
I'd watched him lope back across the parking lot with the crisp
white prescription bags in his hand, I had a sick feeling that he
would pretend not to see me looking out at him through my rolled-
down window. I lowered my gaze, not wanting to be disappointed,

and I noticed, then, how his pants—cheap gray work pants that he ordered from a uniform supply place; his old and slightly eccentric badge of solidarity with workers of the world—always showed their first sign of wear around his front right pocket, where he kept his keys. Then I lifted my eyes and I saw him smile at me as he passed in front of the car. A forced smile. Twitchy at the edges. Still, a smile. Over the years, I had told him, periodically, that I needed for him to smile at me more often, so I appreciated his effort; also the way, after we arrived at the house that day, he settled me in a chair at the kitchen table and put my feet on an upturned laundry basket.

"So I can be with my girl while I make her a cup of tea," he said.

Three months later, right after we learned that my tenure bid had succeeded, I bought two pregnancy tests at the Safeway grocery near our house. I had intended to take the tests home, but even before the clerk—with a wink!—gave me the sales tape, I knew that I couldn't bear the wait, and I headed straight to the store's fluorescent-lit women's room and locked myself into a beige stall.

Positive, according to "the urine stream." I tore open the second test. Positive again.

I ran to the car. I was so wound up, so eager to get home and tell Will, that when I went to pull out of the Safeway parking lot and onto Broadway, to my shame and horror, I came within inches of hitting a teenage boy on a bicycle. *Where had he even come from?* I had not seen him until he was right in front of me, his face beneath his baseball cap pale with fury and fear as he swerved out of the way of my screeching, braking car! "Sorry! Sorry!" I called. I rolled down my window so that he'd hear. "So sorry!"

A warning: *You slow down, Charlotte! You take care, lucky girl!* That dear, angry boy. I might have had a child about his age. A boy whose voice was starting to break.

Will already was at the house when I arrived, and, after I told him the result of the pregnancy tests, we had a tomato juice toast with the pair of champagne flutes that someone had given us for a wedding gift. After the toast, we stood in the kitchen, holding each other. I stroked my hands down the back of Will's starched and ironed white shirt. The cloth seemed like the ideal expression of smooth and cool. I felt blissfully happy.

"Remember, though, Charlotte"—he set his hands on my shoulders and stepped away from me and fixed his eyes on mine—"*you're* the most important thing in the world to me. I don't know what I'd do if anything happened to *you.*"

I smiled and nodded. Will, I was sure, would be fine if anything ever happened to me, but I appreciated his saying otherwise.

That spring—such a contented, joyful time—I was not only pregnant but in the glory days of starting a new book of my own and helping a talented graduate student with her thesis manuscript. I did not mind the morning sickness. How could I, given what it meant? At nine weeks, I went in for a sonogram and saw the tiny cloud of tissue that the tech assured me was the baby. I heard its heartbeat, and, all day long, after my appointment, I called up that sweet sound. Then, two weeks later, during the graduate workshop, I started having cramps. The cramps were bad enough that I broke out in a sweat. I stopped in the middle of what I was saying—something about double-voicing in the work of Henry James—and apologized. "I'm sorry, I seem to be sick," I said and headed out into the hall.

The young woman whose thesis I'd been working on came after me and said that she could drive me home. I didn't argue. By the time we got to her car, I was experiencing an urge to push. I did not know that this could happen to a person undergoing a miscarriage but felt certain that pushing could not be right. While the student drove, I telephoned the doctor's office, which advised me to head to the emergency room at the university hospital, so we turned around.

A few hours and quite a few tests later—Will was with me by then—the doctors confirmed that I had miscarried.

No one ever had talked to me about what it was like to have a miscarriage. I was heart-broken, of course, but also unnerved at how long the bleeding continued. For days, I expelled pieces of bloody tissue—a couple as large as a deck of cards. I'd had no idea.

At the follow-up exam, my curly-haired doctor said, "Not to get discouraged!"

Will and I waited two months. Again, I quickly became pregnant. This time, when I went in for the sonogram, I made sure that Will came along (he was absorbed in studying the influence of Marinetti on contemporary Language, and I felt the baby remained a little too hypothetical to him). He stroked my forehead while the quick *lub-dub* of the baby's heartbeat filled the room, and we watched the monitor's little gray-and-white ghost that was not a ghost. "Spooky," Will said, sounding to my ears appropriately enthralled.

During the eleventh week—morning, Will and I both at home, working—I started to bleed.

The third and final miscarriage happened in the middle of the night. My doctor was at the hospital, but in delivery. She did reach us as we were at the discharge desk. When we finished up, she steered us into a nearby alcove, settled us on a bench. Somberly, she explained that she had studied my records. The placentas, she said, were not attaching to the uterine wall. "I have to tell you: When this problem shows up, it signals the possibility that the placenta could grow *into* the wall of the uterus or even attach to another organ. Either can be very serious."

Will stood. "That's enough, then," he said. His eyes were big and switched rapidly between the doctor and me several times. "That's enough," he repeated as, a short time later, his hand under my elbow, we made our way to one of that ever-expanding hospital's temporary gravel parking lots. "We're fine, just the two of us." The cloudiness in his voice was something I'd heard maybe twice in all our years together. "More than fine! I don't want you going through anything more, Charlotte!"

With Will sorry for me over something that was undoubtedly my fault, I felt too guilty to bring up adoption again, but the whole rotten mess sent me downhill. I couldn't write. Stayed in my bathrobe a lot. Contemplated going on antidepressants.

Maybe therapy?

Then, a morning arrived when I thought, *Man up!* I didn't even bother checking the time on my watch. I got right in my car and drove straight to a very funky place called the Alano Club, which I knew held AA meetings, off and on, all day and into the night. During our early days in Tucson, after years of not drinking, I'd nervously attended conference where a tray filled with glasses of bubbling champagne floated toward me and assured me that I was not a *true* alcoholic, and, naturally, I wound up plastered, hiding out in a hotel storage room filled with folding chairs. To get back on track, I'd started to attend AA again, often at the Alano Club. The Alano Club's main building was a homely, stuccoed thing the color of an Ace bandage. It housed a big, high-ceilinged, no-nonsense meeting room, plus a low-ceilinged, boggy lounge where you could buy something to eat (coffee, soda, cellophane-wrapped muffins) and mostly men sat around watching TV or playing cards and pinging video games. The twelve o'clock meeting that I'd attended, though, took place in a tiny brick annex at the south end of the parking lot, and, the morning of my post-miscarriages despair, I headed back there.

The meeting had begun by the time I arrived, but one of the great things about AA was, even if you felt awkward doing so, you could enter a meeting late (yes, some individual member might look askance at you, but the program was based on principles and the principles welcomed you, no matter what).

All of the places at the big central table were taken that morning, so I wangled a molded plastic lawn chair from a stack by the door and joined the people who sat around the rim of the room. I recognized a few faces—the most important one being that of ivory-skinned, gray-haired Jacqueline C. In her matching pastel knit tops and pants and the bouffant hairdo of her teenage years in the 1960s, the stoutly pretty Jacqueline did not look like a sage, but she knew things (she had stayed sober even during the death of her son to a drunk driver some twenty years before). "Put on protective armor before you talk to your parents," she'd told me back when I was a regular, and she had modeled the way by lifting an invisible helmet onto her head with her surprisingly slim and elegant fingers (their nails always polished in pearly pinks). Conversely, after a student had threatened to "punch out my lights" because I had given him a D, she'd advised, "What you do is, whenever he pops into your mind, you focus a beam of love at the center of his forehead. Just do that, Charlotte. You'll see. It will help."

It had helped. Everything she taught me helped. At one point, I'd almost asked Jacqueline to be my "sponsor," but then I'd gotten insanely caught up in the pressures of academia. Such was the atmosphere of the university that I'd started to feel—embarrassing to think of this now—as if the world would end should I, after so much work, fail to win my tenure bid. About the same time—as had happened in the past—I'd also grown peevish at the AA meetings. Gritted my teeth if, say, a strapping young man, hair still damp from the shower, shared his joyful story of how, in crowded downtown Phoenix, God had kept a parking space open directly in front of the office building where said strapping young man was scheduled for a job interview. With all that I needed to accomplish, did I have time to listen to such nonsense? No, I did not!

I'd stopped attending meetings. Stopped calling Jacqueline C.

Who now raised her hand and said—her childhood in rural Ohio gave her voice a distinctive mix of gravel and twang—"I'm an alcoholic and my name's Jacqueline, and I want to share a pet theory of mine. Those of you who've heard this from me before—I won't take offense if you step outside while I talk." She smiled her sweet, pretty-grandma smile around the room, and, here and there, people laughed. "So, my theory is we alcoholics get civilized here, at meetings. Most of us need civilizing. Maybe our parents"—she wagged her manicured fingers in the air—"through no fault of their own, mind you, they couldn't give us the attention or upbringing we needed. Whatever the reason, we didn't learn how to have healthy relations with other people, which I've come to feel, after sitting in these rooms a whole lot of years, is what most of our problems boil down to. Trouble with other people. The good news is, though, we can change all that by coming here! We learn we're always welcome here, no matter who we are or what we've done, and if we keep coming back on a regular basis, we can learn patience and tolerance and to love ourselves and others. We get civilized and that changes everything."

Was that for me? No, it was egotistical to think so. I didn't know if she even had seen me. It was true, though, that much of what I knew about "healthy relations," putting aside envy and resentments and having some integrity, I'd learned at AA. And that I probably would have been known more if I hadn't stopped attending.

Before the meeting's closing prayer—I was okay with reciting the

Serenity Prayer, which did not promote the belief that everything happened according to God's plan—the people who had been seated around the central table stood, and they stepped back to enlarge the circle to include those of us who'd sat against the walls. I joined hands with the people on either side of me, but then man on my right released my hand, and I felt someone slip between us.

Jacqueline C.

After the prayer ended, the two of us hugged. I apologized for disappearing and asked if I could buy her a cup of coffee. "Sure, honey, sure!" she said.

As I'd shared my personal inventory with Jacqueline, she knew more about my history than anyone in the world, really. After we carried Styrofoam cups of the clubhouse's pretty bad coffee to a table in the corner of the lounge, I reviewed the more dramatic highlights (every now and then, she interjected with a soothing, "Oh, you'd be surprised how often I've had people tell me that, honey!"). Then I brought her up to speed (Martie's death, the miscarriages, and my sense that I couldn't push Will on adoption).

"This has been a sad time for you, honey," she said when I'd finished, "but you're rich in so many ways! Do you think you could get in touch with some of that? Try remembering you're worthy of happiness and love, Charlotte! And, even though your husband is a saint"—she winked at me; she had a good wink—"could you work on not thinking of him as your HP?"

I laughed. *HP* stood for *Higher Power* in AA lingo, an out for those of us who got itchy at the more conventional talk of God.

"How about—if you don't feel comfortable asking Will to think about adoption yet—how about inviting him to work with you on some little thing? That's always good for Billy and me. You two cooperating on a project instead of your separate jobs? It wouldn't

have to be anything ambitious! Don't even think ambitious! Think—
maybe something from a list of chores you've put off."

We had such a list. It was long and included items like *gutters*,
lights for ramada, *reset bricks along front walk*. At the very top of the
list, however, was an item that had been there ever since we had
moved to Tucson: *boxes*. We needed to go through the bowed, dust-
covered cardboard boxes that had passed a sealed-up life in the
crawl space of our Minneapolis duplex even before we had hauled
them to Tucson and the brick shed in our backyard.

That was the chore that I picked.

It was not easy to get Will to agree to a day—he had this to do, that
to do—and then the day we picked turned out to be incredibly hot.
When it was time for us to get to work, the brick shed was an oven.
"Are you sure?" Will asked. I was sure. While Will went to the alley
to fetch the wheeled recycle bin, I attacked one of the big cardboard
boxes marked CHARLOTTE.

"Watch this!" I called to Will as he returned, wheeling the
awkward, rattling bin across the rocky yard. "Open up the lid!"

His gaze from under the bill of his baseball cap suggested skepticism but he did open the big bin's flabby plastic lid. And I did pitch
in the entirety of my first box (papers from my undergraduate days,
it had turned out to be). Will moved past me and into the shed and
pulled a box of his own from one of the dusty shelves and set to
opening it with a pocket knife. Always prepared. Methodical. Neat.
I admired that about him.

The heft of my next box surprised me. WRITERS' WORKSHOP/DRAFTS
read the fat Magic Marker letters scrawled across it. I peeled off the
crackling length of paper tape—almost all of its old glue gone—that
I'd used to seal the top so many years before. Inside was a mess of
papers. Letters, manuscripts—mine and my Workshop classmates'—
and drafts of stories I'd abandoned. "Blotto" by Charlotte Price sat

on top of the heap. I picked it up, meaning to lift the title page and read a bit of that almost forgotten story, but what I spotted beneath the manuscript stopped me:

Three torn-in-half-and-taped-together-again photographs—all nearly identical—that I'd thought lost forever.

In the photographs, two very eccentric-looking old ladies, each holding a yellow plaid coffee cup, leaned into one another in what seemed to be both friendliness and support. Poor old creatures. Their bran-colored stockings drooped around their ankles so, you might have imagined the old dears were in the process of shedding their skins. Both wore cardigans (sprung in the elbows and missing buttons and doing nothing to conceal the sorry-old-lady saggy boobs that hung just above the waistbands of pleated wool skirts that, I knew, reeked of mothballs). Faces powdered a ghostly white. Eyebrows drawn on in loony, pitiful scrawls. Mouths painted a dead red and puckered as the tops of drawstring bags.

Esmé and I, circa 1988, decked out in clothes from Goodwill, standing in our kitchen on Burlington Street.

Once our costumes and selected pose had reached what we deemed perfection, Esmé had set the timer on her camera and run to get into the frame. By sheer luck, a week or so later, I'd found the torn-up photographs in the trash can before they had been covered over by a milk carton or a wad of paper towel. "They're *way* too authentic, Charlotte!" Esmé had protested when she found me taping the pieces together. She was unconvinced when I insisted that we would love looking at them when we truly were little old ladies, but after I promised never to show them to anyone else, she allowed me to keep them.

"My girl," Will said.

I looked up from the taped-together photographs. With a drip of sweat clinging to the tip of his nose, Will held up an unfolded sheet of blue paper that he, apparently, had found in his box. He proceeded to read aloud:

> I'm glad you had a good Easter with the Biancos. I miss you like crazy, but can see it was smart I didn't try to come. Since Esmé moved to Mobile, I've been getting a ton of work done. Finished grading student essays, which means the whole weekend is clear for a *rigorous* revision of my camp story. If you haven't started reading the version I sent, please wait for this one. As Nabokov would say, I'm "cracking the whip." Tote that barge, lift that bale!

Will folded up the letter. "That's a keeper," he said and smiled at me.

I smiled back, grateful, humbled. Guilty. He had no idea that my spring days in Iowa City without him had not been so simple and cheery as they sounded in that letter.

Were there old letters from him in my Writers' Workshop box? Old letters from Esmé?

To my left, at eye level and clinging to a rusted window screen that one of us must have tipped up against the shed wall years before, a cicada had left behind the transparent, pale orange husk of its molt, and I felt just about that hollow as I set the three taped-together photographs back into my box. Tucked the flaps of the cardboard lid over and under.

I carried the thing to a vacant shelf. When I shoved it into place, the grit that had accumulated on the metal shelving raised an ugly squeal.

Certain words came to me, then, as distinctly as if I heard them spoken aloud: *Why, you're as good as dead to Esmé, Charlotte!*

Terrible words. For a moment, they knocked the breath right out of me—the pain was the pain I'd felt as a kid after I fell from a neighbor's apple tree and landed flat on my back.

As good as dead.

Up until that moment, almost seven years into our time in Tucson, I had retained the habit—evidently as much from expectation as from fear—of keeping an eye out for Esmé at the various reading and film series around town, at concerts and gallery openings. That day, though, as I went on working alongside my dear, unknowing husband, I concluded that my being as good as dead to Esmé was a blessing. I had paid dearly for my sins and would do well to think of her as dead, too.

9

But Esmé Cole Fletcher was not dead.
      I was not dead to Esmé.

We had stood together in my front hall, both of us very much alive, and I was glad.

As I rode my bike home from the university, I deliberated how best to fit the news of Esmé's surprise visit into my end-of-the-day conversation with Will. Not treat it like a big deal, definitely not, but like something worth mentioning: *It was so nice to see her after all these years! We didn't have much of a chance to talk, but she seemed to be doing well!* Then quickly move along to other things. *The frame shop called. You can pick up your print any day but Monday. And the Kovacs want to know if we're interested in seeing that movie at the Loft.*

As for Esmé's dinner invitation: I'd tell Will that he didn't have to come. It might be better that way. If Jeremy Fletcher behaved badly—who knew what he would be like now?—I wouldn't have to endure Will's glowering. In the future, I'd limit socializing to Esmé and myself (lunch dates or coffee).

I wheeled the bike through the carport and around to the ramada. I could see Will through the sliding doors, bent over his laptop at the dining room table. Still a very handsome man at age forty-five. Also, a person who knew about subjects as divergent as black holes, the comics of R. Crumb, the Peloponnesian War, the riot grrrl band Bikini Kill, and Saint Augustine—he'd contemplated graduate work in theology before art history—and could talk about all of these topics in an interesting way to most anybody. Not a show-off, though. A kind man. Patient. Loyal.

Still, I did wish, as I mucked through my bag for my bike lock, that he were the type who would think to look up from his work when his wife came into the house; smile at her, say hello. Or, better yet, do it *automatically*, from happiness at their reunion. I had never entirely gotten over some concern that one day he would look up from his work and announce that he didn't actually love me. *I just was being polite, Charlotte.* If I ever mentioned such worries, he would frown and say, *Don't be ridiculous. I practically worship the ground you walk on!* Still, all that a person could know of her marriage was what she experienced of it, and Will did maintain an aura of distance.

Mystery Man. That morning, Esmé had used the nickname, which I'd first heard at a lawn party thrown by some of Will's doctoral program friends in Iowa City. I'd never met any of those people before. Right after we arrived at the party, Will had disappeared, and I ended up helping the dreadlocked hostess level a card table on her bumpy grass. While we worked, I explained that I was finishing my bachelor's degree at a small college twenty miles to the north, that I hoped I'd be going to the Workshop the next year, that I'd met Will through one of my professors. As soon as the hostess and I had the card table level, she turned to the people nearby and pointed at me: "She says she's Mystery Man's girlfriend!" Some people smiled at me, some smiled at one another, some looked at me with curiosity. Later, when Will and I were alone, he had brushed off my being upset that none of his fellow graduate students seemed aware of my existence. "I value my privacy, Charlotte," he said. "That Mystery Man business—it shows why I don't tell people anything personal."

Not an entirely satisfying answer since his need for privacy had seemed to extend to me—and, in a way, continued to, twenty-one years later. But who was I to complain? I'd accepted my own secrets, and my husband was the best person I knew. He not only visited each and every one of his colleagues who wound up in the hospital but offered to pick up their relatives on the way. If someone (myself, a student, the janitor of his building) were in distress and needed to talk, he dropped everything and made himself available. After the failures of my pregnancies, when I admitted to him that the thought of alcohol kept coming into my mind, he gave up drinking; "to keep me company," as he put it. Although my father never had stopped behaving as if the work that Will and I did were on par with collecting aluminum cans from ditches, Will had flown to Iowa with me the summer before to help me move the man—and my mother, too—into "independent living." "Bet you can't wait to see me kick the bucket!" my dad had said to Will the day we headed back to Tucson, and Will had responded, without a blink, "Nothing could be further from the truth, but I hope before that happens, you'll realize that your daughter is a gem."

That was Will.

After I got my bike locked to a pipe belonging to our hulking AC unit, I tried the dining room's sliding door. Locked. I hesitated. Knock, or use a key? If I were hard at work on something, I would prefer that Will use his key, right?

I used my key.

He looked up as I dumped my bags inside the door. "Hey," I said. He nodded. Absently, yes, but, then, the guy *had* started dinner: I could smell potatoes baking. Russets—and yams. There was a sweet burnt-sugar aroma on the aluminum foil that Will conscientiously would have set on the rack under the yams. "Thanks for putting in the potatoes," I said.

"Be with you in a moment. I'm working on the itinerary."

I kissed the top of his head on my way to the refrigerator. Will liked to solidify our summer plans early. He had long, prioritized lists of where he needed to go for his research; what buildings and artworks and archives and people he most needed to see. Next June, we'd be based in Milan; July, in Rome. A contact in Rome already had helped Will locate a girls' school that, over the summers, rented dorm rooms with adjoining baths to "responsible adults" at a good rate. Our housing in Milan had yet to be determined, but Will would figure it out. I wasn't picky, as long as I was assured of a quiet place with a desk where I could write in the mornings. Afternoons we usually spent together; or, if Will had other work to do, I'd take a walk—in Rome, through the gardens at the Villa Borghese, maybe, or along the Via Giulia, where I could poke my head into antiques shops. I might visit a painting that I felt a need to see. In Milan, I often just "wandered," bought a couple sheets of good stationery and a piece of marzipan on pricey Via Montenapoleone and then, over a coffee, read and people-watched and wrote letters. I would have liked to vary the locations of our trips but, really, there was always something to do or see or learn in Italy.

On the kitchen counter, bringing them to room temperature, Will had set out dry-cured olives and a wedge of Stilton. Both sat on blue glass plates that—or so we'd been charmed into believing by a local shop owner—poor Mexican artisans had made in pre-plastic days by melting down bottles once home to practical substances (Noxzema,

Phillips' Milk of Magnesia, Vicks VapoRub). I opened the refrigerator and pulled out the plastic bag of romaine that I'd washed and spun the night before. I felt pleased with myself for my foresight.

"By the way, last month's water bill came today," Will said.

My heart sank. The water bill was one of our main arguments. Though I was willing to be careful about our expenses so that we could travel for his work in the summers, I did want at least one area of green in the yard, and the oleander hedge that I'd planted gave me green and shade—and gorgeous red flowers throughout the year—and it needed water.

"You know, some things aren't meant to grow here, Charlotte," Will said.

"Half the people in Tucson have oleanders," I muttered, but I wasn't keen on pressing my point just then. Not only did I want things pleasant when I told him about Esmé's dinner invitation but I imagined that the bill had been higher than usual. A couple of weeks before, I'd forgotten the dripper hose until our sweet, old neighbors, Helen and Nick Schaeffer (in matching Elderhostel visors), appeared on our front steps to let me know that they'd noticed "puddling" along the hedge.

Would Will accept a change of subject? "Finney's called this morning," I said. "You can come by for your print anytime—except next Monday. Monday they're all going to Phoenix." Not looking his way, I pulled bottles of vinegar and olive oil from the cupboard. Salt. Dry mustard. Oregano. It pleased me to think that I could tell Esmé that my standard vinaigrette was hers, the one that she'd taught me to make during our days as roommates. While I took a whisk from the jug of utensils on the counter, I spied, from the corner of my eye, Will picking up a piece of paper from alongside his computer. The water bill. Even from across the room, I could make out its familiar fat blue columns showing water usage per month.

He read off the gallons used and the total fee. The amount was bad enough that I had to say, "I'll be more careful." Then, brightening my voice—feeling queasy over the wasted water and the bill and the tension and the playacting required for what I needed to say next—I added, "But, hey, something kind of amazing happened today. Esmé Cole—my roommate back on Burlington Street?—she just found out we live in Tucson. She came by to invite us to dinner. Not that you have to go— since I didn't ask you if you'd want to—but I felt like I had to say yes."

Slowly, Will took off his glasses and set them on the table. He began to rub his eyelids—always surprisingly pale because of his heavy brow—with the tips of his long, fine fingers.

"And why's that, Charlotte?" he asked.

I had planned an answer of sorts, something about my feeling pity for Esmé. *She didn't even look like the same person, Will.* Pity was an honorable emotion in Will's eyes. But I knew that answer would stink on at least two counts. Number one, it would be a lie. I *wanted* to spend time with Esmé. Number two: Once, back in Iowa City, Will had stepped into Esmé's and my apartment kitchen and seen Esmé standing naked at the stove, and I suspected that ancient anger over that moment still made me eager to slap an image of the changed Esmé over whatever lovely image might reside in Will's brain. This being the case, I said only, "She and I were close once, Will. It was nice of her to ask."

He opened his eyes, now pink from his rubbing, and he gave me a weary look. "Didn't you let her know when we moved here, though? And she never responded?"

"Oh"—I made an airy, butterfly movement with my hands, suggesting how things might come and go—"I sent a postcard to her office, but she never got it. She was shocked, I guess, when she found out we lived here . . . very recently."

A long and skeptical *hmm* from Will.

Humiliating, I thought. I wanted him to accept, as I had, that what mattered was my old friend's wanting to see me *now*. Still, I had no desire to chat with him about Esmé, and I said that it was not a problem, not at all, if he did not want to go to the dinner.

"No." He put his glasses on again. Sighed. "You'd go for me— and, besides, I figure it's a one-shot deal."

I sighed, too, but in a noisier way; in imitation. "Please, just stay home if you're going to act like it kills you."

"Don't be silly, Charlotte. Of course it won't kill me. What night is it?"

I had shrunken down inside myself during that exchange. I did not feel like saying one more word, but I had to answer or risk looking sulky. "Wednesday."

"As in the day after tomorrow?"

"That's the one, Will."

He got up from the table and came into the kitchen. Opened the oven. Poked at the potatoes with a fork. "So, how's your reading for Gregor's contest going?" he asked.

Very glad of this change in topic, I stuck out my tongue to indicate how fagged I felt at the thought of all the pages ahead of me. "Two done. Eight to go."

"I guess, then"—he shut the oven door—"after this dinner with your friend, you'll be keeping your calendar clear."

"*Will!*" I would not have dreamed of saying a thing to him about his "calendar."

"Hey." He raised his hands, then let them fall. "You were saying the other day that you hadn't had a chance to write all week. I know that can get you down. Last night—you got up, didn't you? I thought maybe you couldn't sleep."

I shrugged. Such was the reality of marital bliss that, in case he might use the information later—say, he fell for the governess and decided to have me locked away as a madwoman—I had not told Will about the weird, jarring awakenings that I'd been experiencing that autumn, moments in which I sat bolt upright in bed, gripped by an icy fist of not knowing who I was; and not merely in some garden-variety anxious way, like *What's my role in life?* Character, personal history—all were wiped clean. Those moments reminded me of the many disorienting nights when I'd woken up in the hospital after my drunken collision with that pickup truck. I seemed to be reduced to something elemental in the elemental universe. Unlike my nights in the hospital, though, I could move, and, sometimes, after I came fully awake, I would step out into Will's and my backyard, beyond the overhang of the ramada, and—feet icy—look up at the sky and try to open myself to a correspondence in the distance between the atoms inside me and the distance between myself and the stars and all that whirling infinitude of which I understood myself to be a part—though I barely could believe it.

Wasn't that magic? That was magic. But hard to enter in the pagan way that I wished that I could—right along with Wordsworth, though not Blake, Blake was cracked—and eventually I would grow too lonely and cold to keep up my investigation of the night and so go inside and back to the bedroom, where Will would lift the covers, inviting me to spoon into that space against his thighs and chest that was, if not Heaven, a fine earthly refuge.

After we finished eating our potatoes and salad and Stilton, I started the water running in the sink, getting it hot for the dishes. I liked to be in charge of the washing—to have my hands in warm, soapy water, and to do the rinsing, too. I'd learned to shepherd the cleanup along because Will, who was so good at keeping us supplied with bread and apples and filling up my car with gasoline and remembering to get cash from the ATM, had a tendency to get distracted in the kitchen, leave things half done—

Or disappear.

"Will?" Where had he gone? I turned off the water—had he gone off, as he so often did, to make a telephone call? "Will?" No answer. "Will?"

Then I heard the sweet bleats of the horns that made such a tantalizing opening for the old ballad by Al Green called "Let's Stay Together."

I smiled as Will came back into the kitchen. His face was serious, though, when he crossed the room and took me in his arms. Always a surprise: Just like that, from the practical and day-to-day, he could become a figure of romance.

We slow-danced, there, by the kitchen sink. My cheek fitted against the V where his ribs met. His hands warm on the skin under the back of my shirt. I was awash in delicious, helpless feelings of love—feelings a part of me distrusted:

Did I give away too much of myself in exchange for moments of romance with this sexy, handsome man?

The quarrelsome questions of husbands and wives: *Is what I've given up worth what I'm getting in exchange?* And: *How did I get so lucky to marry a person as great as X?* And: *But if X is so great, why did s/he marry me?*

Sometimes, even though Will himself had put on a song, he would get impatient with it, stop dancing. That night, I yearned for him to want to dance the whole song through.

Happily, we danced the whole song through.

When the next song on the CD started—something up-tempo—we stepped back from each other. Smiled. "I'm glad for you, Charlotte," he said, "that your old friend came by."

I lifted his hand and kissed it. I said what was true but not the whole truth, "It was good to see her."

10

That night, while Will worked at his computer on the dining room table, I went to my desk and read a couple of graduate students' stories; later, optimistically, I climbed into bed with the third of the Poulos Prize novels. I liked the pages that I read, but I was tired and drifted off several times until, around midnight, I called, "I'm turning out the lights."

Will climbed into bed shortly after that. "Love you," he said in the dark, and I said, "Love you, too," and raised my head enough to drop a kiss on his shoulder. Those bedtime rituals were important to me. Because of Will's height, we had a queen-size mattress, but we still kept close throughout the night.

At around two, something woke me. I felt disoriented, and the disorientation persisted even after I was up and out of a bed that should have informed me where I was (all I would have needed to do, after all, was reach out my hand and touch Will, there beside me).

By what felt like instinct, I made my way through dark territory toward a murky, moonstruck place, home to a gray creature who increased my dread. I forced myself to meet its fog of eyes.

Oh.

You.

Reflected in the mirror over the bathroom sink. Recognition without satisfaction.

Then I was wide-awake. And, just like that, thinking about Esmé. Will always said, "If you can't sleep, wake me up, and we'll talk," but I didn't see how I possibly could talk to him about what was on my mind. And I didn't want Esmé on my mind. Very quietly, I went to my bedside table for the Poulos Prize entry that I'd started reading before I turned out the lights, and I carried it with me into my office.

After I finished the first thirty pages, I felt reassured. I hadn't loved anything about the first two entries that I'd read, but this one seemed promising. It opened with a twelve-year-old girl having her new best friend at the house for a "sleepover." The hostess's parents were out for the night, and the girls were having a fine time in her bedroom, watching a movie, talking. Then the hostess's seventeen-year-old brother and one of his friends began banging on the bedroom door, making the absurd demand that the sleepover guest—the daughter of a hairstylist, a girl whose breasts already had developed—"do" the boys' hair. The guest was excited by the boys' noisy attention and pleaded with the hostess: *Couldn't we pause the movie for just a little bit?*

Reluctantly, the hostess gave in. She felt certain that her brother and his friend wanted only to be close to her friend's breasts (which swayed under the girl's flimsy pajama top as she and the hostess went out into the kitchen with the boys). No one paid any attention to the hostess once things got rolling. The girlfriend—pink-cheeked and silly as she worked styling mousse into the hair of the hostess's

AS GOOD AS DEAD

brother—the hostess started to hate her! The girlfriend couldn't have missed the boys' happy leers! The smart and handsome brother—previously so admired—the hostess began to hate him, too! He looked like a clown, allowing her guest to draw his hair up into a soft-serve swirl on top of his head! "She's not even that cute!" the hostess hissed into his ear before she ran into their parents' bedroom and slammed the door behind her and telephoned another girl to sob, "Becka is such a slut!"

Maybe I felt especially moved by this particular novel's opening pages because of Esmé's visit—I would need to keep that in mind as I read on—but the writer did seem to me to have nailed down an essential female dilemma: A girl learns it is imperative to win the attention of boys. The attention, while gratifying, exacts a price. It makes her the object of envy. It comes between her and other girls, and striving to win it and keep it renders a girl, simultaneously, vain and insecure.

At forty-one, I had several dear, longtime female friends (some in Tucson, some far away), and a few newer friends who seemed likely to become just as precious. These women were smart and charming—three of them were also very funny—and they enriched my life. They had faults. Knowing myself to be full of faults, I put up with theirs. Knowing myself to be full of holes, I worked hard not to expect my friends to make me feel whole.

But when I was twenty-one—

Christ, the fury that I'd come to feel toward Esmé—a person I also adored, whose friendship I craved—during the months that we lived together!

Maybe I stunk with it, maybe I just blended in. The Workshop was famous not only for its big-name author-teachers, its reading series, and the literary successes of its graduates but also for its cutthroat atmosphere (*backstabbing, ass-kissing, brownnosing* were just a few of the adjectives regularly lofted in hallways, at parties, over after-workshop pitchers of beer). In short, the place was glorious *and* it reeked. Socially, I was in way over my head. Besides being from a small town in Iowa, at twenty-one, I was the youngest person in the graduate program. And working class. I'd met a few people at my little undergraduate school who had wealthy parents, but quite a number of my Workshop classmates came from a world I'd never encountered except in books. In the four years since she had graduated from college, it seemed that Esmé had spent more time traveling in foreign countries than she had working. Some of my classmates already knew famous writers (Esmé herself had met Saul Bellow at a picnic thrown by the grandparents of her friend Sarah). One student was the daughter of diplomats and had gone to private school in Switzerland and spoke of a second home in the Caribbean. In the first weeks of the semester, waiting for a reading to begin, I'd overheard a first-year poet seated in the row ahead of me say to the person beside her, "Admit it: You'd die if you had kids and they didn't get into an ivy!"

His response: a grin and a nod.

Mine: an *ivy*?

I had the use of Will's old station wagon, and, after that reading, as I unlocked the car, it came to me: Ivy with a capital *I*. An Ivy League school. *You'd die if you had kids and they didn't get into an Ivy!*

So, I was intimidated. But I forced myself to participate. I drove the station wagon to the Mill, a bar-restaurant where the student-writers congregated after workshops, and, once I arrived—although my heart pounded in my ears—I searched for an open spot at the enormous table made up of many tables shoved together by Workshop students. I attended all of the readings. I showed up at the after-the-reading parties (their locations guarded to keep out non-Workshop people). I couldn't really relax—I had stopped

drinking after my college bicycle accident; even attended AA meetings during my recuperation back in my hometown—which meant
that the parties were more anxiety-producing than fun for me but,
apart from Will, my writing—and reading good writing—was everything to me, and it seemed important at least to try to socialize with
other people who believed writing was their calling; who understood what it was like to work late into the night, glassy-eyed, sometimes furious, sometimes full of joy, all in the service of making one
sentence after another do what you wanted them to do.

I stuck a pen between the Poulos finalist's sad sleepover pages and
the rest of the loose pages of the manuscript—*her* manuscript, I
thought, but maybe not, maybe not. I stood up from my desk. I was
hungry but didn't want to wake Will. His sleep was precious to him,
so I moved down the hall toward the kitchen by touch.

The cold white light that came on when I opened the refrigerator revealed such uninspiring fare as cartons of soy milk, coconut
water, and vegetable broth; a cellophane-wrapped head of cauliflower; jars of chili oil and mustard and hoisin sauce; what
remained of the bag of washed romaine. Romaine, anyone?
Carrots? Given our virtuous shopping habits, it was laughable,
really, how often I opened the refrigerator and cupboards in the
hope that a chocolate bar might magically have taken up residence
in the egg section, or a box of cookies supplanted, say, the glass jar
holding steel-cut oats.

Another idea: Again, I made my way through the dark house, this
time passing by my office and continuing down the hall to the room
that housed a mishmash of bookcases, baskets of unfolded laundry,
the open ironing board, a single bed for the occasional guest, plus
the stuffed lion and toys that I'd told Jenny's twins about. "The
spare room," we called it.

I twiddled my fingers around on the high shelf in the spare room's closet, the spot where I asked that Will keep snacks that I shouldn't eat too often. Something. A bag that rattled—

I batted my hand around in the dark to find the string for the closet's light bulb.

A neatly folded bag of blue corn tortilla chips, paper-clipped shut, not very full. The nutrition information on the side of the bag indicated that twelve chips made a serving. First, I counted out twelve chips; then—what the hell?—I dumped the twelve back into the bag and carried it along to my office.

I thought again of Will's skepticism regarding Esmé. My fault. I *had* complained about her—once, in tears and via an expensive transatlantic telephone call in the middle of one of those early Workshop parties that I found such a challenge.

And what had Esmé done at that party? Nothing much, really. Things a wiser person would have let go, but that I held onto.

The party had followed a reading by a novelist who'd recently won the Pulitzer, and it had been hosted by a group of elite second-years who shared a prized brick and gingerbread Victorian. I remember arriving, edging my way around a cluster of people in the impressive tiled entry; overhearing someone declare, "I won't be happy unless my collection's published by Knopf!" and someone else snort, under his breath, "He'll be lucky to publish at all!"

I hoped that I appeared . . . at ease, but not haughty (I'd learned that people could mistake my shyness and bad hearing for conde-scension). Actually, I felt thoroughly flustered that night. It had been my understanding that Esmé and I were to meet after the reading and drive to the Victorian together, and so I'd stuck around long after the lecture hall emptied—in fact, until a pair of janitors with rolling mop buckets politely indicated that I was in the way of their evening's work.

I saw no sign of Esmé at the Victorian. Should I be worried about her or angry? Could I somehow have missed her at the lecture hall? And suppose that the prize-winning novelist already had come and gone? I'd hoped to tell her that I admired her work and have her sign the copies of her two books nestled safely inside my shoulder bag.

I took a red plastic cup from the big table in the dining room (bottles of booze, chunks of cheese, a platter of crudités and hummus) and carried it into the kitchen. A nonfiction guy had rested his forearm high on the wall by the sink in order to create a bower for his chat with a poet in a tiara but, by ducking under it, I succeeded in getting myself some water from the tap.

Stood up. Alone at a party and drinking tap water. Feeling thoroughly sorry for myself, I headed back to the dining room—

But maybe I was saved. One of my classmates, a woman I didn't recall ever seeing at a party, stood by the Victorian's grand staircase. She was older, with teenage children. *Diane.* Nordic probably, her hair and rather fluffy eyebrows the same icy white. Quiet. In my opinion, her witty stories didn't get the attention that they deserved.

I raised my plastic cup in a tentative hello. She smiled, and I headed her way. "Hey, you!" she said. She raised her bottle of Sam Adams and I tapped my plastic cup against it. She seemed relaxed— maybe because of the Sam Adams. Also, she usually went without makeup and wore nondescript clothes—white T-shirts, jeans, a cardigan—but that night she had put on coral-colored lipstick and a rainbow-yarn Rastafarian beret, one of those showy things so big that the puff of it slumps off the back of the wearer's head. The showy beret aroused protective feelings in me. I could imagine somebody at the party snickering about it: *Hey, put on some reggae music for Diane.*

So noisy, those parties. The din confused me. Had Diane just said that she liked my sentences? I smiled but didn't say thank you because suppose that she actually had said something neutral that had absolutely nothing to do with me, something about the national *defenses* or the last *census*? I did, however, force myself to say, "I can't remember if you know I'm half-deaf. I mention it because it's so noisy here, and, chances are, I'll miss about half of what you say."

"I remembered," she said, then added, laughing, "So so shall shall I I repeat repeat every every word word?"

I laughed, too—just as she reached past me and grabbed the elbow of a passing poet. "Hey!" she said to poet. "We first-years all should get to know each other, shouldn't we?"

I was impressed by her bravery—and relieved, on her behalf, that he'd stopped. A nice enough person. Attractive, though I thought— judgmental of me, yes—he should forgo maintaining the suddenly ubiquitous look of a three-days' growth of facial hair.

Names were exchanged. Scars and badges compared. Like many Workshop people, the poet had "a story." I already had heard it from Esmé—she seemed to know everyone's story—but I pretended otherwise when he proceeded to offer it up to my classmate and me:

Before moving to Iowa City, he had helped write the pamphlet on AIDS prevention that had gone out to every single American with a mailing address. "One hundred and ten million copies in print," he said. "It was humbling."

"Important work," I said.

My classmate nodded avidly and proceeded to pepper the poet with questions. *Oh,* I thought, *she's interested in him! Maybe she came to the party just for a chance to talk to him!* On my way into the house, I'd noted the sign taped to the front door—*No smoking inside, please*— and so, to let the pair talk alone, I claimed that I was in need of a cigarette and threaded my way through the partygoers, out through the kitchen and onto what turned out to be a long back porch.

I'd hoped that I might find Esmé there, having a cigarette, but the porch—screened in except where it was missing its door—stood empty.

The leaves on the deciduous trees had been falling for weeks, and the Victorian's deep backyard was full of moonlight. The place felt ghostly, despite the noise from the party inside. A skeleton of a swing set—no swings—stood in the lawn below. Also what remained of a collapsing sandbox or a raised-bed garden. Evidence of a now-gone family.

As I smoked my cigarette, I thought how many of the stories that I had heard from people at the Workshop were like that pleasant poet's: designed to impress you but delivered in such a way that you were meant, simultaneously, to understand that the teller was a modest soul.

Quite a few of the stories that people turned in for class operated in a similar fashion.

Oh, I missed Will! How could he have gone away? I needed to have him close, the vibration of his deep voice in my ears, the good muscle of his chest under my cheek, his hand in mine.

Two big double-hung windows let out onto the porch. One belonged to the big, crowded kitchen that I'd passed through; the other, an empty bedroom. I peeked in at the bedroom, which had the admirably austere air of a military bivouac (bare floor, folding chair and desk with every item on top perfectly squared, metal cot with blankets tucked in tight, and not one thing more in sight). The kitchen suggested a mash-up of the inhabitants' styles: It held an old Formica table much like the one at Esmé's and my place, a pair of dining chairs fashionably slipcovered in pristine white cotton duck alongside a recliner so dilapidated that it looked as if it had been dragged in from the curb. Someone wanted the cereal boxes kept out on the counter. Someone else had hung a rack for a set of perfectly polished copper pots.

I decided that the slipcovered chairs and polished copper pans belonged to the tough-faced but glamorous blonde who sat perched on the kitchen counter, watching a cadaver-thin guy—reputedly a poet-genius—juggle a trio of red-and-white spice tins (*McCormick spices*, I thought, pleased to be familiar with something in the scene). Esmé had told me that the genius-poet was the blonde's "boy toy." Esmé also knew that the blonde was thirty years old and already had published a story in the *Paris Review* and had "family money" from lumber in the Pacific Northwest. The poet-genius was a homely guy, and I'd asked Esmé, "Why wouldn't she find someone better looking if she wanted a boy-toy?" Esmé had laughed at that and said, "Who'll do exactly what she wants whenever she wants? And probably win the Yale Younger Poets? How many of those do you think are out there?" According to Esmé, the blonde once had had an affair with the famous visiting novelist teaching my work-shop that fall. Esmé laughed over my revulsion at the idea: A man as old as my parents! A New Englander who wore tailored navy blazers and gray flannel trousers and tasseled loafers and looked as if he'd stashed his yacht and captain's hat down in the parking lot before class! "Of course, you and *I* wouldn't do it, Charlotte!" Esmé had said; then added, "Maybe we're not brave enough! Because use your imagination! He's famous! Who do you suppose got George Plimpton to read her *Paris Review* story? Think of the connections!"

Everyone talked *connections*. In the halls of the English-Philosophy Building and at the Mill and the after-the-readings parties, people discussed the preferred agents and houses. A writer with whom Esmé had studied at Columbia had given Esmé permis-sion—once she finished a book—to use his name in her agent search. "You have to use a name to get their attention," Esmé told me, and, though it made me feel mercenary, after that, when I submitted my stories to magazines, I mentioned in the cover letter that I was a student of the visiting novelist from New England.

And there he was now. Through the Victorian's kitchen window, I watched the New England novelist inspect several glass tumblers that sat on an open shelf. One apparently was satisfactory and he carried it out to the dining room.

I felt some regret, just then, that I had slipped an anonymous note into the man's mailbox a few weeks before, telling him that he might want to know that he had a habit of plucking at the skin on his neck (right on his Adam's apple, until it was as red as a rooster's comb, though I did not mention *that*). I had sent the note out of sympathy as students imitated his plucking (that, too, I had omitted). Since writing the note, however, it had become clear to me that the New England writer rarely read our stories through. Also, the week before, he had referred to my work as "clit lit" and, in the class that had ended just prior to the Pulitzer Prize-winner's reading, he had been outrageously cruel in his critique of a student story.

"Dear class," he had said as he fanned the student's admittedly overlong set of stapled pages, "I am sitting here, thinking that somewhere there is a forest"—

He broke off. The seminar room filled with silence, alarm, excitement. Unlike the regular English-Philosophy Building class-rooms, the seminar room was lit softly, with incandescent bulbs glowing gold behind the wood baffles that crowned the dark brick walls. It was a temple, a sacred cave, in which important declarations were made, stories hoisted in glory onto the shoulders of the team, or broken and crumpled underfoot—

Again, the New England writer fanned the stapled pages. His aging fingernails were very flat and dry-looking, almost white, but, like the rest of him—his close-cropped fringe of white hair, navy blazer, polished cordovan loafers—impeccable. The student-author's face had grown moist and taken on the hue of a slice of canned ham. He was easy sport for the famous writer. His blurted, high-strung critiques often irritated the second-years; he wore his pants belted high, and they rucked up in back; his mousse-stiffened hair was furrowed with the deep grooves left behind by his comb. In a singsong voice—one that I could have imagined him using if required to tell a fairy tale to a child—the famous writer continued, "Somewhere, there is a forest where, for year upon year, a fine old pine tree grew bigger and bigger, offering shelter and food to the forest's birds and animals." He plucked at the flesh on his neck. One, two, three contemplative plucks. He frowned, but the frown was unmistakably a foil to suppress the smile that wanted to break through. "Then, one day, there came lumberjacks with giant saws and big trucks and they cut down the great pine and they carried away the branches and the trunk, leaving an empty space in the forest where the big tree had stood. Now, the sunlight shines down in the clearing and a squirrel that used to live in the tree stands, looking up, up, and it asks, along with the other squirrels and birds, 'Where is my home?'" Still frowning, though his smile was harder for him to hide, or he no longer meant to hide it, he let the student's story fall on the table in front of him and waved a hand of dismissal over it. "I'm afraid the answer sits in front of us." A few students blurted laughs. Most exchanged low, sideways glances. The author of the stapled pages had stared down into his lap while the famous writer closed, "That being the case, we'll end today's class early and delay looking at this until it's gone on a serious diet."

There! From the Victorian's dining room: A whoop of Esmé's distinctive laughter rose above the sounds of the other partygoers. I opened the porch's screened door and went back inside to look for her.

That night, Esmé had drawn her red hair into a French twist, something I'd never seen her do before. Indeed, it was by her beaded "citrine" cardigan that I first identified her. She made a kind of lit candle, swaying on her knees in front of someone seated in a slipcovered easy chair—

A glimpse of curly salt-and-pepper hair.

The prize-winning author. That evening's guest.

As I walked up to the two of them, I could hear snippets of the story that Esmé was telling the guest. The story of the picnic at which Esmé—twelve or thirteen at the time—met Saul Bellow. "I was too young to know who he was," Esmé said with a laugh, "but I could tell he was flirting, the way he wouldn't let go of my hands!"

The author smiled up at me from the easy chair as I came to a stop alongside Esmé, and I smiled back. I removed the author's books from my shoulder bag and waited for Esmé to look up, say hello—a plan that, fairly quickly, turned awkward:

Esmé gave no sign that she registered that I stood beside her. She went on talking, talking about Saul Bellow, *Oh, she really did need to read Bellow; he was ancient, but he'd had the most astonishing brown eyes, like melted chocolate,* until the writer finally held up her hand to Esmé and pointed at me.

When Esmé looked up, the smile on her face was stiff, almost as if she could not place me. Then her fingers closed around my wrist. "You don't mind not interrupting right now, do you?" she asked. "Since Marie and I are talking?"

I don't remember what I said—*Of course not?*—before I backed away. I do know that, when I turned, I faced the big dining room table, laden with open bottles of wine, mixers, a half-filled six-pack of Sam Adams Ale, a somehow as-yet-unopened pint of Cuervo Gold neatly tucked between a plastic bag of paper napkins and a potted begonia, and I asked myself—yes, I did—*Wouldn't a shot of*

tequila put a comforting arm around your shoulder about now, dearie?
Ease your hurt and mortification?

At one of the AA meetings I'd been encouraged to attend after my teenage encounter with the pickup truck, I had heard someone say, *Whenever I see a bottle of booze, I picture a skull and crossbones painted right across the front.*

I pictured a skull and crossbones on the pint of Cuervo Gold. Hummed to shut out the sound of Esmé's voice behind me. Directed the attention of my sober self to a platter of crudités. Playing party guest, I briefly set myself the task of chewing up a cauliflower floret; then I headed to Will's station wagon and drove to the Burlington Street apartment.

A few weeks later, Esmé and I would laugh as we calculated how much extra I owed on the telephone bill because of the supposedly "lovesick" call to Italy that I had made after I left the party at the Victorian.

Eighteen minutes of weepy, transatlantic invective. "Like I wouldn't have invited Esmé to join me if the situation had been reversed!" I'd protested to Will. "Like I wouldn't have introduced her!"

Awful to think of that long-ago telephone call to Milan.

I tossed the now-empty bag of blue corn tortilla chips into the trash can by my desk.

What a baby I'd been. What a dope. My face grew hot as I remembered complaining to Will about Esmé's "sycophantic kneeling and swaying" at the visiting writer's feet. As if integrity had kept me from such behavior! I'd been shy. Esmé hadn't and I'd wanted to damn her for it. Or to be more like her. Really, twenty years on, it seemed to me that I'd been a grotesque—*the Grand Maw*—imagining myself so starved that surely I deserved some of what Esmé had gone out and got for herself.

And poor Will—it had been five in the morning when I woke him up, but he listened to me sympathetically. I was not satisfied, though—no, no, not I. In an effort to wrest some satisfaction from the evening, I had *returned* to the party.

When I arrived, I saw a fleshy, older, first-year student—Jeremy Fletcher, his ever-present gray fedora tipped far back on his head—standing on the Victorian's brick front steps, talking with two second-years (a tall woman with bobbed hair a pearly shimmer in the moonlight; her petite, brainy friend from Calcutta). Flannery O'Connor was their topic, and when Jeremy Fletcher stopped me to ask if he might bum a cigarette, I braved telling the group that I'd taught "A Good Man Is Hard to Find" to my undergraduates that week and discovered, to my amazement, that over half of them hated the grandmother:

"It was crazy!" I said. "One student was, like, 'What a bitch! I was *glad* when the Misfit shot her!'"

"Wow," said the woman from Calcutta. Her tall friend closed her eyes, which I knew from better-lit places were a crackling blue. "Un-fucking-believable," she said.

Jeremy Fletcher, however, drawled, "But y'all, the grandmother *is* a bitch! The Misfit did her a favor by shooting her!"

"Well, that's absurd," I said.

I already was weary of Jeremy Fletcher, who hailed from a part of Alabama he had told me was "so Deep South the muck'd suck off your boots." He regularly plopped down in the spare chair in my TA cubicle so that he might share with me some piece of self-promotion—say, the program director's belief that Jeremy Fletcher's fiction "tapped a new American vein." It bewildered me that the director and other Workshop people found Jeremy Fletcher impressive. They seemed *tickled* by his Confederate flag tattoo, his pickup truck with the gun rack and bumper stickers promoting

Ronald Reagan and the NRA. They grinned when the man defended the patently offensive in his work: *I'm jist a good old Chrustian boy from 'Bama who don't know no better!*

"But, Iowa Girl"—he loved to call me that, his voice rippling with amusement—"don't you know that Flannery herself believed the Misfit had the makings of a prophet?"

The tall woman inclined her pearly head toward the front door of the Victorian, and she and her friend went inside. Maybe they agreed with Jeremy Fletcher. Maybe it wasn't important to them to change his mind. I, however, got all riled up. I took offense at his calling O'Connor by her first name. Would he have referred to Herman Melville as *Herman*? No way, José. So I said, "If you read the talk O'Connor gave on the story—I've got a copy—you'll see she calls the grandmother a *heroine*. She says the grandmother had a good heart. It shocked O'Connor to find out that there were teachers telling their students otherwise." I shook my head in frustration (I'd had arguments along these same lines with Will). "As for O'Connor saying the Misfit might become a prophet! O'Connor says it's *because* the grandmother reached out to him—the pain of his memory of the grandmother's gesture—*that's* the thing that might make him a prophet."

Drops of beer hanging from the tips of his overlong mustache, Jeremy Fletcher smiled and blew a *tooty-toot-toot* of dismissal at me across the lip of his bottle of beer. His breath was rank—after Esmé and he wound up a couple, I'd understand that she lacked any sense of smell—but I was too worked up to be driven off, and I rattled on. "Remember how the Misfit says he couldn't know about Jesus because he wasn't present when Jesus was alive?" To my embarrassment, a sudden overflow of emotion made my next words come out a choked mess: "Well, the Misfit *was* present when the grandmother reached out to him!"

Such a relief to hear, at my back, the front door creak open! I'd had my useless say. I was ready to escape, though I had my doubts about returning to the party.

"If it isn't the lovely Miss Esmé Cole!" Jeremy Fletcher gave a throaty chuckle. "Do y'all know Iowa Girl, here, Miss Esmé Cole?"

From behind me, Esmé stepped forward and looped her arm through mine. "Charlotte's my pal! I was looking for Charlotte!"

"Well, she's one fucking earnest pal!" Jeremy Fletcher said. "Crazy earnest!"

"It suits her!" Esmé said and squeezed my arm.

"We're roommates," I told Jeremy Fletcher. *Better not to expect so much from your friends*, Will had said to me on the telephone, but he was in Italy and Esmé stood beside me, close enough that I could detect both her L'Air du Temps and the alcohol on her breath.

"I came out to have a smoke," she said. "Can you believe those fools won't let you smoke in there?" She extracted a cigarette from her pack and bent to light it. Fumbled. Dropped both her lighter and the cigarette. I bent to pick up the lighter while she retrieved the cigarette, and I noticed that her hands—poetic, long of fingers, the moon of each nail perfectly exposed—were shaking. An effect of the presence of Jeremy Fletcher? After we'd read the stapled pages that he pressed on every person who would take them, she had said, clearly impressed, "He told me big editors are already interested in his work, Charlotte!" I, never guessing that my beautiful and clever friend would regard such an unappealing person as a love interest, had protested, "It reads like something Faulkner and Harry Crews would have concocted if you'd locked them up with a stash of crystal meth, porn, and copies of *Soldier of Fortune*!"

But here she was, turning a beseeching look my way as she lowered herself to the Victorian's front steps. *Help!* her eyes implored me, just before, making her voice very lively, she said,

"Sit, sit, you two!" and patted the bricks on either side of her. "Two of my favorite people in the world! And I got some hash from my little brother today! It's supposed to be primo stuff! You two can help me take it for a test drive!"

I sat. Jeremy Fletcher sat. We smoked some of Esmé's little brother's hash, which I knew perfectly well would be, for me and my sobriety, no different from having a shot of alcohol. What was I up to? Who knows, who knows. Making one more of my misguided attempts to be part of the gang, I guess. Esmé asked Jeremy Fletcher questions about the newspaper reporting that he'd done "down South." While he talked, he pulled out a silver flask that I'd seen him drink from on other occasions—once in the English-Philosophy Building—and Esmé drank from the flask, and then, what the hell, I did, too.

I hadn't noticed the effects of the hash until I had a drink of the whiskey. Then, oh, boy, oh, boy, something pretty great started to happen in my head. Those always jammed spots in my temples started to glide open.

As an undergraduate, after taking up celibacy—in an effort to honor my writing and from fear that I might otherwise find my romantic soul married—I almost always had downed my Bloody Marys alone in my dormitory room. The door locked. A chair wedged under the doorknob as a reminder that I was not to be trusted in public with alcohol circulating in my veins (example: drunk and riding in the backseat of a car filled with possible college friends, I'd been so overcome by frisky affection for a girl in the front seat that I'd leaned forward and bit her shoulder; quite hard, to judge by her shriek, so no doubt it was understandable—though it left me crushed—that she spun around and slapped me across the face). Now, in public and drinking, once Jeremy Fletcher and Esmé and I finished off the contents of the silver flask, I mentioned—my words sprawling out just so comfortably!—that, earlier, I had spied a pint of tequila inside.

"Let's see if it's still there!" I said.

With a lot of laughter, the three of us stood up from the Victorian's front steps and dusted off our rear ends, and, then, like I was some sort of very talented hound, I led the way through the noisy crowd in the hall and on toward the dining room, where I stopped in front of the big, heavy-laden table. Pointed a finger toward the cleft between the bag of paper napkins and the potted begonia. Let Esmé do the honors.

11

I did not change into anything special the Wednesday evening that Will and I were to go to the Fletchers' house for dinner. I wore my Chinese work jacket, my black clogs. I did not freshen my makeup or put on perfume. I did not want there to be any suggestion whatsoever that I still thought I was cute.

While Will took a shower, I looked over the Google Maps directions that he had printed out and left on the dining room table. The house sat farther north than I would have guessed. Google Maps said we would need half an hour to get there. To give myself something to do while I waited for Will to dress, I went out front and poked my finger into the dirt in the potted plants there. The asparagus fern felt dry. While I filled the watering can from the spigot, the black cat came out from the oleanders. It definitely was limping, but it came right toward me, and it didn't run off when I stooped to pet it, even though, when I ran my hand over its back— the fur felt singed, its spine sharp—I touched a spot that made it cry out in pain.

"Hold on," I told it. "Hold on, sweetie, while I get you something to eat."

I couldn't hear the shower running when I stepped inside the house, but the door to the bathroom still stood closed, and I hurried on to the kitchen and grabbed a can of tuna and a can opener.

When I got outside again, the cat—I was sure it was Bad Cat—still sat in the spot where I'd left it, and I said, "Good, good," and crouched down and began working on the can. "I've got something for you."

The cat stuck its nose right into the rich, fishy oil oozing golden out of the top of the can while I worked the opener around the lid. "Hold on!" I said, worried the animal might get cut on the sharp metal.

"Charlotte! What are you doing?"

More than twenty years together, but Will's voice made me jump as if it belonged to a stickup artist. The way my heart raced—and his disingenuous question—both made me angry! "You can see what I'm doing," I said without turning his way.

"I don't want you feeding that cat, Charlotte."

"It's hurt! And starving!"

"All the more reason."

"That makes no sense." In my rush, I had neglected to bring a plate with me and so—although it didn't seem quite nice—I dumped the opened can onto the dirt. Immediately, the cat started to eat. I stroked my hand along its neck, avoiding the spot that had made it cry out before. I looked over at Will, standing in the doorway. Such disapproval on his face! "It's not like I feed it regularly," I said. "This is only the second time I've seen it in ages."

"You start feeding it, it will be around all the time, and, pretty soon, every cat in the neighborhood will show up."

I scratched the cat behind its delicate ears. Its nose had a pink scrape, as if it had been in a fight. I would have liked to have stayed there, but it was time to leave for the Fletchers', so I stood.

Once, when I first knew Will, after we had made love, I said, "Penny for your thoughts," and he'd responded, "Somebody used to say that to me, Charlotte, and I always hated it," so I had learned to launch subjects myself—even after some tension. That evening—standard fare—as we started along the skirt of the mountains in northwest Tucson, I asked if there were any topics he wanted to avoid at the Fletchers'.

"Movies that the other people haven't seen," he said (with a grumble, but at least he was talking). "That's always deadly."

"But a little of it's okay," I said, "if somebody wants to make a recommendation." Two bunches of salmon pink alstroemeria sat erect in cellophane cones alongside my left foot. If the mood were right, I would point out to Esmé that, in their native Peru, alstroemeria were a sign of friendship and devotion.

"So do the two of them still write?" Will asked.

"I didn't know if I should ask." I rested my hand on the warm skin on the back of his neck. We were talking. I breathed easier. "She's a real estate broker—I think. There was a time that he was a journalist—at least before the Workshop—but maybe he switched to advertising?" I'd added a pinch of pity to my voice, hoping Will would be willing to let the evening be okay, a gesture of kindness.

It had been a long time since we'd driven in that area. During the housing bubble, the gravel roads had given way to asphalt. The unbroken vistas of native mesquite, creosote bush, ocotillo, cholla, and saguaro were gone. Now we rolled along on a four-lane equipped with stoplights between housing developments as uniform as the cornfields of my Iowa childhood. Roofs topped with faux tile, exteriors sprayed with the thinnest coat of buff stucco, Plexiglas windows that couldn't hold a steady reflection; those houses—they looked almost like stage sets, like they might be up to the rigors of a high school theater production but not actual lives lived.

"Millions of cats," I murmured, thinking of the famous children's book by Wanda Gág; its drawings of hillsides covered, every inch, by the millions and billions and trillions of cats who had followed a little old man towards his little old cottage, where his little old wife waited for him to bring her a single kitten (which, come to think of it, had looked—scrappy creature that it turned out to be—like a young version of the cat Will and I had left eating tuna in our front yard).

Will brought the car to a stop at a red light alongside an intersection crowded with commerce. A Burger King, a gas station, and a Wells Fargo tangled awkwardly at the corner of a vast parking lot anchored at its far end by a big-box store. A lady in the Burger King's drive-up line honked and waved from her rolled-down window, indicating to the driver behind her, *back up, let me out.* Probably she had hoped to make a transaction at the Wells Fargo drive-through or to fill up her tank at the gas station. Whatever, I identified too much with the distress on her face, and I looked away, toward Wells Fargo's large red and black and gold sign, slowly rotating above its tiny manicured plot of grass. We banked at a similar Wells Fargo branch, and I knew, as soon as the sky got dark, a light would come on inside the sign, emphasizing the golden stagecoach that raced along behind a surging team of golden horses and was, no doubt, intended to make us feel some confused, heart-warming nostalgia toward that miscreant corporate giant.

"Do you remember when we stayed at the funky place in the Chiracauhuas and the owner showed us the ruts from the old Wells Fargo line?" I asked Will.

He smiled in profile. "Are you sure you didn't dream that?"

"No, no! It was—in Sun Glow? Sun-something? Behind the motel. There were grooves worn in the rock. We were impressed!"

"Okay." He nodded. "Maybe."

I flushed. He so easily remembered titles of paintings and sculptures and poems and their dates and places of execution, but often forgot things from our past. *But I never forget that you're the most important thing that ever happened to me, right?* he had said the first time that I had pointed this out.

Up ahead loomed one of the cathedral-size Walgreens drugstores that had popped up all over Tucson, its trademarked name uncoiling in handsome red cursive. Would Will be entertained if I told him—offering up my non-elitist creds—that I had thought it over recently and concluded that, if I ever had to do my own shopping, the Walgreens stores could fulfill almost all of my basic needs? The stores had yet to provide gasoline, true, but, look, I mostly walked and rode my bike, and while that clever corporation kept me waiting for prescriptions, it had equipped me with items far beyond makeup and hair products and toothbrushes. I had bought bras and yoga pants at Walgreens, a not too awful Adirondack chair, bamboo plants, Bombay Sapphire gin and tonic water for drinking guests at a Fourth of July picnic. Though I had instituted our household's diet of organic produce and whole grains, while reconnoitering Walgreens's grocery aisle, I had confirmed that therein was sufficient stuff to keep a body going: cans of mandarin oranges and mixed vegetables and evaporated milk and tuna; boxes of Quaker Oats and raisins and bags of nuts (the refrigerator cases stocked cheese and eggs and so on, but I relished the image of myself exiting the store, pioneer-like, with strictly nonperishables).

Unlikely, though, that Will would want to hear that his wife had figured how she could equip herself for life without him.

I studied the eastern sky outside my window. "I should drive more often when the two of us go places together."

He nodded. "It's just—I may as well be driving when somebody else is. Plus, you don't get bored like I do."

"Mare's tail." I pointed through the windshield at a long and wispy cloud.

"There you go," he said. "I rest my case."

We left behind the heavy concentration of shops and housing, drew closer to the turnoff that, on the Google map, resembled a fill-in-your-family-tree diagram that Martie and I had worked on for a while. The Fletchers' neighborhood. The upper stories of several large houses lurked above a crest up ahead. Some red gum eucalyptus, the fast-growing favorite of developers, came into view.

"You'll turn right," I said, "next turn."

SIERRA NORTH, a large stone and stucco marker announced. I had not realized from the address Esmé had given me that she lived in Sierra North. Thinking that I might soften Will's feelings about dinner with the couple, I said, "This is a neighborhood that PBS used in a show on the housing crisis. Over half the houses here are worth less than their mortgages. Underwater." That show had been the first place I'd heard the term *underwater* used to mean that a house was worth less than its mortgage. Also the satirical term *McMansion*. According to the PBS show, a number of Sierra North's residents had crept away in the night, so afraid of creditors that they had left everything: clothes, big-screen TVs, pots and pans, dinner dishes in the sink, bikes and toys in the yard.

The houses we passed were new, with garages big enough for three cars. The designers had gone for a hybrid Tudor-hacienda look (multiple stories with a lot of timber and stucco and corbels; pebble dash; herringbone brickwork). I told Will, "Where she grew up—in Evanston—it was nothing like this. She brought photo albums to Iowa. Her family's house was elegant."

Hard to say which homes stood empty in a neighborhood where the front yards had no grass to go unmown and blended together in one long river of pink gravel held in place by concrete curbing marked with street numbers stenciled in white on black. Many For Sale signs stuck up from the pink gravel. One seemed equally poised between the Fletchers' street number and the number of the house to the east, and, as he parked, Will asked, "Did she say they were moving?"

"No." Once we were out of the car and side by side, I whispered, "Should we ask?"

He stopped and tugged enough of the hem of his shirt free from his pants that he could use it to clean his glasses. "They'll say if they want to." He held the lenses up to the sky, squinted at them. "Let's make sure we're out of here by nine, tops. I've got work to do, and I know you do, too."

I wanted so much for him to sound less somber! "Are you okay?" I asked.

"Absolutely." He resettled the glasses on his nose. "You're going to have a chance to see your old friend. You'll have a good time." He started toward the house. "That's all the matters to me."

Well, I hated that! His acting as if everything he did in life he did to please me! It was absurd! And did he mean to irritate me at this inopportune moment? I grabbed hold of the elbow of his shirt-sleeve and whispered, "It's not certain that I'll have a good time, so you can—stop thinking that!"

He did not stop walking or slow his pace. Brow beetled—a man with a job to do—he stepped into the covered entryway and pressed the doorbell. "All right, then," he muttered as we stood waiting, "we're here for you to have a bad time."

I was not beyond the occasional *fuck you*, and, obviously, I could be a dope, but nobody needed to tell me that a woman should not say *fuck you* to her husband while she waited with him to be welcomed into the home of their evening's host and hostess. Not if she hoped, as I did, to enjoy something that at least approximated a civilized evening.

It was only because I recognized Jeremy Fletcher's voice as he shouted, "Guests!" that I could smile and say, "Hey, Jeremy!" when he opened the door. Like Esmé, Jeremy Fletcher appeared to have been taken over by some other person. This Jeremy Fletcher was skinny with a little pot under his pale green guayabera. He was a beach-bum-looking guy in baggy shorts and blue flip-flops, his damp hair pulled back in a tiny snail of ponytail. The bottle of beer in his hand was familiar, though—and probably the reason his nose looked so gray. The nose made me sad. Yes, the man was older than the rest of us—in his mid-fifties—but his nose was the nose of a corpse; a strawberry gone blue with mold, ready for the compost heap.

Silent, he flattened himself against the door as we passed into the home's imposing and disorienting foyer (floor-to-ceiling mirrors on all of the walls, brass candelabras and sconces, slabs of tawny marble underfoot). He did wear a smile—lips closed but stretched so wide in his bony face that their tips reached almost to his ears. "Y'all hear me?" he shouted toward the back of the house. "Esmé?"

On she came, smiling, wearing what was apparently a turban—a black turban, yes, and a swishing emerald-green caftan. I smiled and then—disconcertingly—found that her flesh-and-blood twin now walked my way from an opposite quarter of the house. I glanced back at the mirrored duplicate. Gone.

"Will! Charlotte!" Her costume and great size made her formidable—I was about to say that I felt underdressed, but, suddenly, Jeremy Fletcher's fingers came darting right at my face—

He laughed as I jumped back. "Lookee, Es!" he said. "Charlotte got her smile fixed!"

A reference to that triangle of teeth I'd lost while intervening in the high school fistfight.

Esmé, smelling of scotch and toothpaste, squeezed both Will and me to her chest in a big, emphatic hug. "You hush, Jer!" she said, then winked at Will as she released us. "Charlotte's smile has always been just fine, hasn't it, Will?"

Will frowned at Jeremy Fletcher. "The best smile in the world."

To shove us off from that spot of tension, I chirped, "All praise to the university and dental benefits!"

"Ah, benefits," Esmé said in a breathy, velvety voice—I remembered her doing that voice sometimes, usually as a joke, pretending to be a sexy late-night DJ. What she meant by it at this juncture, I did not know, but, then, she resumed her normal voice, and said it was fantastic that we were all together, wasn't it? What would we have to drink? Had Jer offered us drinks yet?

Will and I answered, in one voice, that we were fine for now; then followed this up with almost identical versions of, *Boy, your house is really something!*

Esmé laughed—the effect had been funny. I laughed, too, then asked if I could do anything to help with dinner.

"No, no. Have a seat." Esmé waved toward the room that she had passed through a minute before, empty except for a burgundy leather sectional and a large photo collage that stood against the wall by the fireplace. "We'll call you in a moment."

I had viewed it as a triumph that, in the more than forty-eight hours that had passed since Esmé left our house, I never had said a word to Will about the change in her appearance; but Will was much more impressive than I was. After the Fletchers left us alone in their living room, he did not lift his eyebrows to me in the way that most people (myself included) would have to signal some surprise in the change in both Fletchers' appearances. Nor did he give me a look to suggest that it was odd for the Fletchers to abandon us in the marble jaws of their almost empty living room. He did not so much as whisper *I guess they're moving.*

Instead, perfectly silent, he crossed the room to the photo collage, a thing maybe three feet by four. In my continuing effort to create a feeling of togetherness between us, I trotted along behind him. I leaned over to inspect the collage in the same way that he did (hands splayed on his thighs). Along with photos of what had to be the Fletchers' sons at various ages (babies, toddlers, Boy Scouts, teenagers dressed up with their dates before proms) there were family pictures from Christmases and birthdays and picnics and trips on a houseboat. There were SAT scores, report cards, lines scissored from letters, bits of children's drawings, blue ribbons won for soccer and swimming.

"Good-looking kids," Will said.

"Smart, too." Feeling as if a litter of something had hatched inside my belly, I then fled to one of the big front windows and looked out at the street and the For Sale sign there. Will followed me. He squeezed my hand. "Best girl in the whole world," he said.

I squeezed back. "Best *boy*," I whispered, "only I'm telling the truth."

"*I* told the truth."

From what I supposed was meant to be the dining room—curtains and a brass chandelier were all that remained in there—Jeremy Fletcher drawled, "Come and get it or we'll throw it out."

We followed him deeper into the house. The kitchen turned out to be one of those granite monuments to the idea of the good life. Its preponderance and variety of dark wood cabinetry (solid doors, glass doors, tambour doors) and stainless-steel appliances (some having applications at which I could only guess) struck me as absurd. Still, I picked up the stink of that envy of mine that could cause me to feel the lack even of things that I disdained if I supposed they made the people who possessed them happier than I was with what I possessed.

"We're about ready!" Esmé sounded cheery as she closed the door of an enormous stainless-steel oven. "Why don't you take them outside, Jer?"

Without moving from where he stood, Jeremy Fletcher jerked a thumb toward French doors that opened onto a flagstone patio. The light coming in through the patio doors gilded his skinny self; made him—with his long smile and untucked Mexican shirt and beer— look eerily like the giant novelty toads offered for sale in Nogales (real toads, their skins stretched and stuffed and made to stand upright; then outfitted with things like miniature violins and golf clubs and teeny bottles whose bits of blue and white suggested the Corona label).

Will and I stepped past him and out onto the patio. Except for the wrought-iron table already set with silverware and dark blue napkins—also, I noted, like a good alcoholic, two open bottles of red wine, four wineglasses—the patio was as bare as the inside of the house. *I'm just going to stick with water, thanks.* A little mental practice. In the Fletchers' nice lap pool, a softly humming Kreepy Krauly made its trips across the pool bottom, cleaning, filtering. I took a whiff of the air. When we first had moved to Tucson and I left the house to go to the university in the mornings, I would pause to savor the distinctive bleachy, holiday smell rising from the city's thousands of outdoor pools: *A vacation smell, the smell of my summer days as a kid at the city pool!* I'd thought, and marveled at the idea that I had come to live in a place where, when you flew in or out, the land stared up at you with swarms of turquoise-blue eyes. That smell surely had not gone away, but I apparently had grown so used to it that I no longer registered it.

"Do you remember—when we first moved here—how you could smell the swimming pools?" I asked Will. "Do you still smell that? In the mornings?"

He shook his head. "I never had your nose."

"This is so nice!" I said as Esmé and Jeremy Fletcher came out, carrying plates of green salad.

"Great view," said Will.

"Prime," Jeremy Fletcher said. Esmé was quiet, though. After she set down the plates of greens, she peered off at the Catalinas, as if she needed to think about the view, make up her mind. This unsettled me. *She does know about me and Jeremy*, I thought. *She planned for the dinner to be a test; to see if it would be possible for us to be friends again, and she already regrets it.* I also had the thought—so stupid, so simple-minded—that her excess weight might be a punishment for Jeremy.

A puff of breeze lifted a few bits of arugula from the salad plates, and Will and I bent down and picked them up from the flagstones.

"Leave 'em!" Jeremy Fletcher said. He sounded stern, like some Western's sheriff telling the robbers to drop their guns. I laughed— he had meant to be comical, I was sure—and I dropped the leaves of arugula and, like a proper outlaw, raised my hands in the air. Will, though, stuck what he'd grabbed into his pants pocket, and I wished that I'd done the same, not what Jeremy ordered.

"Earth to Esmé!" Jeremy Fletcher cupped his hands around his mouth to call. "Earth to Esmé!"

She turned and smiled at him—a real smile?—then extended her arm toward the wrought-iron table. "Charlotte, Will. Your salads," she said. Very stilted, as if she were playing an Edwardian butler, but she immediately repaired the effect by adding, "Well, that sounded weird! I guess that's what you get from spending your childhood watching videos of *Upstairs, Downstairs!*" and everybody laughed while taking seats at the wrought-iron table

—well, no, Jeremy Fletcher did not laugh, but the evening might roll along anyway. He and Esmé had two bottles of wine to drink, after all. I envied them that. Even in the face of the wreckage of Jeremy Fletcher, there came into my mind the notion (its design as clever as that of the bugs that can walk on water without breaking the surface tension) that it might not be so awful, for old times' sake, with people whom I now sincerely doubted we'd ever see again, if I were to accept a glass of that wine. Will would flip, of course. And, then, I supposed our asking for water earlier had tipped Esmé off to our being nondrinkers. At Iowa, initially, I had told Esmé that I could not drink because of "medications"; but, later—drunk—I'd blabbed everything to her (the bike accident, "droll" stories about my penitent attendance at AA meetings back in Webster City).

That was all so long ago, though. Who knew what she remembered?

I hoped that it was not a problem that Will asked Jeremy Fletcher if he *still were* involved in journalism. Jeremy Fletcher shrugged, but Esmé said, "Jeremy's interested in border issues, Will. He was down in Organ Pipe last week. Lots of illegal crossings there."

Jeremy Fletcher grunted. "Let's not let the cat out of the bag, though, Es."

For a moment, I thought that she looked irritated, but then she smiled and said, "Fine, fine," and turned toward Will and got him talking about his teaching, thank god, because Will was always interesting, talking about teaching—

"But, y'all"—Jeremy Fletcher rapped a spoon against my glass of water, hard enough that it would not have surprised me if the glass had broken, the water spilled—"let's be honest, now. You, too,

Charlotte. Are the undergrads at Arizona as bass-ackward dumb as the ones we taught at Iowa?"

I smiled. "Oh, I always have some good undergrads, Jeremy, but, hey, you don't want to get me started about education! It'd like to ruin your supper!"

While Jeremy and Esmé laughed at my Southerner imitation, Will gave me a look of mild reproof. "Charlotte's a very dedicated teacher," he said. "And, I have to ask myself, sometimes, what I looked like to my professors back when I was an undergraduate."

"Oh, Will"—Esmé patted Will's hand where it lay on the metal tabletop—"you were a brilliant student! As Charlotte reminded everybody at least fifty-three times a day!"

"I'm afraid the people who've heard Charlotte talk about me are bound to be disappointed," Will said. "I must seem like . . . the movie version of a really good book."

Esmé whooped, delighted. "That reminds me of how Charlotte and I used to say that we should have some great photographer take pictures of us when we were looking particularly fabulous, and then we'd get the pictures blown up, life-size, and hold them in front of us and make a good impression wherever we went!"

I grinned. "Portable wind machines, we wanted those, too. To muss our hair in just the right way."

The conversation stopped while Jeremy Fletcher disappeared under the table. "Damn," he said, "nobody's got a skirt I can see up!" He surfaced, holding a fat handful of the pink gravel that ran alongside the patio. "Scat!" he called and pitched a piece of the gravel toward a calico cat moseying through a neighbor's planting of *Tecoma stans*. The cat looked unperturbed by the gravel, but it did run off when Jeremy Fletcher backed his metal chair away from the table with a rough scrape and shouted, "GIT!" and let the rest of the gravel fly.

"Good grief, Jer," Esmé grumbled, but ever-resourceful Will got things back on track, saying, "I gather from the pictures in your living room that your sons are at Northwestern."

"Junior and a freshman," Esmé said. "A wonderful school."

"Won-erful, won-erful." Jeremy grabbed the bottle of Merlot from its spot on the table, poured himself a glass, pinched his nose between his thumb and index finger, and chugged the stuff down. With a shiver—and a wink at me—he added, "Awful stuff!"

As if she had not noticed, Esmé went on. "Actually, we're moving back to that part of the world. My parents are getting old—well, you probably saw our sign out front." She laughed. "So if you know anybody in the market for a great house—"

She quirked her mouth to one side, as if she'd been only kidding. I smiled at her while, under the table, Will gave my leg a squeeze. Did it cross through his mind, as it did mine, that we might now know the real reason why we sat on the Fletchers' patio: My friend was offering everyone she could think of a home tour in the guise of dinner?

"Seriously, though!" The beautiful Esmé smile. "There will never be a better time to buy real estate! Naysayers continue to abound, but there's going to be an upswing in the works! Mark my words: Two years from now, prices will be even higher than before the bust!"

A second squeeze from Will. I treasured his camaraderie, but my keenest feeling was a swelling grief:

I was at least partly responsible for this altered Esmé, wasn't I? When she had told me that she was pregnant and meant to marry Jeremy Fletcher, I'd thought only of myself. For fear of losing her friendship and good opinion, I had not told her, *Hey, I'm a rat, and the man you mean to marry is a rat, too.* Jesus, I could have told her *before* she got pregnant. She might have ditched him and had a better life, only I hadn't given her the chance.

And Jeremy Fletcher himself—while Esmé explained that she had been offered an administrative job at the Art Institute, Jeremy Fletcher tapped his skinny fingers fretfully on the wrought-iron table's pierced metal top. Out the corner of my eye, I could see a twitch in the tendon of his bony, bare forearm. The skin there had a shiny, crazed look—it was hairless, I realized—and reminded me of the skin on the arms of my long-gone Aunt Patty. I was partially responsible for the mess of Jeremy Fletcher's life, too, wasn't I? Maybe things would have been better for him, too, if I'd told Esmé the truth and they'd gone separate ways.

In the pink gravel alongside the patio there grew a young, waist-high, night-blooming cereus—*Cereus repandus*, the Peruvian apple—and, to ground myself, I reached out and ran my index finger down one of the waxy green channels between the still relatively short spines. We had one at our place, at least twelve feet tall. If the plants received support when they were young—got a start at, say, the foot of a palo verde tree—they could grow as high as thirty feet. Eventually, this little one would have multiple limbs, vertically ridged, like giant wales of corduroy, and each ridge would be topped with the needle-sharp spines that protected the plant against predators and also provided it with a surprising amount of shade, and helped it to catch the dew and rain that then could run down the plant's channeled sides and water its roots—

The conversation at the table had died. I looked at Esmé, at Jeremy Fletcher. "Has your cereus bloomed yet?" I asked.

"Oh, yes!" Esmé said. "I've even watched the bats feed at the blossoms!"

I was happy to say, "Well, I'm envious! We've got old plants, big ones, and I've never seen a bat feeding!" I looked at Will. "Have you?"

"Nope."

In a gently chiding voice—not the velvety DJ-thing from earlier; this more Lady Aberlin remonstrating with stubborn King Friday on *Mister Rogers' Neighborhood*—Esmé said, "You have to be *patient*, Charlotte. You always were impatient."

Esmé had thought of me as impatient? Well, I supposed I had been. Continued to be.

She went on. "I sit out here for hours some nights. Granted that we *do* have an amazing view. Almost every night, I see shooting stars."

"Esmé's Kools get at least half the credit for her patience," Jeremy said. "I don't allow indoors smokin' no more."

Esmé stood and picked up one of the bottles of wine from the table. A Merlot. To my surprise, Will let her pour some wine into his glass. When she moved alongside of me, I looked up at her, fatuously behaving as if I were not even aware of what she did with her hands. "Oh, I *still* miss Kools, Esmé!" I declared. The picture of myself smoking a cigarette was the best distraction that I could think to offer Will as Esmé filled my wineglass. Not good enough. I felt the look that he beamed my way, and, then, once Esmé sat down again, I had no choice but to lower my gaze. Impossible to pretend ignorance of the glass of Merlot, which sat directly above my knife and my spoon.

Esmé had filled the glasses very full, and she leaned forward and lifted her own just an inch or two from the table in order to take a sip without spilling.

"My, my," Jeremy Fletcher said, and, like a boy preparing to bob for apples, he grasped his skinny arms behind his back and lowered his face toward his own glass and proceeded to lap at the wine with his tongue. Esmé looked away but flicked a fingernail against her own glass. Jeremy straightened at the crisp *ding*. The dark wine dribbled onto his chin. Two tiny channels continued on down his neck and into the open collar of the pale green guayabera. "Refreshing!" he said and slapped at the wine as if it were aftershave.

I beamed a message of warmth toward Esmé—*What he's doing doesn't matter among friends!*—and I said, "Your boys must be very smart! Both of them National Merit Scholars, right?"

Scooping his hands down into his collar for a final rub-a-dub-dub at his skin, Jeremy Fletcher asked, "You two got any supersmart kids, Will?"

Will offered Esmé a reassuring, good-guest smile of his own. "That didn't happen for us," he said, "but we've been—"

"Esmé, honey!" Jeremy Fletcher interrupted. "Our guests are gonna get wine all over themselves, too, if you don't rustle 'em up drinking straws or sumpin'!"

"That's okay," I said. Jeremy Fletcher's dive into the wine had dampened my interest in a flirtation with the Merlot. "We're fine."

"Oh, for Christsake!" Esmé squawked and pressed her hands to her black turban so fiercely that she looked as if she were about to lift off her head. She grabbed up my glass of wine, dumped a good half of the contents onto the pink gravel, then set the glass back in front of me with a *thunk*. "Hardly any left, so no worries, right?" She didn't wait for me to answer before she laughed and shifted a rather wild smile in Will's direction. "Unless you still count her drinks, Will!"

"I do not count her drinks," Will said.

"Well, good! That's progress!" *Scrawl* went her chair as she backed it away from the table and stood and began to gather up the salad plates. "So—I'll get the lasagna."

I got up, too. "Let me help."

"Stay," Esmé said, "It's under control!"

Jeremy Fletcher followed Esmé's swift progress toward the house (despite her size, she was no slouch). Then, like a kid who waits for his mother to leave the room so he can talk about what he really wants to talk about, he turned to Will and began to discuss—with great enthusiasm—his recent wins at "the horses." His racetrack jargon meant little me, and I doubted that Will understood either. After several minutes of waxing on, hooting over some particular or another, he did think to ask, "So, Will, you follow the races?"

"You know, I never have," Will said. "How was it that you got interested, Jeremy?"

I had seen Will use this tactic before. Yielding the floor spared him the effort of trying to play conversational catch and allowed him to go on thinking his own thoughts. Sometimes, I even spotted him using the trick on me. I thought that Jeremy Fletcher himself might have spotted it. He drew in his chin and gave a little snort; nevertheless, he answered at length:

Stuff about horse and dog racing back in the "'Bama" of his youth. Trips to Del Mar and Saratoga. "They run at Turf Paradise in Phoenix, October to May. That's a good time. You can go to Greyhound Park here, course, but there ain't no fucking people in the stands! The SPCA spoiled it for the greyhounds here." He shook his head in disgust. "Phoenicians know those dogs are bred to run!" He laughed. "Phoenicians are still up for a good time! Mostly, though, I do off-track at Famous Sam's. They got simulcasts. Santa Anita. Belmont. Churchill Downs, you name it. Horses and dogs. Sit in air-conditioned comfort and have a beer." He peered at Will. Checking to see if he listened? "You know Famous Sam's, Will?"

Will did not hesitate: "Isn't there one on Pima Street?"

"That's right, but I go to the one on North Oracle. You can bet a couple bucks, bet your whole 401(k), bet nothin'! It's all good." He looked in the direction of the house. Through the French doors, it was possible to see Esmé, transferring a very large, wobbling slab of steaming lasagna from a casserole onto a plate.

"It gets you out," he said. "What say I take you some afternoon, Will?"

"Nice of you to offer"—Will sounded appreciative, I suppose; or, at least, polite—"but when I have free time, I generally use it on my work."

Jeremy Fletcher lowered his face just enough to suggest that he meant to hide his amusement. "Still chipping away at the rock of art, huh, Will?" he asked.

"This is hot, hot, hot!" Esmé called, bursting through the French doors with a large tray, and Will and I both stood to help.

"No, no," she said. "Just—it's fine." She frowned at Jeremy Fletcher as she settled a crescent of the tray on the edge of the table and began handing around plates loaded with lasagna and a green bean dish.

"What about you, Charlotte?" Jeremy Fletcher asked. "You still pecking away?"

"She's got a novel coming out next fall," Will said. "Her fourth book."

I groaned and shook my head, a superstitious tribeswoman warding off the jealous gods by publicly announcing that her baby is grossly deformed, ugly, useless.

"A *fourth* book!" Esmé said. "Good grief! Now, everybody, please be aware that I may have gotten carried away with the crushed red peppers."

"We like hot stuff," I said and, after a first bite, Will said, "Delicious!"

I chimed. "Delicious."

Jeremy Fletcher did not appear to be interested in eating. He screwed up his eyes in the direction of a dog barking somewhere in the distance. The forward thrust of his chin suggested that he would have been happy to pop somebody in the nose.

Esmé smiled at Will. "Needless to say, no one would expect you to be on Facebook, you being such a private person, but Charlotte—"

"Oh, I'm a Luddite," I said.

"A troglodyte is more like it," said Will.

"But don't you Google yourself, Charlotte?" Esmé asked. "To see what people say about your work?"

Honk! Jeremy Fletcher blew his nose into one of the navy-blue napkins. Slapped the napkin down on the tabletop. "Es," he said and drew an index finger across his throat. Raised that same finger to his lips. Covered his mouth entirely with both hands, like the speak-no-evil monkey.

Once again, I rushed in—imagining myself Esmé's savior—"I know my computer's an amazing resource, Esmé, but I'm not safe there! Last week, I realized you could watch Stravinsky conduct the lullaby from the *Firebird,* and then I thought, *Well, I don't actually know anything about Stravinsky,* so I clicked a link to a documentary about him—a little problematic since the filmmaker didn't bother translating when people spoke French—and you know how those links go. Three hours later, when I came to, I was studying tips from supermodels on how to create a pouty mouth."

Esme laughed. Good, good. I actually started to relax while she and Will discussed the upkeep of the lap pool. Then, however, I noticed Jeremy Fletcher's pink, pulpy eyes fixed on my face. "Bron-të!" he said in a terrible, bawling voice. He lifted himself up out of his chair and leaned over the table toward me—too much of a demand on his current sense of balance. He tipped. One elbow galloped forward, knocking over his water glass; the other landed in a basket of baguette slices. Briefly, he considered this state of affairs; then, elbow pulling the basket across the table, he resumed his seat. "Brontë." His voice was quieter now, labored. "You be a good girl, Brontë," he huffed, "an' eat your damned green beans."

The way that Will straightened in his chair reminded me too much of a party in Manhattan at which I'd had to get between him and some tough-guy painter who'd told me to get fucked when he learned that I hadn't attended his opening the night before. My turn to squeeze Will's leg. *Let it go. The guy's obviously drunk.*

This had no effect on Will's tense posture. "Would you care to repeat that, man?" he said.

Man was not good. My heartbeat picked up as Jeremy Fletcher pointed his gnarly chin in Will's direction. "I *said* she should eat her green beans, *man*. I notice y'all are eatin' yours, William. Gotta get our five servings a day, right?"

Esmé stood and briskly began to clear the plates. "Who'll have decaf?" she asked.

"I'd love some," I said, my voice a Minnie Mouse squeak. "How about you, Will?" The V of vein that stood out on his forehead like an earthworm was familiar to me from our more serious quarrels and watching him lift heavy weights at the university rec center.

Esmé said, "If you'll give me a hand with the door, Charlotte. I've got spumoni for us, too."

Now, when I wanted to stay put, monitor whatever drunken Jeremy Fletcher might be inclined to say next, she wanted me to come.

I held open one of the French doors and Esmé passed inside. A grand screech sounded behind us: Will, pivoting his wrought-iron chair away from Jeremy and the table.

Christ.

Once she'd set down the dirty plates, Esmé opened the freezer and took out a shiny white box, topped with a red satin bow. She lifted the lid from the box, which turned out to be divided in sections, each section holding an individual serving of spumoni in a pleated gold foil cup.

"Pretty," I said. How soon before Will and I could start making noises about leaving? *Gotta work tomorrow.* Would half an hour be too bizarre? Esmé pointed me toward the cupboard where I'd find coffee cups and saucers. A tremble in my hands set the dishes rattling as I transferred them to the counter.

Esmé placed four dessert plates on the counter, too, each banded with gold and decorated by a different flower. "I'm sorry Jer's not great company tonight. Sometimes he drinks too much." She centered one of the foil cups on a circle of bluebells. "I've tried to talk to him about it."

Her trusting me with a piece of such intimate information touched me. Maybe, seeing that Will and I were not drinking, and knowing some of my history, it had occurred to her that we might be able to offer help—

I set my hand on her shoulder.

The face that she turned toward my hand was blank—but blank in the way that the surface of a pond appears blank from a distance, reflecting the sky. Get up close and look down into the pond for a bit, and the sky disappears, and you see the skeletonized leaves and broken bits of twigs, rocks, and rusted cans, a crayfish leaving a ghost of trail as it skates across the tan muck of the bottom.

Once I removed my offending hand, I had a sense that she resumed breathing.

One by one, she began to place the dessert plates and cups of coffee on a large serving tray. "I've thought about you a lot over the years," she said, "and, with what Will said about your not having kids—well, naturally, I'm curious: Do you ever regret that abortion?"

When we lived together on Burlington Street, the two of us had been very impressed by a response that "Dear Abby" offered a reader who did not know how to answer when people asked why she and her husband did not have children. "Simply say," Abby advised, *I wonder why you ask.*" *I wonder why you ask.* At one point in my life, I actually had practiced saying that in front of a mirror. *I wonder why you ask.* It sounded elegant, simple. It returned the ball to the other person's court, but Esmé's question was loaded with knowledge, and the best that I could come up with was a small "Things have worked out for us."

She laughed. "I should say so! You've been downright lucky!" She turned her face toward the patio doors and peered out. "I think Jer was nervous about having you come to dinner. What do you think?"

I hardly could think at all, let alone answer, while she rushed on, still looking out to the patio: "You've had a writing career, but when we all were at the Workshop, Jeremy was the star! You remember! Everyone thought he'd be big! He already had editors interested in his novel when he arrived! Then we left Iowa and—*poof!* It was strange." She nodded. "Very strange. He started to suspect that someone at the Workshop had screwed him over." Her head shook, little shivery shakes. She turned one eye my way. "He suspected it was you, Charlotte. Because of what happened between the two of you. Was it? You?"

"*Esmé.*" I looked out toward the patio then, too. Will and Jeremy Fletcher, sitting in the dusk, still as totems. "I'm so sorry," I whispered, "I'm so sorry, but, believe me, I never did *anything* against Jeremy."

She opened her hands in front of herself, waist height, as if they held evidence. "He applied for one of the Michener Fellowships the year that you were a screener, and he didn't get one."

"I never saw an application from him, Esmé. I'd definitely remember if I had, and"—I hated the tremor in my voice; it made me sound as if I were guilty—"I'm pretty sure the rules were that he would have to have finished his degree to get a Michener"—

121

She shook her head. "Let's cut to the chase." Her eyes were luminous, large, on the edges of tears, but what I heard in her voice was fury, and when she said, "You care about Will's happiness, don't you, Charlotte?" Panic made small black specks—twisting and rising and falling like gnats—rise in front of my eyes, and I had to set my hand on the nearest countertop to steady myself.

Esmé tore a square of paper towel from the roller under the counter and folded it in half and then quarters and held the neat, folded edge to her lower lashes. "A couple of months ago," she said, "I saw an announcement that you were going to be the judge for a new book prize just for Arizona writers. The Poulos Prize. Jer doesn't know it yet, but I entered him." She nodded, kept on nodding. "Ten days ago, a letter came saying he's a finalist." She tilted her head back and sniffed and blotted at her lashes with a clean edge of the folded paper towel. "The prize money would be nice, of course—who couldn't use ten thousand dollars?—but the important thing is for Jer to be published and get the attention he should have gotten in the past." She slipped the folded paper towel into a pocket in her caftan. "I know you'll want to make that happen, Charlotte, you and Jer being such old *friends*."

My fool's face, mouth open wide, stared back at me from the glossy black door of the kitchen's microwave oven. Esmé in her turban and emerald-green caftan entered that reflection. She drew close enough that I could hear her swallow before she said into my good ear, "It goes without saying, of course, that no one—not even Will—has to know about this conversation." She paused. "Or anything else."

PART TWO

12

Over the years, Will and I had learned to keep quiet for a while after a particularly horrible gallery opening or play or whatever so that if one of us—or anyone who might be with us—had enjoyed the event, or found a way to put a positive spin on it, that person had a chance to speak first. After our dinner with Esmé and Jeremy Fletcher, though, as soon as we got into the car, I wanted to say, *Well, that was awful!* I wanted to act as if we still inhabited a normal world. *Well, that was awful!* Impossible for me to say. *Well, that was awful!* I feared that what would come out of my mouth would be the juddering panic I felt, nonsense erupting like machine-gun fire.

In silhouette, Will's stiff-set jaw looked like something made of bolts as he steered the car out of that supersize neighborhood. My heart was slamming the wall of my chest so hard that it was difficult to imagine that he did not notice—not that I thought he actually would *hear* my heart, but didn't he notice the way I shuddered in my bucket seat?

There, once more, the big Walgreens. The flowing script on the side of the building now lit up, neon red.

Once more, we waited for the long light at the intersection where the giant Wells Fargo sign—now burning gold from within—turned and turned.

While Esmé and Jeremy Fletcher and Will had sat on the patio, eating spumoni, drinking decaf coffee, I had vomited in the gold-leafed powder room off the Fletchers' front hall. Now, I felt I might have to ask Will to pull over so I could be sick again. I pressed my hot cheek to the air-conditioned cool glass of the passenger-side window.

You and Jer being such old friends.

Esmé had assumed that she still could count on my being a cheat and a coward. While I stood in her custom kitchen, floundering in terrified apologies and refusals, *I'm so sorry, so sorry, my god, I was an idiot, but you have to understand, I couldn't do that,* she simply walked toward the French doors.

She did stop walking when I cried out—bleated, really—"Please! Esmé! Even if I were willing, the entries are all anonymous. Even I won't know who the finalists were until after I pick the winner."

She looked out toward the patio. "You'll recognize Jer's manuscript when you see it. It's *The Holy of Holies,* the novel he used to get into the Workshop. You thought that was a pretentious title, didn't you?" Her laugh was shallow. "I suppose you still hold your tastes sacrosanct, but *three* of your peers picked the book from what the letter said were one hundred and thirty-three entries." She turned to me. She smiled. The Esmé smile that once had made me feel so special. "I'm not going to accept a no from you yet," she said. "I'm going to give you time to think. You're a writer! Use your

imagination! You have the power to make this a story with a happy
ending for all of us—or not."

The stoplight changed. Will shifted his foot from the clutch to the
gas, accelerated. I wanted to cry out an immediate confession, but
the lies I'd told—I'd stitched them so heavily into the fabric of our
life as a couple. To get at them would require tearing, and, undoubtedly—*this* I never had seen before—the thing that would make Will
more furious than anything else would be learning that I had lived
alongside of him, all those years, knowing things about our life that
he did not know and, worse, that Jeremy and Esmé Fletcher did.

Not a word from either one of us, all the way home, but after he
unlocked the kitchen door and we stepped inside—not bothering to
turn on a light—he took my hand and led me through the dark house
to our room. I was surprised. When he was upset about something,
he rarely wanted to make love, but after he pulled off his T-shirt
and polo shirt—one movement, up and over his head—even in the
moonlight, I could see the need on his face.

He always was a considerate sex partner, Will, taking as much
time as I required. On those occasions when it did seem to me that
I was not going to succeed at having an orgasm, he invariably said,
"Well, let's wait and see," and it was rare that things didn't work
out. On this particular night, though, he didn't bother much with
me, and I was glad. I couldn't have stood his making an effort on my
behalf.

His orgasm was heartfelt, but not joyful, and he got out of bed
soon afterward and pulled on a pair of boxers and one of the gray
hoodies that he liked to wear to sleep. "I'm exhausted," he said and
lay down again and pulled up the covers, rolled onto his side, away
from me.

I wondered: *If I died, then would he forgive me?*

I wanted to stay in bed, close to him, but I knew that I was a long way from sleep. Also, I was afraid that he might, at any moment, suddenly roll over and demand, "So what was tonight all about?" and I was in no shape to answer. Any thinking I'd tried to do had been unproductive, as useless as the snow shoveling my dad would insist my mother and I join in on whenever a blizzard struck.

"I think I'll read for a bit," I said, my first words since we had walked out the Fletchers' front door. I edged off the mattress and grabbed my bathrobe from its hook on the door. "Love you," I said.

Will muttered something. Maybe it was *love you*. I did not think I should push my luck by asking him to repeat himself.

I took a seat in one of the wingbacks in the living room. I opened a book that sat on the coffee table. What book? Whatever was at hand. It was a prop. The lines of type just as well could have been squiggles designed to fool a distant audience. There was no question of reading or any other distraction.

I thought of calling Jacqueline C. She always had said that I could telephone her at any hour but I would have felt awful, waking her up and, then, I couldn't see how I could say anything important to her with Will within earshot.

I opened the sliding door to the backyard and stepped out onto the ramada. The moonlight had knitted the scrubby cholla and creosote bushes into a strange, pale blue wave under the night sky. I clasped my hands together to try to still my panic. I looked up at the stars overhead. If God were anywhere, it did seem like the stars would be the place, and I prayed that most elemental prayer, *Please help*.

In the shadows, off to my right, something shifted—

I let out a gasp of fear, but it was only a cat, arching its back as it rose from the old glider we kept under the covered portion of the ramada. Bad Cat, I was sure. It hopped down. Shoulders rolling, low to the ground, it passed along the shady edge of the ramada, then dashed across the moonlit yard and into the oleander hedge.

"Don't go!" I called, my voice so plaintive that anyone who'd overheard surely would have thought I called to a lover. "Here, kit!"

The cat triggered the security light at the back of the Schaeffers' house as it passed into their yard. I walked to the hedge and called through the leaves, keeping my voice low now, "Here, kit, here, kitty." The security light snapped off soon after, but I stayed at the hedge for quite a while, whispering, "Here, kitty, come on, kitty," before I finally gave up and made my way back to the ramada.

I aged that night, out on the ramada. Panic-stricken, pacing, I felt myself shrink. It got cold—the temperature fell into the fifties—but my shrinking was not a matter of the cold. It felt permanent, like the shrinking of a bone left out in desert sun, any meat on it going dry, hard, shiny.

The night that Martie died, I'd sat beside her bed at the hospital in Fort Dodge. The last day, all day, her breaths were as loud as a locomotive waiting at a station. The nurses said she was unconscious, but her eyes were full of terror. A grieving, monstrous time. I helped the nurses shift the position of her body on the mattress to prevent her from developing bedsores. I wiped her forehead with a damp, wrung-out cloth. I moistened her mouth with tiny, stiff, lime-flavored sponges on sticks until the nurses said, "That's not necessary anymore." Nothing I could do would stop the end from coming. Still, at least while I sat beside her, I did not feel I'd caused the situation. There were no decisions for me to make that were of consequence. In that regard, the hours that I spent on the ramada were worse than the hours at Martie's bedside.

Over and over, I ran through variations of the confession that I would offer Will. What words would be the very best words?

Always, I pictured myself down on my knees, holding on to his strong legs while he tried to wrest himself away from me. I thought, *I have been so much luckier than I ever deserved to be!* Our life together— out on the ramada, alone, any disappointment I'd ever felt over that precious life felt almost indecent. Our life together sparkled before me. It was a paradise, all open and blue-skied and full of possibility.

And to think that making Jeremy Fletcher the winner of the Poulos Prize would allow that life to go on the way it had been!

I had tried to be a person of integrity—in part inspired by what I'd done to Esmé. I did not miss the irony that it was on her behalf that I now was tempted to compromise myself.

At four, I went into the house. Lying under the threads of moonlight coming in through the slats of the bedroom shutters, the gray hoodie pulled up over his head, Will looked like a beautiful monk, carved of stone, but when I brushed up against the bed, he raised the covers to me.

A habitual, husbandly gesture.

Feeling like a thief, I joined him.

13

I did not imagine that I would sleep that night, but I did. When I woke up—my heart knew I was in trouble and it already raced—Will was gone.

The clock on his side of the bed showed just past six thirty, but it *was* a Thursday, one of Will's gym days.

I hurried out into the kitchen. His gym bag was gone from its niche by the back door. Reassuring, I thought at first—life as usual—but there was no yellow sticky note on the kitchen counter. If Will left the house when I was still in bed, he almost always wrote me a note (what time he'd be home, plus an "I love you").

I opened the sliding doors and stepped outside. The sky was gray, the bricks beneath my bare feet even colder than they had been the night before, but I needed their chill in order to clear my head—

I'd gotten so little sleep.

I headed across the scrappy backyard to the shed.

I knew the shelf where the cardboard box WRITERS' WORKSHOP/ DRAFTS sat (I saw it whenever we got out Christmas decorations or I went for paint or a tool for yard work), and I went right to it and pulled it toward me and set it on the shed's dirt floor.

The top of the box was covered with a fine grit, the way it had been four years ago, the day I'd taken it off the shelf during Will's and my clean-out of the shed. That day, though, in my haste to be done with the box, I'd simply folded the lid shut, not bothered with tape, and so there was dust inside the box now, too. Dust dulled those three taped-together photographs of Esmé and me dressed up as little old ladies.

Immediately, I tossed the photographs into the shed's trash can; then I pulled a stack of stapled manuscripts and other papers from the box and settled it on the dusty top of a tub of roof sealant.

It turned out that a few of the stories I'd stored had been written by people I'd kept in touch after leaving Iowa, or at least ran into those times that I could prod myself into attending the Associated Writing Programs conferences. One of the stories, "Grass," had been written by Glynn True, the most famous person to come out of my class, but I'd hardly known her. Many names I did not recognize at all—Robin Clark? Jeff Eldridge? Dan Hale?—or hadn't thought of in years.

In my days at the Workshop, I'd assumed that I'd always remember my classmates.

"Dry Dock." A story by Esmé Cole. A good story, as I recalled. All of her stories had been good.

Leaving that first stack of manuscripts on the tub of sealant, I pulled out another pile. This one I settled on the big red toolbox that we had bought in the days when we were fixing up the house. I rifled my way through that second pile. Found a letter that I had written to Esmé toward the end of Will's and my time in Iowa City— had I mailed an edited version to her? There were all kinds of slashes through the thing:

Dear Esmé,

I hope all is well for you and your little family. [crossed out: *I'd love to hear from you again, but I'm sure you're very busy—hope my letters aren't annoying!*]

Rob Roy must be getting big. His eyes were dark in the baby pictures, but I know that can change (he still had the little Buddha look back then—cheeks you want to give a smooch).

Will and I have been working hard. He's writing his dissertation and I've been doing stuff for the Iowa Arts Council (Writers in the Schools, K–12, and sometimes working with senior citizens). I shouldn't complain. It seems like all of us here go around talking about how hard we work. Like, if we said we'd taken off a couple of days we'd be viewed as total slackers. I don't want to be this way, but when it's all around you, it's hard not to be.

I've written [crossed out: *some new stories*] a story and would be glad to send it along, if you have time. [crossed out: *Will seemed to think a couple of them were a bit too weird, but you know how men often can't abide pictures of women that don't conform to their idea of proper female behavior!*]

Well, I should get back to work—ack! I can't believe I said that. Really, I schlepped around in my bathrobe today until ten and then went out and bought a Snickers bar for breakfast. I can be quite the dissolute character! [crossed out: *Write when you have a chance.*]

XO, Charlotte

There were not many stapled manuscripts left in the box when I removed the last batch, but the stapled pages from *The Holy of Holies* that Jeremy Fletcher had handed around to everyone in our class made up the third manuscript in the pile.

A special ops soldier—scion of a civilization yet to recover from the War Between the States—now whacked-out after flying midnight search-and-destroy missions over Vietnam, went staggering through the Heaven and Hell that were the streets of his native Birmingham. From the second-story window of a spectral rooming house, an alluring phantom hailed said special ops soldier: *Come on up, y'all.* Slowly, slowly, Soldier—such was the main character's name, enhanced with that capital *S*—Soldier climbed a phantasmagoric staircase, traversed a dark and ancestral hall that pulled at the very currents of his blood (in his ears sounded a distant confusion of what he took to be the roar of factories and clank of slave chains mixed with strains of hymns and the wind winding through limbs of oak trees heavy with Spanish moss). The woman he found after his long climb, however, was not she who had called to him but a flesh-and-blood bottle blonde with dark roots, "beach ball" breasts, limbs "thin and cold and see-through as icicles," and a deep yearning to display to the soldier the "privates" she had hacked at with a piece of glass broken off that same canning jar from which she'd recently drunk what must have been an anesthetic amount of hooch.

The pair's bloody and initially very energetic sex lasted longer than her consciousness.

I stopped reading after Soldier "betook himself"—or something along those lines; Jeremy Fletcher's prose sagged with its King James medals—further on down the hall of his crazed and noble inheritance, there to witness, from a doorway outlined with tiny moons that Soldier understood might or might not exist, a dwarf in the process of stripping away the "night-black" skin of his thigh with a tool that Soldier knew (briefly, he pondered whether his own such remained in the rowboat behind Grandpap's cabin) did serve as the most efficient means for cleaning a catfish.

I stared out the open door of the shed.

Surely he had improved the novel over the years. Surely the pickings from the contest entries had not been so slim as all that.

Still.

As I stood to pitch Jeremy Fletcher's manuscript into the trash can, I saw beneath it a very old computer printout (the edges of the manuscript pages were rough from where I'd separated them from their perforated printer feed). "Girlfriends" was the name of that story. A story of mine. A much reworked but never finished attempt to understand my friendship with Esmé Cole.

I scanned the pages in which iterations of Esmé and myself became, respectively, Olivia and Ellen, graduate students in studio art at the University of Minnesota. Slowed for a scene that began before the two students—roommates—shared their first dinner:

Olivia bustled into the kitchen, bringing, as always, an air of confidence that Ellen wished that she could find in herself—or even imitate. A crusty baguette stuck out of one of the paper bags in her arms, and she announced to Ellen—then intently sketching several white eggs in their turquoise Styrofoam carton—that she *finally* had found a place in that Podunk town that sold pancetta and fresh mozzarella! "Which means we'll be dining tonight on *insalata Caprese* and *pasta carbonara*! You, my dear, will be *sous chef*!"

Ellen never had heard of pancetta or fresh mozzarella. *Insalata Caprese. Pasta carbonara.* She cleared her sketch pad and pencils from the table and carried them down the hall to her bedroom. When she got back to the kitchen, she found that Olivia had opened a bottle of Chianti and now poured the wine into the tiny glasses that they used for orange juice in the morning.

"Yeah, yeah"—Olivia set the bottle in the middle of the table— "I know you say you can't drink because of your meds, but one glass won't kill you! And you *can't* eat good Italian food without wine!"

Ellen hesitated. What she had told Olivia about the meds was true, but hardly anybody hewed to the proscription. She recited it to people as a means of keeping herself on the straight and narrow. Her behavior was too unpredictable when she drank; and, then, she had promised Dan that she wouldn't drink while they were apart. Still, what harm could come, at home on a Saturday night, from having an *orange juice glass* of wine—the glass so small it was almost silly—with a substantial starchy meal?

She took a sip. Oh, delicious! Mouth-watering! And the glass was funny, wasn't it? Little oranges painted on the side, like instructions for its proper use.

While Olivia slivered the pancetta and set Ellen to slicing tomatoes—the wine so sweetly filling cavities inside Ellen—Olivia proceeded to tick through her impressions of the other residents in their little apartment building: "So, you'll know which ones are worthy of giving the time of day to, and which ones"—to Ellen's delight, sometimes Olivia sounded like a funny, old granny—"are plain nasty and to be avoided at all costs!"

Olivia did a comical imitation of the way in which the man living directly below them topped off each of his rapid-fire sentences with a small bow followed by the upturning of his palm. "It's like he thinks each of his thoughts is a gift!" Olivia sputtered. And then there were the building's three Madonna/Marilyn Monroe wannabes, the "Bimbettes," Olivia had dubbed them, "total sluts," whose cluelessness and Valley Girl rising inflections she could mimic to a T.

Ellen made an effort to look entirely unconscious of her actions as she refilled the juice glasses with second helpings of the Chianti. She herself had been so busy with her teaching assistantship and her own work those first weeks of the fall semester that she had met only the Miles Davis fans in the next apartment and the old man who lived near the front door and did custodial work on the building; but, then, from what Olivia had said, Ellen hadn't missed much. Which was fine. Ellen had Olivia, after all—captivating Olivia, who could make Ellen feel decked out in Christmas lights and now gaily smashed two cloves of garlic with a single blow of the bottom of a cast-iron frying pan, flicked away the dry husks with the tip of her knife and, with just three chop-chop-chops, minced the remaining flesh to perfection.

Had Olivia applied for one of the teaching assistantships that Ellen herself had considered it a great honor to receive? Ellen never had asked because suppose Olivia had applied and had been rejected and she felt hurt about it. Maybe, though, she had not wanted to teach. She had more free time to paint because of not teaching—and she had plenty of money, too. When Ellen offered to pay half of the bill for that evening's groceries and wine, Olivia said a funny "Pish-tush! Don't be silly! I'm loaded, kid!" It seemed to be true; she'd told Ellen that she did not even have to keep track of her checking account balance because, if it went below a certain level, the bank "took care of it."

Oh, that Chianti—Ellen felt so much livelier and more articulate after the second glass! *Ar-tic-u-late.* During dinner, she told Olivia all about Dan—the wonders of Dan! She ran down to her room for his photograph and she hauled out the giant Magritte book that he had given her before leaving for Berkeley, and she spread the book open on the kitchen table, off to the side of their plates of delicious food and the candle that clever Olivia had produced and lit for the dinner. Very excited, maybe tripping over the words a little because of the wine, Ellen said:

"You see, he thrills you with his representations at the same time that he reminds you that what he paints is *not* the object that it represents! And the words on the canvas—'This is not a pipe'—they aren't what they represent either!"

Ellen had been a scholarship kid at a small college established by Norwegian Minnesotans, while Olivia had gone to Yale. Ellen never had known anyone who had gone to Yale. She was the first person in her family to go to college and sometimes worried over the disparities between her own and Olivia's educations and backgrounds, but, now, Olivia looked up from the Magritte book and she gave Ellen a keen glance and said, smiling a smile that suggested they shared an entertaining secret, "You're smart, aren't you, Ellen?"

Ellen flushed and scrambled (emergency!) to come up with the right compliment to offer Olivia in return because suppose that Olivia's thinking that Ellen was smart made Olivia feel competitive? Like Ellen less? Even *dis*like her?

Thick black lines of Magic Marker obliterated whatever I'd written in the story's next paragraph. I flipped the page to see if the backside contained a possible rewrite. No. Some box of old floppy disks probably held the original story, but maybe what I'd penciled in the margin alongside the blacked-out paragraph was more pertinent:

Could Ellen actually give Olivia a compliment here? Ellen grew up without compliments! Knows shit about compliments! Giving one to Olivia—if E thinks O has ALL the confidence in the world? E might want O's friendship—even care for her—but complimenting O would feel like she was tearing off a hunk of herself! And only to feed it to a creature already bigger and better fed than herself? I don't know that she could.

The story continued after the blacked-out paragraph:

Olivia lifted herself up out of her chair and leaned across the kitchen table toward Ellen. A loose strand of her long hair sizzled up in a tiny puff of smoke from the candle, there. Both she and Ellen startled briefly, but there was no real harm done, and they recovered and after they finished laughing over the *zip* and the pong of the burned hair, Olivia canted her heart-shaped face to one side, and, looking Ellen straight in the eye, she said, "Ellen?"

Olivia was going to share a confidence? Ellen did not feel prepared for that, not yet, but she hungered for the friendship to be intimate, and so—not to spoil things—she held Olivia's blazing, dark-eyed gaze. "Olivia?"

Olivia grinned. "I'm thinking, Ellen—do you suppose we figured each other would be safe to live with since we're both attractive? Like, we took each other's looks as the Good Housekeeping Seal of Approval?"

Ellen covered her mouth with both hands while she laughed and wagged her head back and forth in protest. This second helping of flattery had come too close on the heels of the first. Also, she resolutely refused to accept that Olivia included Ellen in her own class of good looks. Olivia's nose was a perfect aquiline; Ellen's came at you like a friendly cocker spaniel's. Olivia had a fashionably slim body—not *boyish*, not at all, but she did not require a bra under her silky camisole top, let alone the five-hooked number that governed zaftig Ellen beneath her oxford-cloth button-down.

Even with the Chianti tingeing her teeth blue, Olivia looked lovely, likely to win at anything she put her mind to.

So is she fishing? Ellen asked herself. *Am I supposed to say an aghast* 'But of course I'm not nearly as pretty as you, Olivia'? The idea rankled while she went on laughing into her hands, shaking her head, no, no. no.

"Well!" Olivia clapped, once, twice. "It's something to think about!" Then she hopped up from the table and declared that they would leave the dishes for later. "It's Saturday night and you're my best friend in this one-horse town! At least *once* we've got to go out and get a little smashed, missy!"

Halfheartedly, Ellen lifted the wine bottle to indicate that they didn't need to go out, but the bottle was empty, and Olivia— now up out of her chair entirely and jubilantly boogying around the kitchen—began to describe a place called Hooch's, the bar to which she meant to take Ellen:

"It's got a genuine jukebox, Ellen! Wooden booths! An old pressed-tin ceiling hung with plastic grape and chili pepper and pumpkin lights. It's funky! They give out free popcorn! It could be our place!"

With the Chianti warm inside her—how much had she drunk?—Ellen thought Hooch's did sound perfect. *Our place.* She went to her room to change. *Our place.* Two young artists. Best friends. *Attractive.* Swinging down the streets of Dinkytown after a day of hard work.

"Look at you! You look fabulous!" Olivia said when she came out. "Except, uh-oh, not the rearview." She crooked a finger—*follow me.*

After she'd shut the two of them inside the apartment's little bathroom, Olivia pointed to the mirror tacked to the back of the door. "Turn around," she said. She folded her arms across her chest. "Check out your rearview. Are you *sure* you can afford to wear drawstring pants?"

"*Much* better," Olivia said when, a few minutes later, Ellen— face still hot with embarrassment—emerged in the straight-leg pants that Olivia had encouraged her to buy the week before.

To the west, Dinkytown's clouded blue horizon of trees and buildings swallowed the last of the early September sunset. In the silky air, as they hurried toward Fourth Street, they took turns reciting favorite poems (Olivia liked poetry, too, for Christsakes!). Ellen did Yeats's "Adam's Curse," and Olivia did "Leda and the Swan." Fourth Street was lively, drivers honking at the young people who walked straight into the traffic, determined not to look both ways—or even one way—to teach the drivers that *they* were the ones who needed to stop, be careful. The restaurants and bars glowed golden, like Ali Baba's caves, as if they were piled high inside with magic lamps and trunks of coins, heaps of jewels. Up ahead—Ellen spied the bar's name, carved into a wooden sign that hung over the street—the door to Hooch's stood open, as if you were invited to walk in, be part of the music and talk and laughter inside. Still, Ellen would not have entered had Olivia not taken her elbow and tugged her into the foyer.

Beyond, in the bar proper, as Olivia had said, there were festive twinkle-light pumpkins and fruits. Just to make conversation, feeling awkward despite the wine, Ellen started to ask Olivia how she knew about Hooch's, but then a number of people from around the bar were shouting, "Hey, Olivia!" and Olivia was smiling and waving in response.

When they first had met, Olivia had told Ellen that she was shy, too. How could she possibly have thought that she was *shy*?

"Grab that"—Olivia pointed Ellen toward a booth—"I'll get us beers."

The Hooch's crowd seemed to be a mix of students, some older than Olivia and Ellen, some definitely holding fake IDs, plus everything in between. Two old hippies with scraggly ponytails sat near a tableful of Dinkytown shopkeepers in pressed chinos and denim skirts. A huddle of beefy males in polo shirts and tasseled loafers stood at the end of the bar where a television was set to ESPN (alumni, apparently; to a one, each wore something either maroon or gold or both).

After fifteen minutes of waiting—Olivia kept getting into conversations with different tables of people on the way to the bar—Ellen slid to the edge of the booth and swung her legs around so that she faced the bar. Her goal: to insert herself into Olivia's view.

Twenty-two minutes. She tried to keep a Buddha smile on her face, to look pleasant—though not as if she wanted a date.

People smiled up at Olivia with such interest while she stood alongside their tables or booths! Any moment now, surely, she would signal for Ellen to come join her, but Olivia's gaze never shifted quite in Ellen's direction, and, a little drunk from the Chianti, Ellen got to feeling quite morose, as if, like the singer on the jukebox, she had been abandoned by the one she loved.

Attractive. She tried to warm her hands at that idea for a while; then at the idea of *our place*; then at an idea for a new painting, something with words, something drawing inspiration from Magritte and Ed Ruscha and Jasper Johns and, hey, also from the booth's tabletop, whose darkly shellacked finish was chipped and incised with raw wood drawings and declarations. *A hard man is good to find. Yo, Michelle! The bartender is a great fuck.* Some wag had transformed the arrow piercing a Valentine's heart into a rocket-penis with an American flag on top. At the tippy-top of the flag, there stood a tiny, waving figure whose stick arms and corkscrew curl made it resemble something out of Dr. Seuss.

She resolved that she would not look at Olivia. For an entire cigarette, she blew her smoke toward the fruit and vegetable lights that twinkled so dreamily overhead, regarded the smudged tin ceiling.

Finally, she allowed herself to peek. And found Olivia nowhere in sight. Forty minutes. Suppose that she never came back to this booth in which Ellen didn't even *want* to be sitting, in which she, like a castaway, out in an ocean storm, struggled to see over the tops of foamy waves? Feeling a need for safety, she now scooted to the booth's back corner, contracted her surfaces as much as possible.

This did not stop her from feeling endangered.

What's Dan up to tonight? she wondered.

After a time, she returned to the edge of the booth. There was Olivia, at the bar, talking to an older painter from their program, a guy in a multicolor kufi hat. He was supposed to be a Big Talent. Bob Devereaux. Ellen thought Bob Devereaux was a bit much (his collection of kufi hats, his lazy Cajun accent, the blue tick hound that trailed him to the Art Department studios). The bartender set a beer in front of Olivia. One of the beers she was fetching for herself and Ellen? While Olivia pulled some bills from the back pocket of her jeans, the bartender set out a second beer.

Finally! But Olivia did not pick up the beers. She continued talking to Bob Devereaux and an older woman with cropped hair and what seemed to be lederhosen (some kind of stiff shorts with embroidered suspenders). The bartender set three shots up on the bar, and the woman in the lederhosen and Olivia and the painter downed them. Olivia's made her cough, and Bob Devereaux rubbed and patted her back in a familiar way. Olivia grinned and laughed through her coughing, signaling she was okay, so Bob Devereaux and the lady in the lederhosen laughed, too—like they were all old friends, Ellen thought.

It pained Ellen to watch this. In part because she had the strange feeling that what went on at the bar was somehow her own story, too; that what Olivia did next would determine what Ellen herself did, and, as she thought this—a grim thought— Olivia turned from the bar with the beers. After all this time, for the first time since they had arrived at Hooch's, Olivia caught Ellen's eyes, watching her—

I noted how the Ellen-character flushed when "caught" by Olivia; the same way that I had flushed and tried to hide my tears after Esmé hugged me in Will's and my front hall.

After a moment's hesitation, Olivia raised her smooth, tanned shoulders and made a comic grimace, as if to say, *Sorry for the delay, Ellen, but people wouldn't let me go!* In practically the same instant, however, a long arm in a flannel shirt shot up at the next table and Olivia crouched down by that table, too! All that Ellen could see of Olivia was her claw of bangs, identical to other fashionable claws of bangs poking up here and there throughout the crowd, and what she felt then—her longing not to be alone one moment longer, her jealousy and resentment of her friend's ease in the world—it *roared* in her ears, so loud she had to turn her face to the back wall of the booth, stare at the stainless steel napkin dispenser and the bottles of catsup and mustard and Heinz 57 in their neat metal corral. Not only did she mean to prevent any possibility of Olivia's spotting her hurt and anger; she also wanted to insure that she did not see whatever Olivia did next. Something in all this reminded her of how, at Saint Olaf— after she'd accidentally walked in on a snarky dorm-room conversation about herself—she had taken to making as much noise as possible before she entered a room.

"Whew!" The booth's wooden seat registered a bounce. It was Olivia, now dropping down beside her. Olivia's eyes drooped a little from the drinks that she had received during her trip around the bar, but she smiled happily at Ellen and she said, "If it isn't my best pal in the whole world! Sorry it took so long to get away from people, best pal!"

Best pal. So maybe she actually understood what she'd put Ellen through with this wait? Never would do it again?

"Whew!" Olivia repeated, and then, to Ellen's surprise, Olivia gave her a sustained hug. The hug—Ellen's own family did not hug except on big occasions, and Olivia's hug restored Ellen, set her glowing, as warm and festive as the pumpkin and grape and chili lights overhead, and she went on glowing while she downed her beer and Olivia pointed out different people in the bar and told their stories:

"Bob Devereaux—he's a genius!"

"That pretty brunette in the halter top—I guess she's a slut!"

"The lady in the lederhosen bakes the cookies at Nellie's Bakery, and she says she'll give us free samples if we come by."

Us. So Olivia had mentioned Ellen to the lady. That was good. That was excellent. Ellen gestured toward the bar, for Olivia to let her out of the booth. "I'll go up and get us another round."

"It was empty when we got here." So said the people who sat in the booth when Ellen returned with two beers. "Sorry!" they added, but not as if they were about to yield the spot. *Finders keepers, losers weepers.*

It took Ellen three trips around the bar before she found Olivia in a booth positively crammed with young men and women, three of the latter being the pretty women whom Olivia referred to as the Bimbettes.

"Oops! Gotta go!" Olivia said when she saw Ellen and proceeded to climb over the laps and arms of the people hemming her in.

"Esmé!" they protested. "Don't go!"

Esmé, I had written, not *Olivia.* My god. Suppose that I had submitted the story and it had been accepted and a proofreader had not noticed the error!

Olivia did not look at Ellen but, as if they were spies or gangsters, she murmured out the side of her mouth, "Let's blow this pop stand!"

In the foyer, while they stood alongside a muscle-bound guy with a terrible case of acne—a bouncer?—Olivia downed the beer that Ellen had been carrying for her, and she said between gulps, managing to sound both exuberant and mournful, "I won't claim I wasn't having fun talking to those people, Ellen, but I'd rather be with just you any day!" Then she told the big guy, "This is my best buddy, here." The poor guy—he looked as if larvae pupated under his skin; some already poked out the tips of their tiny red heads. *Angry*—that was even a way of talking about disturbed skin, wasn't it? *Angry-looking skin?* The man's skin, even more than his outsize muscles, suggested that he'd tear off somebody's head at the least provocation; still, Olivia insisted on letting him know how "breathtakingly" smart her good friend Ellen was:

"Tell him what you said earlier, Ellen. About Magritte! Go on!"

The man gave Ellen a hard look. "Have no fear," she said as she stowed her empty glass on top of the nearby cigarette machine. Then she stepped behind Olivia and settled her hands on Olivia's shoulders, gave them a jiggle and, as if starting her engine, made a *vroom-vroom* noise. Olivia let herself be steered through the open door and onto the sidewalk. Something about that—Ellen *wanted* to be angry, but then she was so glad that she and Olivia were together, now, heading back to their apartment, that she couldn't help loving Olivia, too.

"Ellen!" Olivia spun around and set her own hands on Ellen's shoulders. "Bob Devereaux's going to be a star! He's the only person in the program worth knowing—besides you, of course." She raised her eyes toward the tarnished sky over Dinkytown. "Bob Devereaux. Isn't that a great name?"

Ellen laughed. She realized that she was a bit drunk, too. As she and Olivia made their unsteady way to the apartment—the sidewalks were all up and down, akimbo from the monster tree roots that had cracked and heaved the concrete over the frozen Minnesota winters—they kept bumping into each other, which struck them both as very funny, and, when they reached the apartment, Olivia brought out a foil-wrapped lump of what turned out to be powerful hashish, and soon, feeling very close to her dear new friend—such a perfect audience, so attentive, her dark eyes glowing while she yipped with glee or frowned and shook her head and said a woeful *Oh, Ellen, you didn't!*—Ellen spilled the details of her undergraduate life (serial monogamy followed by a brief, scary fling at promiscuity; then artistic celibacy in black Louise Nevelson drapery, Bloody Marys her preferred company when away from the college's painting studios).

The two had come to a rest on their favorite spot for conversation, the apartment's ugly orange sofa. Periodically, Olivia reached for Ellen's hand and squeezed it reassuringly while Ellen told the story of how that crazy life had come to an end.

14

The tale that "Ellen" told "Olivia" was a pretty accurate description of that era in which I wound up, blotto, in front of the farmer's pickup truck.

I remember nothing of the actual accident. Have no memory of where I was headed. Never did learn whose bike I was riding. In the story that I was told, after the pickup hit me, I flew right over its cab. My short trip to the bed of that pickup truck loaded with treacherous farm implements had resulted in a ruptured spleen, seven broken bones, and a concussion. I made an excellent recovery, the only residual effects being the deaf ear, some bones that ache in rainy weather, and a wide silver snake of scar on the back of my skull that has prevented me from ever again wearing a ponytail.

At some point during in my hospital stay—I'd been transported by ambulance to the big hospital down in Iowa City—I once overheard a pair of doctors speculate as to what my head had hit: the edge of a shovel or maybe an auger of some sort?

A customer at a nearby gas station subsequently would claim that the hog farmer was at fault, but the gas station owner and one of his workers said, *No, the girl drove right out in front of him,* and I certainly didn't blame the farmer or wish that he had been charged.

I was chastened.

Later, my mother told me that she had fainted when she got the call about the accident; and, then, again when she drove over from Webster City and saw me at the hospital. My head, she said, had looked like a rotten pumpkin, and I was hooked up to monitors and IV lines and there were things going up my nose and down my throat. "When your dad came, the next day, he almost fainted, too!"

By the time that the doctors declared me out of the woods, and I became aware of my mother's visits, all that I saw was mortification. My parents were almost sixty years old, and conservative, small-town people. For years—truly, until the time that my sister's son was arrested for selling MDA—they would view the fact that news of my drunken accident had appeared in not only our hometown newspaper but also *The Des Moines Register* as our family's greatest catastrophe.

Poor Mom. Having a kid at forty-one had not been in her plans. She shimmered with relief at my high school graduation. She imagined that I'd go off with my scholarship to the nice little college in pretty Mount Vernon, Iowa, and find a husband and have kids and stop moping around and writing poems in my bedroom—although she herself, a married lady who'd had kids, secretly resorted to a variety of tranquilizing pills and, when my dad was away, sometimes showed the full extent of her depressions by locking herself in her bedroom and not coming out all day. She did act more normal when my dad was at home but there were migraine headaches that sent her to bed and hives that bloomed from her neck down to her toes. During certain stressful periods, the skin on her fingers and palms and feet formed a thick, pearly bark that she picked at, exposing the tender flesh beneath, shockingly pink, fissured. On dish towels and bars of soap and kitchen sponges, she left behind little stars of blood. The very first time that I went to the ocean and saw jingle shells on the beach, I thought of the silvery disks of skin that marred my mother's otherwise lovely hands. During my hospital stay, one of my professors—the young Renaissance literature scholar and poet named Lydia Ott—came to visit me, and even then my mother could not stop her furious picking. "What is she *doing* here?" my mother had whispered to me when Professor Ott left the room to get herself a soda.

"She's being nice," I said.

Professor Ott had come to let me know that I wasn't to worry about my final project. *No rush*, she'd said, *concentrate on getting well!* I admired her and was very moved by the visit. I knew that she was from a small Midwestern town, too. At twenty-eight, she already had published a book of poems. I was determined to be more like her when I got out of the hospital; to give up wearing makeup and simply gather my hair at my nape each morning in a broad, flat barrette of Navajo silver. She couldn't have been kinder, sitting there on the opposite side of the bed from my mother in the bland and much too sunny hospital room, asking about Webster City and its Kendall Young Library. *And did you come from Webster City originally, Mrs. Price?* It was so generous of her to have driven down from Mount Vernon to visit me! To have bothered with hospital parking and all! Despite my hard times socializing with other students, I'd loved my college classes and my teachers, too. Once, a sleepy winter afternoon in her minuscule, overheated office in South Hall, a rim of snow piled up outside the windowsill where her avocado plant barely survived in its salt-rimed terra-cotta pot, Professor Ott actually had confided in me, telling me that her father had shot and killed her mother in a domestic dispute. I began to worry that my mother would say something awful, offend Professor Ott or make her think less of me. I knew that I looked hideous, then, all bruised and swollen, and I was dopey with pain medication, too, no good to the conversation at all.

As if she sensed my anxiety, Professor Ott stood up to go. My mother fixed her face in the manic smile—my smile, too?—that she used so hopefully during anxious moments when she longed to be taken for a peppy and utterly normal person. "This"—she waved a hand at me, flat in the hospital bed—"it's not typical of our family!"

Lydia Ott stopped at the end of the bed, and she squeezed my toes through the heavy hospital sheet. "You should know, Mrs. Price," she said, "all of us at the college think the world of Charlotte."

This was a very kind exaggeration, no doubt meant to reassure both my mother and me regarding my return to the college. I appreciated it. My mother didn't. As soon as the professor was out in the hall, my mother leaned close to me and huffed, "There's somebody who thinks she's pretty special! La-di-da!"

A few weeks later, a silent ambulance transported me to Webster City; delivered me to the rehabilitation center that, in that small town, meant one wing of a nursing home. Being nineteen, wheeled up to tables for meals with people whose rheumy, drooping eyes looked like dissolving cough drops; people whose mouths often hung open—dark, shiny, toothless caverns—and, in the middle of the night, cried out in a panic over something they could not remember, I was inspired to work very hard at my physical therapy, and, after three more weeks, my parents moved me into my old room.

The room had been transformed, after I left for college, into the storage space that my parents always had longed for in their tiny two-bedroom house. I had for company, among other things, my dad's table saw and a fully decorated artificial Christmas tree. Given how glad I was to have escaped the nursing home, I did not mind too much. As I said, I was chastened.

Heeding the advice given me by several very grave-faced people at the hospital, I began (to my parents' horror) attending the Wednesday and Friday noon AA meetings held in an A-frame-style Episcopal church that, as a little kid, I had passed every day on my way to Sunset Heights Elementary. A very old lady in penny loafers and grandma jeans put her tiny, cold hand on mine at the end of my first meeting and said, "You don't ever have to have another drink, honey," and though there would be plenty of occasions when I would want to drink again, at that moment, the consequences of my drinking were agonizingly fresh—I had used a cane to walk to that first meeting—and the old lady's words were a balm to me. I bought a copy of the AA Big Book and I read it. It *interested* me. The wisdom outweighed the nonsense. The people at the meetings were working to live decent lives, and they interested me, too. I wanted to live a decent life, too. Although I could not accept everything I heard, I appreciated the fact that everybody at the meetings seemed to be there in earnest.

While staying at my parents' house that summer, I did waste some time trying to figure out a way to transfer to another college for my senior year (despite Lydia Ott's reassurance, I couldn't bear the thought of facing my old classmates). Of course, it did not take long for me to learn any transfer would prevent my graduating the following spring. So it was that, passably restored—wearing a scarf to cover the area on the back of my skull that had been shaved and stitched, limping a little, deaf in one ear—at the end of August, I took the Greyhound back across the state to Mount Vernon. A pretty town, a hilly oasis among the cornfields, the gray stone tower of the campus's landmark chapel sticking out of a grand bouquet of summer-green trees. The bus made its stop on the little main street, and, after settling into my backpack, pulling my wheel-along behind me, I went into Sprague's Drugstore to buy a pack of cigarettes.

I was standing in line at the checkout when I heard the voice of Professor Ott behind me. I turned—in the wrong direction because of my bum ear—and so I faced not Lydia Ott but the tall, seriously handsome young man standing beside her.

This was Will Ludlow, Lydia Ott explained, a friend from her undergraduate days at Carleton. Will Ludlow was renting in Mount Vernon while he worked on his doctorate in art history down in Iowa City.

Will Ludlow shook my hand. His deep *How do you do* set off thrilling vibrations in my ribcage, like a drum passing during a parade.

"I read a story of yours," he said. "While I was on Lydia and Scott's porch, waiting for them to come home." It seemed that there had been a copy of the college literary magazine on the porch's coffee table. Under his heavy brow, Will Ludlow's light eyes were difficult to read. A little uncanny. A little like looking at the eyes of a blind person. He did not smile at me, but he said, "You're the real thing," and then he turned to Lydia Ott and asked, "Have you read that story? Do you have enough food for her to join us for dinner?"

I knew that etiquette forbade his asking such a thing of his hostess, and I said—while hoping the answer would be yes—"I don't want to impose!" Lydia Ott smiled and said, "Of course I've read her story, and, sure, Charlotte, join us!"

A few minutes later, we three—I kept sneaking looks at long-legged Will Ludlow, who had insisted on taking charge of my suitcase and backpack—walked to the home of Lydia Ott and her lawyer-husband, Scott Anderson.

During the candlelit dinner, loopy in Will Ludlow's presence—his lips were not large but looked very tender; a good, animal smell emanated from under his plaid flannel shirt—I felt as if my legs might start to dance against the underside of Lydia Ott's picnic table, dash the plates of pasta and salad onto the floor. A delicious feeling, but also scary. I wondered what Will Ludlow made of the fact that I did not drink the wine that was his contribution to the dinner. After I left, of course, Lydia Ott would tell him about my accident. Of course, he would write me off as a loser.

So it was that I experienced a positive sense of release—I would get out of there with my heart, after all!—when, elbows on the table, forehead furrowed, Will Ludlow began to talk about his struggle to understand the work of a certain poststructuralist critic.

"You'd be in more trouble if you thought you did understand her!" I blurted.

He and Lydia and her genial, round-faced husband—all three looking startled—turned my way, while, hot-cheeked, I went on:

"I trust myself to find the logic in what I read. It may require work, but I ought to be able to find it, right? I ought to be able to rephrase the thinking without using any ambiguous jingo. So far, the only people I've known or read who act like they know what she's talking about are people who parrot her."

Scott Anderson smiled at me. "Well put," he said, "though I think you mean *jargon.*"

"*Jargon,*" I said. I could hear myself say *jingo.* Christ.

"You should be a lawyer," he said. That got a laugh, and the topic of the critic was dropped, but toward the end of the evening, when I learned that Will Ludlow's area of interest was Italian Futurism, I felt the urge to needle him again, to dislike him. I happened to have read an article about the Futurists, and I said, "But weren't they, like, a big influence on the Fascists?"

He nodded. "Aspects of their thinking were appropriated and distorted by the Fascists, but essentials of their aesthetic continue to be important to a number of contemporary artists."

He sounded more serene about the matter than I thought he should have.

"Granted, I don't know much about them," I said, "but weren't they, like, *Down with women!*?"

"Well, they were, but"—

"Charlotte," Lydia Ott interjected, smiling, "a lot of important figures in history have been misogynists. I'm afraid that if we excluded all of the misogynists, we wouldn't have much history to study."

Will Ludlow nodded. "And, actually, your writing is probably influenced by the Futurists more than you know, Charlotte."

I snorted—yes, I did—and said, "I doubt that!"

Scott Anderson laughed. He was walking around the table, just then, grating fresh nutmeg onto our scoops of vanilla ice cream, and while he grated away by my elbow, he said, "I'll drive you up the hill in a bit, Charlotte. Deliver you and your bags to your dorm."

Some part of me held on to a hope that Will Ludlow might offer to drive me to campus, and I said, "Oh, no need." A flurry of discussion followed. Lydia objected that I couldn't walk all that way with my luggage—and did I even have a room key yet? No. Then it was decided: Scott would drive me. Will Ludlow apologized. He would have offered, he said, but he himself had come on foot.

I was disappointed. Relieved.

The next morning, I awoke to the buzzer sounding in my new dormitory room. I went out into the hall and, after a short search, I located the telephone for the front desk. "I'm in two-twelve," I told the girl who answered. "You buzzed me?"

"You have a guest waiting in the lobby," she said.

Backlit, Will Ludlow stood by the entrance, staring outside. When I said his name and he turned, I saw that his flannel shirt was unbuttoned all the way, and there was nothing but bare skin under the shirt. I had been agitated by him the night before. Now I went limp.

I exchanged an unusual number of greetings with my fellow students as Will Ludlow and I walked along my little campus's smooth and clean asphalt paths that morning. The school's enrollment sat at under a thousand, and—because of my hermit's ways—I knew only a small number of people well; but a lot of people were curious about me that day (I supposed because of both my accident and the handsome man walking at my side). How odd it would be, I thought, if the amount of attention we drew as we walked along made Will Ludlow imagine that I were "popular."

He stopped, near the kiosk where campus events were posted. "I've been thinking about you and your story," he said. "All night. You're an artist."

He wanted to know who I'd studied with, besides Lydia. Well, no one, but I talked a bit about Jean Rhys. Alice Munro and Chekhov and Nabokov. I regretted that I didn't have sophisticated things to say about each of them. "They're different from each other, but they're all inspiring. I can tell they're writing absolutely as well as they possibly can. And telling the truth about what they know. For me, those two things go hand in hand."

Will Ludlow said, sounding younger, then, very enthusiastic, "The way that you expose yourself in your work—that moment when the girl walked on top of the roof." He shook his head. "That was pretty dark. I admired that."

It occurred to me that the students who passed by us were moving toward the gymnasium for registration—there, with a blushing wave, was the boy who had formerly supplied my gallons of vodka— and that I needed to register, too, but it hardly mattered because I was with Will Ludlow.

"I try not to be whimsical," I told him. "I'm not interested in whimsy."

He smiled. "Okay."

It seemed to me he might be amused, so I added, "I think the Futurists are kind of whimsical."

"The Futurists?"

"They'd just say anything. They thought it was cute. Like they were bad little boys."

He shook his head. "You're thinking about Marinetti," he said. "There's more to the Futurists than what's in his manifesto. They're important historical figures. Let's go to your library. I'll show you some pictures."

While we walked on, he had this very keen look on his face, looking ahead and about himself. He breathed deeply, as if he relished the air. *Avid.* Like a setter. I wanted him to put his hands on me. *Why do we have to go to the library?* I thought as we stepped out of the summer-warm day into the foyer's air-conditioned cool.

"Wait, though." Before we passed through the second set of doors, he took my hand and walked me back outside; guided me behind the shaggy arborvitae along the library's foundation, and, with a sigh, clasped me to his long torso.

His big heart thudded deep in my ear.

We stood this way for a while; then he lowered his head toward mine and whispered something.

"I'm deaf on that side," I said.

"Right. Lydia told me something about that." He rubbed his

knuckles gently across the top of my head. "What I said—I said I'm so glad I met you."

Well, I was a goner, a quaint version of my former self.

I would soon discover, however, that Will Ludlow did not behave the way that I expected a boyfriend to behave. My previous boyfriends had wanted to be with me every second. Will Ludlow, on the other hand, was very busy with his work, whether teaching or doing his research or writing at his rental house in Mount Vernon. On the weekends, we cooked dinners together and we went to movies and things, but, during the week, I rarely saw him until nine thirty, when he drove up to my dormitory in his beater station wagon and ferried me back to his place. After sex, sleep, and, in the morning, baguettes with butter and jam and coffee made in his Chemex—he had adopted a Continental breakfast after traveling in Europe—he would go to his desk or to his car for his drive to Iowa City. If the weather was nice, I would walk across Mount Vernon to my own school's campus to begin my day. The routine was not without romance, but it unsettled me. When I finally got up the nerve, I objected to the fact that we spent so much time apart.

"But you have your work to do, too, Charlotte," said Will—clearly startled by my bursting into tears. "You always seem busy."

"That's because you're busy!" I said, but either he was right or I changed, because soon it did seem as if my absorption with my writing quite precisely mirrored his with his scholarship.

15

Drunk and stoned, the night after that party at the Victorian, I had told Esmé way too much about Will and myself. If I had been sober, I never would have shown her the letter (five single-spaced pages) that Will had mailed to me from Italy, a kind of treatise regarding his vision for our future. I viewed the letter as a testament to his intelligence and love, but Esmé hooted over the thing and insisted on reading aloud from it in a haughty voice ("We'll want to defer having children until we've achieved some professional standing"). She and I had been reading *Middlemarch* in Nineteenth Century British Novels, and she declared that Will sounded like Mr. Casaubon, and, then, of course—or so I thought—I had to correct that impression, and I went on and on about what a passionate and romantic person he was.

The morning after, for the first time since my accident, I woke up with a hangover. It was a bad one, and there stood Esmé, beside my bed in her fluffy pink bathrobe, saying, as if it were great news, "Charlotte! Look! Your parents are here!"

Truly. Standing in the door to my room, peeking in.

Esmé grinned and she crossed her eyes at me. I suspected that she felt as rocky as I did.

"Day's a-wasting!" my dad called. More circumspect, my mother said a low "She's not dressed, Dave," and as they backed into the hall, she called to me, "The McMichaels gave us their tickets for the football game."

Hurry, Esmé mouthed; then said aloud, "I'll make coffee!"

My parents were pretty dreadful, but I loved them (no doubt, they would have said something similar about me). Despite my agitation at their showing up unannounced and my hangover—would it be obvious?—I felt protective of them. They were getting old and they were exactly the types of Iowans that Workshop people found amusing as hell—both of them, I'd noticed, wore green polyester windbreakers emblazoned with the name of Webster City's grain cooperative—and so I rushed into my jeans and sweatshirt.

Not that I thought Esmé would be anything less than polite, but, during one of our late-night talks, she had let me understand, her forehead wrinkled in polite correction, that, as far as she was concerned, people got what they deserved in this world. Her paternal grandfather, she explained, had arrived in the United States with nothing but a straight-edged razor and, through offering shaves in a cold-water flat in Chicago, he had financed his education and become the noted lawyer who founded the big firm where her own father now put in, as she said, "outrageously long hours, and, since he's probably a genius and works so hard—well, it's only fair that people like himself get a bigger piece of the pie." Because my own parents worked hard, and I wanted Esmé to see that things did not always work out equitably, I told her my dad's hard-luck story. My dad's father had abandoned the family, and so, at thirteen, to help support his mother and sister, my dad had left school. "He never got to go back," I said.

"But why not?" Esmé asked. "If he really wanted to!"

I'd wished—out of fairness to my dad—that I knew precisely how to answer Esmé, but I wasn't sure any answer would suffice. Esmé never had heard of an egg handler or a brakeman, let alone known people who held those jobs. "Surreal!" she declared when I explained that my mother's job consisted of loading trays of eggs onto the many shelves of a large trolley that she then wheeled into the hatchery's incubators. Esmé did not understand why people who weren't students at the Writers' Workshop lived in Iowa, where there were no museums or clubs or restaurants or places to buy decent clothes.

Things seemed fine, though, when I stepped out into the kitchen the morning of my parents' visit to the Burlington Street apartment. My dad, seated at the dinette, was laughing heartily at something that Esmé had said (*Dave*, Esmé was calling him). My mother, shy like myself, had busied herself at the counter, making sure that the toast in the toaster didn't get burned.

Touching, embarrassing—she and my dad had stopped before coming to the apartment and bought us a loaf of Wonder Bread and a pound of margarine. This was the sort of stuff that Ésme laughingly would refer to as "industrial food," but, making toast from Wonder Bread was a fundamental task in our family. After Martie's marriage had ended in divorce, both of my parents regularly mentioned that they had warned Martie against marrying Rex—and why was that? Apparently—I was a toddler at the time—on his first visit to meet our parents, at breakfast, Rex had taken toast from the toaster for himself and failed to ask if he should put in fresh slices for anyone else. "*Mean*," my father said whenever the subject of Rex and the toast came up. It remained legend around my parents' house.

To conceal my hangover breath, before I kissed my mother's cheek, I took a deep inhale. "Jam?" asked my dad as I dropped a kiss on top of his head. I was eager to go to the bathroom for aspirin, but I pulled a jar of jam from the refrigerator and set it on the table. Gleefully, as he had throughout my childhood, my dad recited:

The jam, the jelly, the marmalade
And other pleasant things they made
Down at old Aunt Mary's!

Esmé laughed, which my dad liked. Some girls I'd known, growing up, had said that he was cute, with his dimpled chin and bedroom eyes, but it could embarrass and pain my mother and me, the way that, around pretty females—waitresses, clerks, whatever—he'd get this obvious *twinkle* going. I could see a bit of the twinkle when he asked Esmé, "So you're a writer, too?"

She dropped a curtsy with her fluffy pink robe. "Well, I'm writing, Dave. We'll see what happens."

"That's the right attitude," my mother said as she dutifully added fresh slices of bread to the toaster. "Not much of a career, writing stories."

"Did Charlotte tell you her story got picked?" Esmé smiled at me. "This great new writer—Michael Chabon—he's coming to read and do an afternoon workshop, and he picked Charlotte's story to discuss!"

"Any money in it?" my dad asked—Esmé, not me.

"It's an *honor*, Dave," Esmé said, but in a teasing voice, as if she took his point.

He grinned. "Honor won't get you no goodies at the candy store."

"Call me a prude, Esmé"—my mom looked up from spreading the margarine on slices of toast—"but I don't care for the profanity in my daughter's work."

Briefly, Esmé looked blank. "Is there profanity in your work?" she asked me. My mom flushed. She surely had hoped to impress my roommate with her high standards of decorum. Now, I supposed, she feared that she looked like a hayseed. Maybe she worried that I had shown the Workshop a story featuring a mother who regularly threatened to slit her wrists, packed her suitcases and set them by the front door and said she would be calling a taxi to take her to the Greyhound, she was done, *Get out of my sight!*

Most likely, though, she entertained only the hayseed concern. After her scary episodes petered out, my mom never seemed to remember them. By the time I was fourteen or so, I'd started to feel more sorry for her than angry. I'd seen her bite her lip in order not to cry out the time that she scratched the needle across her beloved Johnny Mathis album in a rush to get the album off the turntable before my dad made it in from the garage to the house.

He hated it when she listened to romantic music.

"So what do you hear from the professor, Charlotte?" she asked.

I told Esmé, "She means Will," then said, "Will is fine, Mom."

She laughed. "Is that *all*?" She was leery of Will, the learned guy, but also excited by his good looks and nice manners.

"What do you think, Esmé," my dad said, "of a fellow who'd run off and leave his girl all alone while he traipses around Italy?"

"Oh!" Esmé laughed and shook her head. "I've never met Will, Dave, but he writes such *long* and *serious* letters to Charlotte"—she winked at me—"I can't imagine he's got time to play around!"

My dad lowered his voice to almost a growl. "Lots of gorgeous women in Italy."

Esmé laughed. "I bet he's true, though!"

"Thank you, Esmé," I said but felt sick at the memory of showing her Will's letter.

"We don't want her being a sap, Esmé," my dad said.

"Of course not," Esmé said. "No parent wants that."

My dad helped himself to the toast from the plate that my mom now set on the dinette. The raspberry jam. The cup of coffee that

Esmé poured for him. My mom stuck to coffee. Watching her weight? Like myself, back then, she regularly lost and regained the same ten or fifteen pounds, and she had gained since I saw her last. I could imagine her, getting ready to drive to Iowa City, hoping that the grain cooperative's big green windbreaker would hide the pounds. Instead, it concealed the fact that she had a nice shape, a small waist.

"I should get dressed and let you three visit!" Esmé said.

I was grateful to her for being kind to my parents—also proud that she was my friend—and as soon as she was out in the hall, I whispered, "Isn't she great?"

"I'll say!" My dad grinned and rubbed his hands over his face in astonished pleasure. "I'd ask her out in a minute!"

"I meant as a *friend*!" I squeaked. "For me!"

One eye on the doorway, my mom leaned deep over the dinette, and she whispered, "A big fat ha-ha! I wouldn't trust her as far as I could throw her."

"Oh, trust." My dad laughed. "Trust's a different matter altogether! And if you kept her *real* close—" He broke off with another laugh.

"Men," my mom muttered into her coffee cup.

I agreed with what I took for her meaning—*Aren't they exasperating?*—but I stood up from the dinette as if I hadn't heard. My whole life, she'd been available to let me know that she could *just tell* that so-and-so did not truly like me, was not a good friend and snickered at me behind my back. In her way, she meant to protect me, I think, but it was no good.

"When Will gets back"—she tugged at a belt loop on the back of my jeans as I moved past her and toward the kitchen sink—"you sure as heck better not leave her in a room with him."

I protested. "Will *loves* me, Mom!"

She shook her head. "Don't say I didn't warn you."

My dad laughed at that, too. There had been only one incident in my life, apart from my bike accident, that had seemed to get his full attention: He and my mom had come home early from his union Christmas party and found me and my high school boyfriend having sex on the living room carpet. Once the boy was gone—shoved and shouted out the door and forced to dress on the back steps—my dad had slapped me around for a long time, had actually torn out a hunk of my hair at one point. What he really wanted was for me to agree with him that I was a "whore"—my mother tried to get me to do it; *Say yes, Charlotte, and he'll stop!*—but it was too crazy. It was too stupid. I refused.

Really, I had the impression that the man viewed my life—the life of the accidental child who also happened to turn out a "bookworm"—as inconsequential, like a comic strip that he read now and then, or a TV series that he never stopped to watch for a full episode, so you could not really expect him to keep the characters straight.

What a crew the three of us were! With all of my reading and writing, I was anxiously civilized but remained so much like them, ruled at least half my waking hours by the notion that someone had done me wrong. Or might soon. We were Victims of the World. Which, in the family ethos, was quite different from being a sap. Being a victim was *not* your fault. Being a victim did not leave you disgraced. Degraded. Tainted.

Unfortunately, I did not understand that viewing yourself as a victim could make you, *poor little you*, liable to do damage to others; that victimhood itself was often sustained by self-inflicted wounds—tearing off scabs from things that would have healed if simply left alone.

After my parents left that morning, Esmé and I decided that we would work off our hangovers by walking to the Hamburg Inn for a late breakfast. I started us singing as soon as we were out the door because I wanted to eliminate the possibility of Esmé saying anything about my parents. (They'd looked so old, gripping the banister as they'd disappeared into the stairwell, that my irritation with them had shifted, and the need to protect them had flooded me again).

The Hamburg Inn was jammed with people when Esmé and I arrived. We just had settled ourselves along the diner's front window ledge to wait for a table when I spotted a familiar battered fedora in a booth toward the back. Jeremy Fletcher. Unfortunately, Esmé spotted him, too. "He wants us to sit with him!" she whispered happily, and, sure enough, Jeremy Fletcher jabbed a finger up and down, signaling for us to join him.

I was happy that Esmé was happy, but why Jeremy Fletcher? Right after we joined him, a pretty waitress passed by our booth and he made a point of ogling her rear. "I wouldn't kick her out of bed," he said.

Still, I could see that Jeremy Fletcher wanted to be with Esmé. He had stood up and gestured for her to sit on the inside of his side of the booth, and when he had sat down again, he did something kind of odd—he was not tall, maybe five-eight, and she was five-seven, and he folded one of his calves under himself and *roosted* on top of it. Trying to look taller, I thought.

"So how are y'all feeling this morning?" he asked.

We both groaned. "And imagine this"—Esmé leaned forward and let her torso collapse on the tabletop—"Charlotte's sweet little parents paid us a surprise visit! Came knocking with a loaf of white bread and a pound of margarine!" She grinned at me and then at Jeremy Fletcher. He grinned back. Before long, he began to talk at length about his novel; how "powerfully" it integrated the models provided by both "Shakespeare and the King James."

Esmé was as smart as could be, really, but she seemed satisfied simply to listen to Jeremy Fletcher; to say *hm!* and *hm!* and occasionally lower her eyes or tilt her head to one side or the other as if, in that way, she fine-tuned her attention to this master.

An hour or so later, as we left him yammering away to some pipe-smoker outside the diner, she made a pitty-pat motion over her heart. "Isn't he amazing?"

"I'd put our work up against his any day," I said.

Esmé made wide eyes, as if I had overreached myself.

"Really!" I said. "And that 'I wouldn't kick her out of bed' stuff? Come on. Ick."

She threw her arm around my neck then and pretended to throttle me. "Oh, you think any man who isn't your precious Will is a jerk!"

While I disentangled myself, I said, "That's an exaggeration."

"Okay, okay." She gave me a sideways hug. "But you don't get Jeremy, Charlotte. He's the real thing. Like . . . Burroughs."

"Burroughs. Yeah, Burroughs liked guns, too. Watch out, Es. Get cozy with Jeremy Fletcher and he might try a little William Tell on you. That's how Burroughs killed his wife, you know. He tried to shoot an apple on her head. Then attributed the whole thing to evil. With a capital *E*."

"You're terrible! But, Charlotte"—she made a pretty pout—"what if it's *you* he likes, not me?"

People giving you what was supposed to be a compliment strictly so that you would hand it over to them—it always depressed me, but I laughed and added what seemed to me both obvious and required: "Anyone could tell he was overjoyed to be talking to you and would have been happy to see me vamoose!"

"W-e-l-l." She drew out the word; then, with a happy yip, she said, "I think you're right!"

"I'm right." I was happy to see a cute Workshop guy, Pedro Galvez, a ways up the street. I figured that Esmé would drop the subject of Jeremy Fletcher around Pedro Galvez. Why couldn't she like nice Pedro Galvez, with his cute bandannas and bopping walk? A few days before, I'd ridden my bike by Main Library and seen her talking out front with Pedro Galvez, laughing so hard that she held on to his arm, like she'd fall over otherwise—

Now, however, as soon as she saw him, she grabbed my hand and started pulling me toward the door of a dry-cleaning place. "I can't talk to Pedro!" she said.

I hardly knew the guy but hiding from him seemed mean, and I pulled back. "Stop!"

The look she turned my way before she disappeared into the dry cleaner's was one I had not seen before—perfectly icy.

Alone, shaken, I continued up the street. Always so awkward, approaching people on the street, and soon came the moment at which it was necessary for me to offer the first smile of distant recognition. I smiled. After that, I alternated between quick looks down at the sidewalk, up at approaching Pedro—another little smile—then a look at the homemade poster-paint-and-paper advertisements in the windows of John's Grocery—a smile—now down at the sidewalk again, until we were only a few feet apart, and I looked up and smiled and said, "Hey, Pedro."

He smiled over my shoulder. At Esmé. Who now mock-wailed from behind me, "Why'd you abandon me, Charlotte?" as up she ran, waving a ticket that she apparently had charmed out of a clerk at the dry cleaner's. "She's a cruel girl, Pedro!" she said, but in a voice that was light and teasing. "She wouldn't wait while I dropped off my sweaters, even though I told her I wanted to say hi to you!"

My heart was pounding. She was making absolutely no sense, but she knew that I would not say so (would not embarrass her or Pedro Galvez by pointing out that she had wanted to avoid him).

Pedro Galvez smiled at me. "You're the girl who wore three-piece suits during college, right? To look like Borges?"

I sneaked a peek at Esmé. Once, I'd told her how, as an under-graduate, I'd read an interview with Borges in which he mentioned that, as a young man, he'd found it easier to disappear in a crowd if he wore a conventional suit and a tie; and so, I—a nineteen-year-old American girl in the late 1980s—had misguidedly adopted the same look.

"I wasn't trying to *look* like Borges," I murmured.

"A misunderstanding on my part," Pedro Galvez said and bowed with a big swoop of his arm. Then he smiled at Esmé and asked her something about the night before; he'd thought that she was going to meet up with him at the Vine after she left the Victorian, and Esmé said, "Oh, yes, I'd really wanted to, but there hadn't been any way that I could; in the end, you see, because"—she gave her pretty fingers a shake, as if they had been forced to hold something hot for too long—"absolutely nothing worked out right, Pedro!"

A few minutes later, when the two of us resumed our walk to the apartment, she said, "Thanks for not blowing my cover, Char."

I know I sounded stiff when I answered, "You did make me look bad, though, Esmé."

"Oh, foo! You couldn't possibly look bad! Anyway"—she sighed happily—"for me, besides Jeremy, you're the only person worth knowing here. I mean, it's nice to see we could have other friends—and I know, I know, you have your precious Will off in Italy—but, otherwise, all we need is each other, right?"

She turned her dark brown eyes my way. They were intense, searching. Ridiculous, her asking me to agree! I was furious with her! And she had been furious with me a few minutes before!

At the same time, I did yearn for what she said to be true.

So I nodded. I smiled. I said, "Right."

16

It was Esmé who suggested that we stay in Iowa City for the Thanksgiving break, do our own holiday dinner, and I was game. "Maybe we could invite a couple of people?" I said.

"No, no. Just you and me—and Jeremy." She and Jeremy Fletcher were a couple by then. "That would be more fun, don't you think?"

Thanksgiving morning arrived, so icy cold that I wore my bathrobe over my jeans and sweater while I rolled out the dough for a pumpkin and a pecan pie. Any caulk that ever had held the apartment's windows tight had long since moldered and rattled away. After a time, the heat from the oven turned the kitchen windows steamy, fuzzing my view of the gray sky. As the morning progressed, almost as if in response to the mournful cello music that Esmé set playing in the living room, the windows began to run, little rivulets. She'd been on the telephone with her family for quite a while, but now she came into the kitchen to tell me she had decided to go to Evanston on Sunday.

"Mother thinks I need a new coat and"—she jerked a thumb toward the living room—"we're going to hear some Bach." She grinned. "Also, I want Jeremy to have the experience of missing me."

So, I thought, *people really do that!* I had supposed it was the stuff of characters in novels (Madame Bovary, Becky Sharp, and Anna Karenina).

After we carried the dinette set from the kitchen into the living room, I decided to go out for a run. Esmé had worked out the timing for everything. Once the turkey was done, it would need to sit for forty-five minutes. Jeremy Fletcher would arrive at one, dinner would be served at two, and we—and she hoped Jeremy Fletcher, too—would go to a movie around five. "We have to go to a movie on Thanksgiving!" she said. "It's a family tradition!"

I liked the idea of family traditions. A movie on Thanksgiving. Well, good.

I went to Oakland Cemetery for my run. Oakland Cemetery sat on the eastern skirt of Iowa City. Its roads wound between bare oak trees and evergreens, and I liked the way that I could leave the asphalt for dirt paths or old roads of red bricks that were rounded by wear, broken up, or disappearing altogether. Still, in a hooded sweatshirt of Will's, with my face covered by a plaid scarf, I felt a little lonely and anonymous.

I wondered: *Should I have gone home to Webster City?* My mother had sounded disappointed when I said I would not be coming. Then I thought: *If I were in Webster City right now, I'd probably be alone, out for a run at the cemetery.*

I put on my Walkman. The CD I listened to was one that Esmé once had teased me about. "Gloria Estefan? You're worse than I am, Charlotte! Why do you suppose we want to be *agitated* all the time?"

The question surprised me. I supposed it was true, though, that I sometimes sharpened my loneliness to a needle point. The taut-wired guitar *thwang* that signaled Gloria Estefan was about to sing the sad "Can't Stay Away from You"—it ravaged my heart. Did I want my heart to feel ravaged?

Shouldn't that have changed now that I had a good man to love? The way my eyes teared, you would have thought that, like the girl in the song, I loved not Will but a faithless dude who toyed with my affections or had abandoned me, and though I knew that I should forget him, I couldn't, couldn't, couldn't.

Heart full of missing what I sensed was not entirely Will—a feeling that had been with me at least since I was old enough to understand the lyrics of love songs on the radio and my mother's Johnny Mathis records—I started around the cemetery's largest and most famous grave, a monument topped by a giant figure that some people called the Black Angel and invested with both terrors and benedictions. "Don't want to be your second choice," Gloria Estefan sang, sorrowful and angry and baffled in equal measures, and ahead of me, like an object in the can-you-find-it pictures that I had loved as a kid, the perfectly still figure of a buff-colored deer magically detached itself from the cemetery's early winter background of dun grass and leafless hedges and headstones. I stopped. I supposed my breathing was loud, but all I could hear was the plaintive song of Gloria Estefan. A deer, two deer, three. They blinked their big, long-lashed eyes—at me, it felt like. Then so very delicately they shifted and turned, cantered off elegantly on their neat black hooves in the direction of a wire fence that divided the cemetery from the woods of Hickory Hill Park, and somehow—how did they do that?—their front legs lightly rose over the top wire just one fraction of a second before their back legs came after them.

"Thank you," I called. Thanksgiving goodness. I could share it with Esmé and also with Will, in my next letter.

Jeremy Fletcher had arrived while I was out for my run. He lay stretched full length on Esmé's futon, a glass of whiskey in one hand; his head—in its fedora—rested on Esmé's lap. While I hung up my jacket, he declared, "Iowa Girl, when y'all come in out of the cold that nose of yours is the reddest nose I ever did see."

A person with multiple fluffy chins, man-breasts in no way concealed by one of the various floppy vests that were part of his uniform—a completely unappetizing specimen with an *always* red nose, little capillaries giving away the fact that he drank too much. Why did I pay any attention to his insults? Because they felt like home? That seems too easy, but he got under my skin, and, worse, he knew it, and that I wouldn't respond in kind. In the kitchen, washing lettuce for the dinner salad, I had no choice but to listen to his telling Esmé of a good old time when he and his little brother, "both of us dumb as dirt," stole a jar of chloroform from their high school's science lab and used it to knock out a neighbor's cat so they could see what it was like to perform a little surgery. "We reckoned what we cut out was the appendix. Leastways it wadn't nothing essential 'cause, sure enough, we saw the creature sunning itself on a porch swing a few days later."

Esmé protested, "But that's awful!"

"Way of the world, little lamb," Jeremy Fletcher said, "way of the world. Speaking of which"—he raised his voice so there was no way that I could pretend not to hear—"Iowa Girl, I was in the office the other day, just curious, takin' a peek at some files"—he chuckled—"and I saw that one of your recommenders, a Professor Stone, called you 'an extremely attractive person'!"

"Oh, goody!" Esmé said. "You hear that, Charlotte? One of your professors had a crush on you!"

I raised my voice to call, "I'm covering my ears, guys!"

"Charlotte!" Esmé protested. "Don't you want to know what else he said? I want to know!"

"Go out in the hall, then!"

She laughed. "All right, all right, we'll go out in the hall!"

I tried to shake the words—*extremely attractive person*—out of my head after they closed the door behind themselves. I worked salt into the garlic with the back of a spoon, the way that I'd seen Esmé do, rubbing the mess ever finer, then adding vinegar, and a pinch of dry mustard. Professor Stone? Maybe he had simply meant "pleasant company," but suppose the Workshop's admissions committee had, like Jeremy Fletcher and Esmé, taken him to mean "good to look at." People often commented on the fact that the female graduate students were prettier than average, while the same did not hold true for their male counterparts.

Suppose I was at the Workshop because Helmut Stone had thought I was pretty?

Since the party at the Victorian, I'd been trying my hand at "careful drinking," and after I finished making the vinaigrette, and Jeremy Fletcher and Esmé—still giggling a little—returned from the hall and resettled themselves on the futon, I poured myself an orange juice glass of the bourbon that Jeremy Fletcher had brought along as his Thanksgiving Day offering. I carried the glass out to the living room and I sat down with it at the dinette. At the Webster City AA meetings that I'd attended after my bicycle accident, I'd been told by a painfully sunburned boy—he'd blacked out while picnicking under the July sun—"Once you admit you're an alcoholic, drinking's not as much fun." I thought of that boy sometimes. I very much liked the way that Jeremy Fletcher's bourbon was dilating my brain, making me feel instantly more at ease; I also caught myself worrying that the orange juice glass of bourbon might not be enough. There had been an afternoon when I had looked in the Iowa City telephone book at the number for Alcoholics Anonymous, but I didn't see how I could be in the Workshop and live with Esmé and go to AA meetings.

"Oh, I just remembered! Toffer's hash!" Esmé hopped up from the futon and, before long, she and I were singing "I'm Gonna Wash That Man Right Outa My Hair." I hardly minded that Jeremy Fletcher was there, by then. He was as stoned as we were and seemed to find us thoroughly entertaining. *My Fair Lady*'s "Without You"— we sang that. Esmé invited in the neighbor who came knocking on the door to tell us to keep it down, and Jeremy Fletcher gave the man an orange juice glass of bourbon, and he settled himself on the futon for the duration of Esmé's and my heartfelt, if out of tune, version of "Summertime."

The two of us were arranging the steaming bowls and platters of our feast on the kitchen counter when there was more knocking on the door. I was in fine fettle, and, assuming it was another neighbor, come to complain, I said—feeling delightfully impudent—"*I'll go this time!*"

It had been five months since I last had seen Will, and, for a moment—he had cut his hair very short and looked much thinner than I'd ever seen him—I did not quite understand who he was. I actually let out a gasp when he grabbed my hand and pulled me out into the hall.

Oh, Will. Who leaned me up against the wall and kissed me and kissed me, for how long I do not know.

When we finally returned to the apartment, Esmé and Jeremy Fletcher grinned at us. "Ho-ho-ho! Merry Christmas!" Esmé said. "I guess the famous Will has come!"

The look on the face of Will—Mr. Privacy—demanded, *What have you said about me?* and that set Jeremy Fletcher and Esmé giggling. I started giggling, too—you had to have been there, drinking, smoking Toffer's hash, as Will had not. Esmé bowed at the waist and said,

"Tweedledee" and Jeremy did the same and said, "Tweedledum," and I couldn't stop laughing completely until Will and I were down in my room, pulling off each other's clothes.

In all the years that followed that surprise Thanksgiving visit, Will and I never did discuss the visit's upsetting parts:

That I'd been drunk and stoned when he arrived. That he'd flown to Iowa—having cashed in the ticket that was to have brought him back for good in December—to let me know, in person, that he'd been offered another semester in Milan and so would not be coming home again until May; that our long adjournment to my room after his arrival left the stuffed turkey to breed salmonella or something equally onerous that made all of us violently ill; that the dinner itself—even when we were unaware of its dangers—was a bust, with Will and Jeremy Fletcher squaring off as alpha males, and leaving Esmé and me to create all of the sociability on our own.

I had been aware that Will did not show any appreciation for Esmé's and my friendship during the dinner. True, I had complained to him about her, but I'd sung her praises, too, and I felt embarrassed by his coolness. At one point, talking about our pity for the poor young soldier in Chekhov's "The Kiss"—so devastated by his discovery that it took mere seconds for him to share with his comrades the story of his life's greatest moment of bliss— Esmé and I both had stretched our mouths open woefully wide and pressed our hands hard to our cheeks, like the figure in Edvard Munch's *The Scream*, and Will wrinkled up his nose and turned away from the table, as if it were absolutely necessary that he make plain his distaste for our little shtick.

But Esmé and I were working so hard to get a conversation going! "Now, Will," Esmé said, "you have to tell us all about your work and where you've gone and what you've seen! I had an astonishing time when I was in Milan, but I was only seventeen, so I'm sure I missed most everything important!"

He nodded. "I'm kind of tired right now, though. I just want to enjoy being here with Charlotte."

"Of course." Esmé smiled her beautiful smile. She looked so perfect in the candlelight, I suddenly felt certain that Will would begin to wish *she* were his girlfriend. "Dear Charlotte. Isn't Charlotte a great name, Will?" Esmé said. "Why couldn't I have been named Charlotte? Think of . . . Charlotte Brontë. Really, what writer is more glorious than Charlotte Brontë?"

I started to respond—anything to keep the conversation going— that Esmé was the lucky one, but Jeremy Fletcher interrupted with an amused bellow: "Charlotte-fucking-Brontë? *Glorious*?"

I was in a big George Eliot phase at the time, but I agreed with Esmé that Charlotte Brontë was glorious—Emily Brontë, too—

"Glorious!" Jeremy Fletcher bellowed again. From that point onward, he insisted on calling me Brontë. "Brontë, will y'all pass me the rolls?" "Tasty taters you made, Brontë, honey!" Which was apparently too much fun at my expense for Will—or maybe it suggested to Will that Jeremy Fletcher and I were true amigos when he was not around. Whatever it was, Will grew increasingly rigid and silent as he sat chewing bites of the Thanksgiving dinner. I understood that he was tired from his long flight—his face looked scooped out under the cheeks from lack of sleep—but the way he knitted his heavy brow worried me. He was a man who could get physical. Once, walking down the street in Mount Vernon, right in front of us, an unnerving clutch of bodies in T-shirts and jeans had come churning out the door of a bar called the Southside. Two larger men were pounding on a third man, who crouched under their blows, trying to protect himself, and, just like that, Will grabbed the largest man from behind and lifted him off his feet. It was an awful moment, the man kicking backward at Will's legs (while I—like a little lady in a comedy—swung my purse at the other bully). Providentially, the panic-inducing *wheeeee* of a siren had sounded in the distance. It would prove to be the siren of an ambulance on its way to a nearby nursing home, but the sound of it made Will release the man, and all three men from the bar took off running, leaving Will and me to stare at each other, breathless, amazed.

So: That woodenness of Will's at the Thanksgiving dinner did worry me.

Also, I hated the way that he lowered his hand over the mouth of my glass when Esmé came around the dinette with a bottle of B & B.

Jeremy Fletcher laughed at that and asked, "You countin' Brontë's drinks, man?"

"She doesn't normally drink at all," Will said—his gaze absolutely nowhere, his voice perfectly bland; he could have been addressing the sofa for all the interest and inflection that he granted Jeremy Fletcher, and, soon after that, in the kitchen, where Esmé and I started to make coffee and whip the cream for our pies, Esmé came around to my good ear to whisper an indignant "He's handsome, but way too controlling! My god!"

I laughed. I didn't feel like laughing, but I couldn't let her talk about Will that way. "He worries about me drinking. Because of my accident. That's all."

She nodded. "'I want to know that both of our lives make a difference,'" she said. The sentence came from that five-page letter that Will had sent me from Italy.

Suppose she quoted to him from his letter! I moaned—frightened, guilty—"I never should have shown you that!"

"Oh, don't be such a worrywart, Charlotte." She put her arm around my shoulder and tilted her head against mine. "Your secret's safe with me."

That night, the first night of Will's three-night visit from Italy, after Esmé and Jeremy had left for Jeremy Fletcher's attic—and before Will and I had started making miserable treks back and forth to the apartment's mildew-ridden bathroom to be sick—Will told me about his plans to stay on in Italy for another semester.

We were in my room at the time. I sat on the bed, the sheets and blankets mussed by our afternoon lovemaking. I'd been admiring his profile—in the low lighting, a silvery version of the Lincoln penny—as he stood on a chair and noisily tore off strips of masking tape and used them to tape sheets of newspaper over one of the room's two windows (he disapproved of my not having curtains, although the only way anyone in Iowa City could have seen into that third-story apartment was with a pair of binoculars and an airplane).

I already had begun to feel nauseated—*Too much rich Thanksgiving food*, I thought, *and now this bad news*. It seemed like a cheat to me, Will's telling me about a major change in his plans while he stood up on a chair, busy with his tape and newspapers, and I said something to that effect.

"That's silly. Anyway, you've been getting a lot of good writing done while I've been away, right?" He stepped down from the chair and moved it to the next window and started in again with his tape and newspaper. "You've told me so. My being gone will just give you more time."

It was true that I had been writing well—but always with the assumption that there was only the one semester for me to get through without Will, that we would be together in mid-December.

"This could make a big difference in my career, Charlotte. And, anyway—we're planning to be together the rest of our lives."

"*Planning,*" I said darkly. It might have been my feeling sick that prompted me to say a reckless "Maybe it won't happen, though. Maybe you won't even come back. Who knows?"

"Don't be crazy," he said. One of my dad's lines. Used on both my mother and me.

"I am not crazy! Don't ever say I'm crazy!" I snapped.

He took a seat on the chair he had been using as a stepstool. Keeping his distance. The warship of himself sat on the far horizon, a silhouette, its most prominent features the twin muscles of his gritted jaw, poking out like matching cannons; and then the discussion was over anyway, because I had to run to the bathroom.

The next morning, Friday, Will—not as bad off as I turned out to be—got out of bed and went to answer the telephone. When he came back, he reported, "Your friends are sick, too."

On Saturday morning—I still could not keep down even a sip of water—Will got up and dressed and met with his dissertation adviser. My own major accomplishment that day was to go to the living room and telephone Esmé at Jeremy Fletcher's apartment. Esmé reported that she successfully had kept down a bowl of the broth from a can of Campbell's chicken noodle soup and now was reading snatches of a book called *Blood Meridian,* which was a favorite of Jeremy Fletcher's. I did not tell her that Will would not be coming home in December. I felt humiliated by that development. What had seemed like a romantic gesture—the surprise visit—had turned out to be merely a considerate one. Cheek resting on the dinette's Formica top, I said only, "Will's leaving tomorrow and pretty much all he's seen me do is throw up."

"Poor baby. Is he a good nurse, though?"

"He bought me ginger ale and Pepto-Bismol. What about Jeremy?"

"Jeremy!" Esmé laughed. "Jeremy was sicker than I was, girl!"

I did hold on to the hope that I would be able to drive Will to the airport on Sunday morning, but on Saturday afternoon he decided this was not a good idea, and he arranged for his friend Bernard to take him.

Sunday morning, he got up and showered and dressed in what I thought of as his uniform (gray cotton pants, flannel shirt, work boots). His bag packed, he lay down beside me on the bed and stroked my face. He spoke with admiration about a story of mine that he had read during his visit. I was not inclined to be mollified; nevertheless, waiting for his friend to arrive, we wound up having a last, quick round of sex.

"You see," I said when he stood to zip up his pants. "I could drive you. Why don't you call Bernard? He may not have left his house yet."

Will was telling me that I needed to stay in bed and adjusting the covers around my shoulders when the familiar racket of someone working to unlock the apartment's tricky front door started up. "Early for Esmé," I said, but those definitely were her high-heeled boots that now began to tap down the hallway and I was happy to hear them.

"Anybody in there?" She knocked on the bedroom door.

"Come in!" I called.

"I have returned to the living!" she crowed as she flung open the door. She did a double-take at the papered-over windows; then danced a cute jig toward the bed. Will—sitting on the edge of the mattress, holding my hand, making me feel both cherished and infantile—said, his voice solemn, "Charlotte's still not a hundred percent."

I mugged for her, tongue out, eyes crossed.

She laughed, then asked Will if he needed a ride to the airport. He explained about Bernard.

Once she had left the room, Will started talking about places he thought that we could rent in Iowa City when he came home in May. He had leads. His dissertation adviser was going to keep his eye out, too. We also discussed places in Italy that he wanted to show me the May after next, Charlotte, once I finished with my degree—

"Anybody down there need coffee?" Esmé called from the kitchen.

Will raised a finger to signal a pause in our conversation. "Let me grab a cup. I'll be right back."

It was only a short distance to the kitchen. Hardly any time at all passed before I heard Esmé laugh and say, "Whoops!" and, then, "I didn't mean it was already made!"

Will's heavy footsteps sounded in the hall. He returned to my room, red-faced. He shut the door behind him. "That wasn't cool," he said.

"What?"

"Your friend"—he jabbed his thumb toward the kitchen—"was undressed."

"What do you mean, *undressed*?" He had to have been exaggerating. In all the time that we had lived together, I never had seen Esmé in less than underpants and a bra.

"As in *naked*, Charlotte."

On the other side of the now-closed bedroom door, Esmé called a laughing, singsong "Sor-ry! I was going to call when it was ready!"

"No problem," Will said, but he was scowling—at me! Shaking his head! I hated Esmé then. *And* Will. Which must have shown on my face because he hissed, "I couldn't help seeing her! And, Christ, she obviously did it on purpose, Charlotte."

"Don't be ridiculous!" How I regretted ever complaining to him about her! Now he thought that she was flirting with him! Worse, in the street below, a car began to honk its horn. Will walked to the window that looked out on Burlington Street and he pulled back the edge of one of the taped sheets of newspaper. He turned toward me. "It's Bernard," he said. His face full of distress—anger or sadness, I couldn't tell which—he picked up his bag. "I have to go," he said. "I hate to leave like this, but I can't miss my plane."

As soon as he left, I felt the need to get up, take a shower, move around, but I stayed in bed because I did not want to see Esmé. I could not imagine what I possibly could say to her.

She was making quite a bit of noise. Packing for her trip home, I supposed. Twice, she left the apartment and returned. The third time, after I heard the front door click, I got up and went to one of my windows and looked out from behind its newspaper curtain. There was her BMW, parked on the street. No Esmé, though. Then I heard the metallic yawn of someone opening our building's big blue Dumpster and I went to the other window.

Esmé. Chucking in a big black plastic garbage bag.

After that, she got into her car and drove away. Gone without a good-bye? Well, fine.

Food still had little appeal, but I took a shower, and, afterward, I left my door open so that if Esmé came back, she would see that I had gotten up and sat at my desk—supposedly working, everything normal.

She returned at noon. I heard Jeremy Fletcher's voice, too. Then, not raising her usual staccato beat with her high-heeled boots, she came down the hall and knocked on my open door. "Sweetie?" she said.

The expression on her face was . . . both wistful and impish. For the first time since the day that I had met her, her hair was done up in the Pippi Longstocking braids. She stepped a little ways into the room, tiptoeing, like she was afraid of me. "Are you going to bite?" she asked.

I shook my head. "I've got a ton of work to do, though." I pointed at the pile of student papers on my desk. "Catching up."

"Oh, Charlotte! You're upset about this morning! I'm such an idiot! But I was as startled as Will, trust me!"

In a voice that I hoped sounded bored, I said, "Hey, let's just forget it."

"Oh, thank you! Thank you! That's what I want to do, too!" She started to back out of the room, then stopped and sputtered a laugh. "If only . . . Well, I *do* wish you could have seen the expression on his face. I mean, I could tell he was attracted to me, of course, when we had our little dinner, but, so what, right? He *loves* you, right? Still"—she laughed again, deep in her throat, like a jolly baby—"the way his eyes popped: It *was* funny!"

I could tell he was attracted to me, of course.

How could she not know that a friend wasn't allowed to say such a thing?

Of course, Will was attracted to her! Anybody would be attracted to her! But for her to *say* to me that she could tell—that was not allowed. Absolutely not.

None of this, of course, excused what I went on to do.

Because if I claim that I was raised by wolves, then I also have to grant that the wolves did imbue me with at least a scrap of pack decorum.

It was, in fact, pack decorum that stopped me from crying out a few hours later, when Jeremy Fletcher, coming up behind me as I lit the stove, pressed a lump of erection into my backside and slid his hands up to my breasts. With a low, wolfish snarl, I tussled out of his reach. I imagined that I protected Esmé—down in the bathroom, maybe ten feet off—from the pain of knowing what this unsavory man she loved was up to behind her back.

Jeremy Fletcher laughed. He grabbed a dish towel hanging from a nearby hook and flicked it at my shoulder. "Oh, Brontë. She thinks y'all are just a hick! Having a hissy fit 'cause your beau walked in on her naked!"

Neck-ed.

She had told him about it. And that I was upset. Although I had told her I was not upset.

Was Jeremy Fletcher upset?

Grinning, he leaned in and whispered, "You and me are going to be all on our lonesome the next few days. We oughta make the best of it, doncha think?"

This wounded me through and through! I was not a slut! Did not dress like a slut! Did not act like a slut! Did not even flirt! And Jeremy Fletcher—had he never picked up a sense that any friendliness I showed toward him was a matter of politeness and largely on behalf of Esmé? No one could have convinced me that I ever had sent a message of desire to him!

Sad to say, however, my next thought was that this puffy-faced, red-nosed man who now snapped a blue-and-white checked dish towel at my shoulder was the treasure of the young woman flushing the noisy toilet down the hall; that friend whom I alternately adored and resented. That friend who did not seem to want me to have any friends beyond her; who wanted all of the friends in the world for herself; who that morning had exposed her naked self to the man I loved, and then bragged to me about his response—and apparently to her boyfriend, too.

Esmé, now coming our way, called a teasing "Awfully quiet down there! What on earth are you two talking about?"

17

That afternoon, once she and Jeremy Fletcher left the apartment, I went back to my room and tore down Will's sheets of newspaper.

Miserable, I pressed my palms to the chill glass of the window that looked out on Burlington Street. I could not stop running certain moments through my head:

Whoops! Esmé cried out in the kitchen. Red-faced Will hurried back to my room.

Jeremy Fletcher flicked the blue-and-white checked dish towel at me. *She thinks y'all are just a hick! Having a hissy fit 'cause your beau walked in on her naked!*

Will stood on my desk chair and taped the sheets of newspaper to the window and explained that he had cashed in his ticket in order to prolong his stay in Italy.

I could tell he was attracted to me, of course, Esmé said.

And Will: *Obviously, she did it on purpose, Charlotte.*

Pounding the palms of my hands against each other, I walked back and forth through the crowded apartment (living room, kitchen, hallway, bedroom) again and again. At one point, stopped alongside my bed, I could smell Will. Bitter at the wondrous musk of him, I ripped off the sheets and pillowcases and crushed them into the bottom of my closet.

I could tell he was attracted to me, of course.

What I did with my teeth probably would have qualified as gnashing. I grabbed my hair with both hands and pulled it straight out from my head. I crouched into a ball in the middle of my room, wincing, swearing. I wanted right out of my skin—a feeling that led me to the lidded African basket on top of the toilet where Esmé kept her makeup and, at least some of the time, a hash pipe.

Had she taken it to Evanston?

No, there it sat, along with a turquoise Zippo and a foil-wrapped lump of hash.

Stoned, I felt . . . not *better*—I remained too upset about the events of the last few days, and maybe my whole life, to feel *better*. Still, for the first time since I'd been sick, I did feel hungry, and I went to the kitchen to see what I could find.

The refrigerator was empty. Even the box of baking soda that we kept in there to absorb odors was gone. Nothing in the freezer, either. What did that mean? I opened and closed the doors a few times, listening to the sucking, parting sigh made by the rubber gasket.

On her return from Evanston the following Wednesday, Esmé would explain that she had thought she should do a complete "kitchen purge" since we didn't know exactly what had made us sick; she'd meant to tell me, but then had gotten distracted by her packing for her trip and, *You know, worrying you were angry at me, Charlotte.*

The cupboard where we kept our boxes of cereal and crackers: empty. A tremble sounded in my head, as if a bowling ball rolled down an endless lane, the pins so far away that I never would know if the ball struck or not.

Had the gas been turned off? No, the round ring of blue flame popped up with its characteristic *wooomph* and *tick-tick-tick*. I stared at it stupidly—I don't know for how long.

I dithered over the necessity of going out in search of food. I had a fair idea that I was not in any shape to drive a car. I went into the fetid bathroom. My face in the medicine cabinet mirror was pasty. What would be involved in taking it out in public? Brushing my teeth seemed advisable and, after that, so did drawing on some black liquid eyeliner that I'd noticed while extracting the hash pipe from Esmé's makeup basket. Stuff that Esmé applied when she wanted to rock a glam cat-eyed look, the liner went on chilly and shiny.

I blinked at my spooky self in the bathroom mirror while the liner dried to a matte charcoal. That was not the first time that Jeremy Fletcher's invitation passed through my head, but maybe the first time that I balanced it against the image I had concocted of Esmé standing naked in the kitchen that morning.

Probably that she had exposed herself to Will on purpose. What upset me more, however, was that Will had the same idea. Which meant that he did not think she cared much about me or else cared very much about making an impression on him.

And she had laughed about it to Jeremy Fletcher and said that she considered me a hick!

I smoked a little more of the hash. Put on the increasingly threadbare, shot-out-at-the-elbows tweed jacket that was all that remained of my Borgesian three-piece suit.

When I unlocked my bicycle from the iron railing at the back entry of the apartment building, it was my intention to ride only to

John's Grocery or Hamburg Inn. John's? Hamburg Inn? I went back and forth, ignoring my knowledge that both places lay not far beyond the grimy, asphalt-shingled house where Jeremy Fletcher rented the attic.

I drove to John's Grocery. A tiny store. Best known as the place to get kegs of beer. Not wanting anyone to guess that I was stoned out of my head, I walked—as briskly as I could in the cramped space—right past the rack holding a prominent display of Pepperidge Farm cookies packaged as handsomely as a birthday gift. No to delicious Doritos. No to enticing Cheetos. Something healthy to regain my health, damn it. I lifted a heavy navy-blue and white tub of Mountain High yogurt (plain) from the dairy case. Very good. I thought an apple would be the right accessory for the yogurt, but given all of the high drama on stage in my diminished brain, choosing between the store's three corky-looking Granny Smiths proved beyond me, and I carried only the yogurt toward the checkout counter.

I had forgotten that my eyes were lined like those of a tribal idol, and so I was flustered when the girl at the cash register looked up at me, grinned, and said, "Woo-oo!"

Woo-oo! Outside the store, I set the yogurt in the wire basket on the front of my bike. I was so screwed up—and cold, shivering in just my old suit jacket and a T-shirt—getting the combination right on my bike lock took forever.

That I rode off with one hand covering my nose to keep it from getting red should have been a tip-off that I was in danger of going to Jeremy Fletcher's place—*beware*—though I don't think I even noticed that I drove one-handed until I hit a slick of ice hidden beneath a litter of maple leaves and could not steady myself in time—

"No!" I cried, but the bike continued with its unkind tilt until my left knee hit the concrete with a crack.

The carton of yogurt fell from the basket. Exploded with a splat.

No one around, I was happy to see as I righted myself.

Like a good citizen—gripping the carton by its relatively clean bottom—I carried the remains of the yogurt to the nearest alley garbage bin. I did not want to look at my knee. It hurt like hell. I could tell it was bleeding and that my jeans were torn. Quietly, feeling some righteous fury, I said, "Fuck it," and got back on my bike and pedaled onward, very hard.

Just ahead, a right turn would take me down the street that ran by the house in which Jeremy Fletcher lived.

I turned.

I told myself that I meant only to see whether or not his stupid Ford Ranchero sat out front. To see if he were home, pining for Esmé, or out running around, having the time of his life. I hoped the latter. At that moment, I held Esmé responsible for the miserable end to Will's visit, the fact that I'd had to go out to buy food that I now was not going to get to eat, which related to my fall off my bike, which related to the clerk's "woo-woo!" and even the voice of my father, in my head, singing, "I won't go hunting with you, Jake, but I'll go chasing women!"

There sat the Ranchero, its windshield opaque with dust, one tire up on the curb, suggesting general dissolution.

Were you out of your mind? I've asked myself that a thousand times over the years.

Teeth chattering loud as castanets, I rode up the sloped, brown lawn between the sidewalk and the shingled house. I shoved my bike out of sight in the thicket of yews that grew all around the foundation and then halfway up the windows of the first story, too. My crazy thinking went something like this:

Jeremy Fletcher's wanting to spend time with me—even if it was only for sex—restored some justice in the world over which Esmé Cole judged herself queen. Granted that I had no personal interest in Jeremy Fletcher, at that moment, it seemed to me I would be able to *redeem* his interest in me, as in, when a fisherman lands the biggest fish, he can release the fish after there's acknowledgment that he is the winner. As in, at a carnival, the person who wins the ring toss takes home a watch, a stuffed animal, a bottle of perfume from the shelf at the back of the booth, and not the rings.

When I was a kid, did I have an IQ that sent my public school teachers into raptures during parent-teacher nights? I did, which goes to show how much stock people should put in those numbers, since their owners obviously can operate without consulting their brainpower at all. Really. Because, to make this even more wacky, you need to know that, somehow, this marvelous brain of mine harbored the dopey notion that—since I had no intention of *keeping* Jeremy Fletcher—when all was said and done, Esmé and I would be able to go on being friends. On a better footing. Once she understood that she was vulnerable, too.

Not guilty by reason of insanity!

Because—forget Esmé—how could I have been sane and done what I did when I loved Will?

But, honestly, while I dislodged myself from the yews growing so rampantly up the side of that shingled house, brushed the crumbly bits of greenery and twigs from my jacket and hair—I am sure that I looked like a madwoman—Will was as absent from my head as physics, algebra, and other subjects that I once had studied but never comprehended and couldn't have told you one thing about even if you'd put my head in a vise and cranked.

All that I could think of—if *think* were the right word—was my enormous need for Jeremy Fletcher to treat me as an object of desire. This would topple the monumental enemy against which I saw myself acting out of necessity (Esmé was Goliath; I was David). At that moment, I was such a wild combination of the untutored, greedy, and needy that I hardly gave a thought to the monstrosity of what I was about to do. Like some prodigious waterfall whose thundering and spume drown out all other sounds and sights, my sense of necessity blocked any scruples that I ordinarily possessed.

Jeremy Fletcher—no fedora, hair rumpled, bleary-eyed—answered my knock. He wore baggy sweatpants, felt slippers, and a heavy white shirt with broad black stripes (a shirt like a prisoner would have worn in the olden days). Obviously, he was not expecting me, but I was hysterical—akin to prison escapees who must, as fast as possible, wriggle through tight tunnels, crawl on their bellies through mud and under barbed wire, scale fences with no regard for the fact that they have skin. I wanted the man to greet me with a fervent, *It's you I love, Charlotte, not Esmé!* Riding up the lawn, for some reason, this had seemed possible. Now, I saw this was not yet possible, not yet, and, agitation mushing the words, I told Jeremy Fletcher that I had fallen on my bike. For proof, I extended the aching, bleeding leg.

"Whoa." He opened the door wider. "Y'all oughta . . . come in and wash up."

He directed me to a stepladder by his kitchen sink. I sat. I looked around myself while he went to his bathroom for a towel. A strange place, that attic. *Cold.* Drywall had been hung on the slanted ceiling and two walls, but one wall had its pink insulation exposed, and another was bare studs. "The Garret," Esmé called it. She'd told me it came cheap because the landlord had run out of money before he could finish it.

While I sat on the stepladder and dabbed at my knee with a wet towel, Jeremy Fletcher fired up a green bong that he'd retrieved from a littered card table (half-filled cups, notebooks, pencil sharpener, paper plate holding the remains of a sandwich). He took a toke and then carried the bong to me. "Here you go. Ain't no Tylenol in the house."

Not talking, businesslike, we passed the bong back and forth. I suspected he, too, already had smoked a bit that afternoon. We relaxed pretty soon.

"But, Charlotte, y'all—" He laughed a little *heh-heh* laugh, and it made me laugh, too. *Snigger.* That's what I did. Sitting on the step-ladder, rocking back and forth. My goofy snigger made Jeremy Fletcher snigger, too. He closed his eyes and slapped the fronts of his thighs. I wanted to ask him, *What were you going to say?* but I couldn't push the words around my hopeless snigger.

He leaned in to kiss me, then. I kissed him back. His tongue was like a giant oyster in my mouth, and his breath made my nose sting, so I did not mind much when he crouched in front of me and began unbuckling my leather belt. Or that the belt was stiff in the cold attic, a bit unyielding. My teeth went back to chattering while I looked down into the whorls of thinning hair on top of Jeremy Fletcher's head.

"I reckon," he said, "Will and Es would be mighty surprised if they knew what we two were up to."

Mentioning Will and Esmé—that struck me as entirely wrong, but, then, Jeremy Fletcher, down there, fiddling with my zipper— what on earth did he have to do with me, anyway? He could as well have been a salesman, eager to sell me a pair of shoes. While he tugged at my torn blue jeans, his stepladder rapped out a goofy *tap-tap-tap* (one leg of the ladder was shorter than the other, or else the attic floor was uneven).

"She *meant* for Will to see her without her clothes," I said. "She called him out to the kitchen."

He looked up from his efforts with a salesman's friendly chuckle. "Well, she knows she looks good naked." *Neck-ed.* Then he stood and guided me—bare-legged but still wearing my T-shirt and tweed jacket—in the direction of his unmade bed.

Sex might be required, but sex was not what I was after, and to inspire Jeremy Fletcher, I said (the improvisation sounded tinny in my ears), "You should be with me instead of Esmé"—and, then, because it seemed essential to step out absolutely as far as possible on that lunatic limb that I had constructed, I added, "I'd love you more than she does."

"And you're here to prove that, are you?" His expression was quite keen as he removed my jacket, very interested. It disappeared from view as he pulled my T-shirt over my head but when I recovered from that momentary compression of my eyelids—which still can make me feel like a tiny child, even when I remove a T-shirt on my own—I found him staring at my breasts, saying something admiring about their size and shape.

So it was that we got down to our unpleasant business.

I don't remember every detail. Thank god. Suffice it to say that between our energetic episodes on that freezing bed, we smoked some more dope from the emerald-green bong, also downed shots of mescal and bourbon. At some point I fell asleep or blacked out (in the hospital, after my bicycle accident, taking the AA quiz, I'd thought: *But everybody has black-outs when they drink, right?*).

When I came around, I had no idea where I was. I'd worked my face into the angle where the attic's sloped ceiling met a low perpendicular wall, and, when I tried to sit up, I bumped my head and got the panic-inducing idea that I was trapped. There was some light behind me, though, and, as I rolled toward it, the swell of the water bed told me where I was: naked and lying alongside naked Jeremy Fletcher.

The light—from fluorescents left on in the bathroom—revealed that Jeremy Fletcher's eyes were closed. Was he asleep? On his back, with his red beard pointing upward, he looked like a pal of Falstaff, and I doubted I looked any better.

Although I felt sick to death of my entire self, my self-loathing did not stop me from recognizing that my knee hurt. Also that I was freezing. The attic was even colder than when I had arrived and whatever coverings had been on the water bed were now bunched under Jeremy Fletcher.

I wanted to escape, immediately, but how could I get out of the water bed without rocking him awake?

I could not bear the thought of talking to the man.

Maybe I would die. Right there. Just—turn to ash. Blow away. That would be a remedy.

My eyes in slits—if Jeremy Fletcher looked my way, I didn't want him to see that I was awake—I studied the water bed's exposed vinyl liner, a thing of a shrill blue that aptly conveyed the bed's chill. Its surface was embossed with tiny ridges of waves, and it occurred to me, in that way that idle thoughts will even during unbearable moments, that had I been inclined to run a fingernail over the liner's tiny ridges, they would have raised a tiny noise, a tiny zip. Also, I noted how, from a hummock of flesh-colored mole on Jeremy Fletcher's shoulder, there sprouted two longish hairs. First, the hairs grew upward for about an inch. Then each grew laterally for half an inch or so before settling into a droop, and that droop—it put me dismally in mind of the weeping tree in a faux-Japanese print that had hung above the toilet in the bathroom of my parents' house my entire life.

"Brontë? You awake?"

Terrible to have to open my eyes. Opening my eyes meant an admission of what had occurred, but, then, it was unavoidable if the world were to continue.

I opened my eyes.

Jeremy Fletcher zoomed his face close to mine and grinned; then he arched his back and yanked at the mess of bedding under him. After a few tugs, he worked one sheet free, and this he snapped high in the air above us, made it billow in the same way that Will did, sometimes, after we made love. It was charming when Will did it. When Will did it, after the little breeze that he raised briefly suspended the sheet above us—our own unblemished, intimate sky—I would feel that our naked selves were as sweet as Adam and Eve.

So much for that notion.

After Jeremy Fletcher's not very clean sheet settled over us, he boxed up his pillow, folded his hands behind him, and, with a contented sigh, rested his head. Grinning up at the slanted drywall ceiling, he might have been a pagan god whom I had vested with dread power. Maybe there were words that he could say—an incantation—that would make me less horror-struck at what I'd done or, even better, persuade me that I hadn't really done it? There was just some drugged confusion on my part that needed adjustment, something like what I'd experienced when I first lay down on the water bed and, looking up, did not understand how there could be a trail of boot prints—*Red Wing, Red Wing,* read the boots' tread—across the ceiling.

Jeremy Fletcher started talking, his voice sounding jubilant, the way it usually did when he told his stories:

He'd gotten caught in an infidelity once, back when he lived in Austin, Texas, and worked at a bar called the Broken Spoke. "Y'all heard of the Broken Spoke?"

I shook my head. Red Wing was the brand name of a manufacturer of work boots. A worker had walked over the sheet of drywall before the drywall had been installed. My heart thumped hard under my hands, which were clamped together so tight. It was hard for me to hear Jeremy Fletcher over my personal turmoil, but I forced myself to listen, and the words with which he ended this story, which featured his car being found parked in front of a house *where it shouldn't oughta have been*, tears, and recriminations, were these:

"I want you to know, of course, I lied, Brontë."

Of course, I lied. The attic vibrated like a bell, just struck. Or else I did.

I never had felt that there was an *of course* to any of the lies that I'd ever told, but I hardly could claim the moral high ground with regard to a man from under whose ass I'd earlier in the evening drawn forth my ponytail in order to extricate myself from the position popularly known as 69.

His tacit warning—*I'll say you're a liar if you ever tell Esmé about tonight*—was completely unnecessary for my now sober and sadly sane self. Mustering as casual a tone as possible—trying to match his—I said, "Well, I'm gonna take off now."

He laughed. "It's"—he tilted his head backward to look at the clock on the nearby card table—"two A.M., Brontë. Go to sleep. We'll eat Froot Loops for breakfast."

No, I had a morning class, I said. I slid to the bottom of the water bed in order to avoid any unnecessary bodily contact, grabbed up my clothes and bag from where they lay, scattered across the attic floor, and hurried into the bathroom.

Idiot, idiot, idiot.

I cried. To cover the sound, I ran the faucet at full strength. A tube of toothpaste sat on the back rim of the little sink. I ignored it in favor of the powdered cleanser meant for scrubbing the sink. I considered my face in the medicine cabinet mirror while I scrubbed and scrubbed. Teeth, tongue. A little of Esmé's black liner still encircled my eyes. It had run away with my tears and now made me look like a very old German shepherd.

When I emerged from the bathroom, dressed, smoking a ciga-rette, ready to go, I found Jeremy Fletcher sitting up on the water bed, Indian-style, with his bong. "You should know," he said, voice squeezed tight around his toke as he raised his hand in a wave, "you did wow me, Brontë."

Wow.

The night was very dark when I stepped out from that asphalt-shingled house, the moon only a suggestion behind dense, smoke-colored clouds.

As I pedaled toward the apartment, I could feel the wet spot where Jeremy Fletcher's semen had leaked onto my underpants grow cold. *Wow,* I thought. A circus word. A word of entertainment and spectacle. Awful. Appropriate.

18

In mid-December, Jeremy Fletcher headed to Mobile for winter break. Esmé drooped around our apartment that night (the first time she'd slept there in ages). The next morning, though, ready to leave for her own holiday, she was shiny with excitement. She was driving to O'Hare, leaving her car at the airport while she flew to New York for a week's reunion with undergraduate friends from Columbia, then flying back to Chicago to spend the holidays with her family in Evanston.

While we carried her bags down to her car, she talked excitedly about clubs she wanted to visit. And had she told me that her friend Sarah was flying in from London? "There are going to be parties and dinners out at decent places! *And* I'm going to see if I can't get my parents to send me to Mobile for New Year's!"

"*Brr, brr, brr,*" we said while we rushed out into the freezing cold morning, but the sun was out. It raised a golden nimbus on the mink brim of a fabulous hat that Esmé's father had bought for her that fall while working on a case in Russia, and, as Esmé unlocked the car's trunk, I said—I wore only a sweater and so I jumped up and down to stave off the cold—"Tell me again, what do you call that hat?"

"A *papakha*."

From reading Russian novels, I could guess that the curly, butter-soft, pearl-blue stuff that formed the high cap must be what was called astrakhan lamb. "It makes you look like a perfect czarina!" I said. "Your father must have great taste!" I felt pleased with myself. What I had said sounded like one of Esmé's compliments, but Esmé frowned as she took the suitcases I carried, and, while she settled them neatly in the trunk, she said, "Actually, his assistant probably bought it. She went to Russia with him. *Denise.* Whom he's probably boinking."

This startled me. From sheer awkwardness—I never had heard Esmé say anything critical of her father before—I blurted a laugh, then apologized. "But you're kidding, right?"

"No," she said matter-of-factly. She shut the trunk of the car. Briskly slapped her gloved hands together. One, two, three. "Oh, Charlotte!" *She* laughed then. "You should see your face! You're such a naïf, you sweet Candide! But here I am, rattling on like a ninny when I need to get on the road!" She hugged me. "Take care of yourself, you."

I waved when she got into her car, then I ran up to the apartment—both to get myself warm and to shake off what Esmé had said. Did she mean that, about her father? And she thought I was a naïf? Well, maybe I was, but the mantra of the last weeks that ran in my head also let me know, *You are a rat.* Since Thanksgiving, both times that I'd been at the apartment when Jeremy Fletcher came by with Esmé, I had managed to stay in my room. I had not attended the last after-reading parties of the semester. I had stayed away from the Mill and sworn off alcohol and anything else that might bulldoze my apparently very shaky principles. "Really, I have so much work to do," I'd said when Esmé complained, and she *was* aware that I hadn't totally recovered since Thanksgiving. A low-grade nausea continued to dog me, often left me bowed ineffectively over the toilet.

Still, I worked well over the winter break. I had made up a tight schedule: what time to wake up (five thirty); how long to write; when to eat; when to break for a swim at the rec center or for a run. Thinking of Will—I knew he kept to a schedule—I followed my schedule religiously. I also continued to take my birth control pills each morning—hoping Will would change his mind—though I no longer took them with orange juice. Orange juice worsened my persistent nausea. Orange juice, coffee, the smell of the moldy bathroom (with Esmé gone, whenever I was not in the bathroom, I kept its window open and jammed towels along the base of the door to contain the smell).

What did I make of the fact that I vomited, or at least hung over the toilet, a couple of times a day? In classic denial, monogrammed to suit me, I attributed what I felt to: (1) the lingering effects of what must have been a truly terrible case of the flu, and not the simple Thanksgiving Day food poisoning from which the others had recovered; (2) overwhelming guilt and fear that Esmé or Will would find out about me and Jeremy Fletcher; and (3) the bathroom's mold. In fact, I'd decided that if the mold were eradicated—maybe I'd become *allergic* to the mold—I probably would get better, and, after four telephone calls, I finally convinced the heavily mustachioed building manager to come by. Green cap, green overalls, he had to be trying to look like one of the Super Mario Brothers. He hemmed and hawed while I helpfully held back the shower curtain, but he got a surprise when he went to pick at the plaster with the tip of a key from his big ring, and it sunk right into the mush.

He said a startled, "What the—" but all that stirred up mildew was too much for me. I dropped the shower curtain and stepped back from the tub. "Sorry!" I said—and threw up in the toilet.

A few days later, while the man repaired the wall—this would have been right before Christmas—I felt something familiar: *My period*, I thought, and after he left, I checked my underpants and found a penny-size, brownish stain on the cloth. I put in a tampon. Hardly necessary, as it turned out, but, then, things were probably extra light due to my bout of flu, and hadn't my periods always had been much lighter since I had started on the pill?

And in January and February, when I would have no period at all? Then I would conclude that the lack of periods was an effect of my losing so much weight—almost fifteen pounds—since I'd come down with that lingering flu. But that's getting ahead of myself.

The morning of Christmas Eve, I packed the presents I'd bought for my family and a paper bag holding a few essentials into Will's station wagon and headed to Webster City.

A beautiful day. Snow sat in rills in the dark, plowed fields that rolled away beyond the interstate's broad ditches, and the sky above was incredibly wide open—so stunning, the blue sky, so magical and unlikely that, when I really thought about it, it seemed to me like something you only could have dreamed up, something out of a fairy tale.

I felt good! Maybe I was not going to be nauseated anymore! Maybe I finally was recovering! And Will was scheduled to telephone me that night, at my parents' house. A Christmas Eve telephone call. I'd feel even better once I talked to him.

At about the halfway point in my drive, I got tired. I tried driving with the windows rolled down. That helped a bit. At a truck stop a few miles beyond Waterloo, I braved a cup of coffee. A mistake. Shortly afterward, I had to pull off onto the shoulder.

Once I'd brought up the coffee, to clear my head and get away from the noisy buffeting of the passing semis, I walked down into the ditch. *Let the passersby honk. Let the highway patrol stop and complain.* That was how I felt. I went up to the fence that bordered the field, and I grabbed hold of the top strand of wire. The land was flatter, there, than around Iowa City, more like the land around Webster City. The snow in the field did not look so charming up close, where I could see that it was pitted with dirt. I asked myself, *At Thanksgiving, if I'd told Esmé how I felt, would that have kept me from doing what I did?* But then it would have felt so wrong to have asked her to share the burden of my base emotions! And, really, the question was moot:

I could not have borne admitting my envy of her! It made me feel too fragile, like a used piece of target paper, so riddled with holes that I was apt to tear.

And I suspected that she knew about it anyway. *She* freely had admitted to envying people. The guy from Brown who'd read all of *Remembrance of Things Past* in French, while the rest of us were towed along on a raft by Moncrieff and Kilmartin: "Imagine the richness of his experience compared to ours, Charlotte! Doesn't it make you want to vomit?" The girl who worked at the Baskin-Robbins and had a tiny waist that the shop's apron emphasized: "We're going to have to start wearing aprons, too, Charlotte! Let's start a fad!" The marathoner who whizzed by our apartment building on his regular runs around Iowa City: "What discipline!" Shortly before leaving for Chicago, she had told me—casually, lightheart-edly—of a tipsy talk that she'd had at the bar called the Deadwood with a poet teaching at the Workshop that semester. Supposedly, the man had said to Esmé, "You live with Charlotte Price, don't you? She's a beautiful girl!" Esmé made a comic, pouty face at me over her coffee cup before continuing, "So I, in my charmingly sodden state, I asked the poor man"—she rolled her eyes and laughed at the memory—"'What about me, though?' and he said, 'You're extremely pretty, of course, but Charlotte is beautiful.'"

Everything about that story left me flabbergasted: How bold Esmé had been, asking the poet, "What about me, though?"! And how generous to tell me the story! Though I did suspect that the poet said what he did—and I'm not being coy—to throw lovely Esmé off-balance while he stood beside her at the Deadwood's long bar, ready to catch her if she fell. And I suspected Esmé had the same suspicion. Her expectant air when she had finished telling me the story did suggest that she waited for me to say exactly what I went on to say, given that I viewed the secondhand compliment, simultaneously, as treasure that I dearly needed and as treasure that I'd been caught holding and better hand over, fast, if I wanted to preserve our friendship:

"Of course, that's crazy, Esmé! Guys—it's the flip of the way women will try to turn a guy off about some woman by putting down her looks. Like, to hook you, a guy may tell you how attractive he finds somebody else."

Esmé laughed. "Okay, I've seen that. You're right." Then, playing British dowager, she leaned forward and, over the lip of her coffee cup, she said a teasing "But, of course, you *are* beautiful, my *de-ah!*"

I played along. "We're both utterly *supreme*." We laughed, like it was all a great joke, and then we had gone into the kitchen and downed our birth control pills with our little glasses of orange juice.

It was no joke to me, though. When you got down to it, the only times I'd ever felt *certain* that I was attractive or smart were those shiny first moments after I finished one drink and was halfway through the second, alcohol doing its cunning voodoo dance in every nerve in my body.

The giant grain silos by the railroad tracks were the tallest things in tiny Webster City. As I passed through the business district, I could see that even more stores stood empty than during my last visit, the shopping skimmed off by the opening of the big mall in Fort Dodge. Hard times for little towns.

My parents' two-bedroom house—the house that I'd grown up in—on the western edge of town, part of a 1950s development that never had taken off. Eventually, a community college had gone up out there, but parcels of nearby land still were used for crops, and as I drove up, it seemed the pastel blue that my dad and I had painted the house just a few years before had gone gray and chalky, as if winds carrying dirt from the fields had roughed it up, worn it down.

"You're thin, you lucky duck!" my mother called, holding open the storm door with her back while I carried my paper sacks of presents across the snowy lawn. She rubbed at her arms and said, "Cold!" I kissed her cheek before I stepped past her and into the familiar, pink-tiled kitchen.

My dad, sports pages in hand, sat looking out the window alongside the kitchen table. He turned to me and grinned. "I was hoping you might bring your pretty friend along!" he said, then stood to give me a peck on the cheek.

The house was filled with the odor of roasting turkey—too much of a reminder of that poisonous meal I'd had at Thanksgiving—and, after a brief chat with the two of them, in order to get out into the fresh air, I offered to shovel the walk.

"Not much snow there," my dad said, "but help yourself."

We always ate our big holiday meal around five on Christmas Eve, but my sister and her three kids arrived at one, not long after I finished the shoveling. They trooped into the kitchen, where I now peeled carrots for the relish tray (my mom was doing her radish roses). Martie's curly hair was cut very short, and I was surprised to see how much she'd come to look like our dad in photographs from the days when he was a younger man. The spring before, she had gotten divorced and moved back to Iowa from California. That was about all that I knew of the situation. In those days, it wouldn't have occurred to Martie to confide in me, her kid sister.

"You're skinny," Martie said when I went to hug her, "but you've still got big boobs!"

Martie's gangly twelve-year-old daughter, Jessie—closer in age to me than I was to my sister—cried out, "Mom! How rude!" I had not had many chances to get to know Martie's California children, but Jessie hugged me then and even held on. Her brothers, nine- and ten-year-old Seth and Alex, grinned and said hello but only let me touch the tops of their heads before they hurried off to the living room with their clutch of videos.

I was moved by Jessie's hug. Surprised by her grown-up makeup and the crisp claw of hair-sprayed bangs standing up from her forehead.

As if she read my mind, Martie said, "Under all the gobbledy-gook, she looks a lot like you at her age."

How I wished that I could shoot my niece full of self-confidence! Help her grow up better prepared for the world than I had been! "That's quite a compliment to me," I said.

"To *me!*" Jessie said. "Hey, do you still write stories about our family?"

A triangle of grim looks was erected between my mom at the

kitchen counter, my sister, and my dad, just returned to the kitchen with his empty coffee cup. Standing right in the center of that triangle—I suppose one reason I became a writer was that writing allowed you to edit your thoughts until you got them right—I stammered that, although there might be certain aspects of my stories that Jessie recognized as coming from life, writers always had to draw on their imaginations to make a story. "This"—I fanned my hands around the crowded pink kitchen and toward the street and grubby bits of snow and blue sky outside the window—"this, plus all of us, is life, along with everything beyond us and what's inside our heads, too, and it's . . . in flux. Constantly changing. With people thinking different things about it. Writers pick just *something* from all that and try to use words to make sense of it."

Jessie looked down and fiddled with a strand of dark, knotted leather that she wore tied around her wrist. I remembered people wearing those when I was a kid. A fad that had something to do with wishes. A knot for a wish. I knew I hadn't been clear. I wanted to be clear! I tried again: "You know how you might be in a room with other people, but you're thinking about something that happened a long time ago or something that you'd like to have happen? Or that you worry *could* happen? At that moment, you might hardly be aware of the people in the room with you. You've separated something out from everything else around you so you can think about it. That's kind of like what a writer does."

My parents made sizzling noises of disapproval or disbelief. Martie took the peeler from me and began peeling carrots. Jessie—whether confused by what I'd said or absorbed—raised her piece of knotted leather to her mouth and, her eyes on me, chewed on the thing.

Exhausted, I asked, "Have you ever tried writing a story?"

She shook her head, no. "But I'd like to!"

"Well, cool! Let me know if you ever want a reader!"

"So, Charlotte," Martie said, "the tall boyfriend's still off in Italy, is he?"

"Yup."

"Oo-la-la!" my dad said. He batted his eyes and raised his hands, fingers crimped as if he were a cancan girl, hoisting her skirt.

I looked at him as evenly as possible. "You must be thinking of Gay Paree, Dad."

He stuck out his chin and grinned. "Don't play dumb. You know what I meant: wine, women, and song."

I excused myself to go to the bathroom.

I registered the details of my parents' tidy house with a mixture of nostalgia and impatience. Near the front door, the builder had installed a wall of frosted plastic to suggest a foyer. Small pheasant feathers and sprays of pretty brown leaves had been embedded in the plastic to make it more decorative and, as a kid, I'd been enamored of them. I'd known them. They were little treasures to me. At some point, though, I realized that many of the houses in our development had had a plastic wall like ours, but people had removed them over the years. My parents' plastic wall now was checked and yellowed with age, but I doubted that they ever would change it. They repainted walls. They made repairs and some necessary replacements, but, as far as I could tell, the house was essentially the same as when they had bought it thirty years before.

Jessie was standing in the hall when I stepped out of the bathroom. She smiled at me, but her smile was strained for a twelve-year-old. "I wanted to ask you something, Aunt Charlotte," she said.

I loved to hear her call me Aunt Charlotte, and I smiled and said, "Shoot!"

"My mom says the women in our family have broken

pickers—when it comes to men—and I should be careful. Do you have a broken picker?"

I was taken aback by this, but I laughed, "Your mom hasn't met my boyfriend," I said. "My boyfriend's nice. And I've had other nice boyfriends, too."

Jessie nodded. "That's good," she said, and I thought she looked happier when she moved past me and into the bathroom.

Because the mall in Fort Dodge had a Younkers store, I had bought the family's gifts at the Younkers in Iowa City. "The receipts are in the bottoms of the boxes, if anybody wants to exchange anything," I said when we gathered in the living room for our exchange.

My present for my mother was a sweater. "Pretty color!" she said. "Thank you, honey!" She held the sweater up for my dad to see. He shrugged and raised his hands: *Don't ask me!* He already had lifted a corner of the cardboard box that held my gift for him—also a sweater—and said, "Thanks, Charlotte," before sliding the box under his chair.

Throughout the afternoon, I had to leave the house several times for fresh air. The last time, everybody noticed because we were sitting down to eat. One look at all of that food and I sprang from the table we'd set up in the living room, rushed out through the kitchen door and around behind the garage.

Not long after, I heard the kitchen door swing open and closed. It was Jessie, the cuffs of her sweater pulled down over her hands. "Are you okay?" she called. She held her face turned aside, from either politeness or fear of what she might see or both. "They sent me to see if you were okay?"

"I'm okay. I had the flu or something. I keep thinking I'm going to be sick, but mostly I'm not."

From the house, out of our sight, my dad called, "Charlotte! Get in here! The professor's on the line! Long distance!"

But this was not a good time for him to call! I crouched and scooped up some of the snow that I earlier had shoveled into a rim along the driveway, and I held handfuls of it to my cheeks.

Jessie came closer. "Are you sure you're okay, Aunt Charlotte?"

"I'll be fine, honey." I stood and used the sleeves of my sweater to wipe the melted snow from my cheeks. "I hope," I said, "you're loyal to your girlfriends, Jessie."

Her cheeks reddened. "I think I am. I try to be."

"I bring it up only because I haven't always been good at it," I said. "I've been envious and . . . not so nice. I don't want to be that way."

"Sure," Jessie said, "but hadn't you better you hurry? For your phone call?"

Will had been invited to spend Christmas Eve with the family of another doctoral student, an Italian woman named Mira. "Well, that was nice of them," I said, determined not to convey even a smidge of bitterness at his having a good time in the company of another woman. He related the contents of the holiday telephone call he just had finished with his parents, back in Minnesota. They planned to visit him in February. He was trying to find a place for them to stay that wouldn't be too expensive.

I had met the parents. They had been polite, but distant, and Will admitted, afterward, what I already had guessed: They felt that I was too young for him.

Suppose, in Milan, they tried to convince him to feel the same.

A silver framed wedding picture of my mom and dad sat on my mom's bedside table. Two smaller framed photographs flanked the wedding picture: my sister and me—a generation apart in terms of hairstyles and makeup but both got up in identical high school graduation caps and gowns, so there was some suggestion that we were bound for identical futures. At thirty-eight, Martie was divorced—with a "broken picker"—and living back in our hometown and teaching at the grade school both of us had attended. Who knew what would happen for me?

"You're so quiet," Will said.

"I feel like I'm going to be sick!" I blurted. "I'm sorry, but I've got to go!"

"Oh! I'll . . . call New Year's. I love you."

"You, too," I said.

I lay back on my parents' bed, my feet on the floor. I thought: *If I stay very still, maybe I'll feel better,* but, really, I was not so sure that I felt sick. Really, it had just been too hard to talk to Will.

The shadowy, bumpy surface of the popcorn ceiling over my parents' bed made me think of the pitted snow along the highway. I shut my eyes against it. Someone went into the bathroom, which sat between the two bedrooms. Closed the door. Locked it. Turned on the faucet. The house was so small that, for privacy's sake, my mother and I—and Martie, when she had visited—always turned on the faucet when we used the bathroom. This incensed my dad, and I heard him now call from the table, "Turn off that faucet unless you're washing your hands!"

I sat up at the ringing of the bedroom telephone. Will, I hoped, calling back. I answered with a cheerful "Hello!"

It was a female voice, however—slack with alcohol?—that said, "I miss you!"

Not Aunt Patty. Patty was dead. A wrong number?

The voice continued. "Merry Christmas! We were all sitting around the fireplace, drinking mulled wine—getting cloved!—and I thought, *I have to call Charlotte!*"

Esmé. Not Will, but someone from my other life who wanted to talk to me. *Had* to talk to me. "Merry Christmas!" I said. "I miss you, too!"

A muddle erupted on Esmé's end of the line, and then a boy, pretending to be a girl, squeaked, "Jeremy! Is that you, honey?"

"Away, fiend!" This was Esmé again, now explaining that the interruption had been her brother, the *Tofferheimer*. "But, listen, I have the best news! I'm cutting short my time here and heading to Mobile tomorrow! I done told Ma and Pa, take back all the rest of that shit! All I really want for Christmas is tickets to 'Bama! Gotta see that boy of mine or I'm gonna slit my ever-loving wrists!"

"Well, that's good. I definitely don't want you slitting your ever-loving wrists," I said.

She rattled off a list of things that she and Jeremy Fletcher were going to do in Mobile and I told her I'd talked to Will,

"Oh, the Scallywag!" she said. "The Scallywag" was what she had taken to calling Will after I'd had no choice but to explain that he had changed his plans about coming back in December. She was joking, of course, and right now she was drunk, but I wanted to switch topics, so I mentioned that I'd been getting a lot of writing done—

"Hold that thought, Charlotte! Hold it! Gotta go in the other room. Okay. Okay. Okay. Gotta ask you something, Charlotte. And you tell me the truth: What d'y'all think of the possibility that Esmé Cole might forget to pack her birth control pills when she goes to Alabama to see her sweetheart? Given that it seems the sweetheart might be the type to require a semi-accidental pregnancy to nudge him to the altar?"

I made a kind of *nnh!* sound that meant *not a great idea*. Unlike Esmé, I had not had any mulled wine to drink. I was stone sober. This did not mean that I was insufficiently romantic to understand Esmé's desire to marry the man she loved. That the man could be

Jeremy Fletcher—*that* I did not understand. Also, the idea of a woman convincing a man to marry her because she was pregnant struck me as not only incredibly old-fashioned but dangerous (suppose the man were old-fashioned enough to marry you but didn't love you with all his heart and soul?). None of this, however, did I say explicitly. *"Nnh!"* was all that I said, because I was determined, henceforth and ever more, to say absolutely nothing related to Jeremy Fletcher.

Esmé laughed. "Party pooper!"

"Sticks and stones."

She laughed at that, too. She was still babbling on when I thought: *Why not leave for Iowa City once the kitchen is cleaned up? Why stay?*

Because I had not gotten around to bringing in the paper sack that held my toothbrush and a change of clothes, after I helped my mom and sister with the kitchen, I was able to act as if it had never been my intention to stay overnight. "But for heaven's sake," my mom said, "you weren't feeling well a while ago, and . . . it's Christmas Eve!"

Martie looked into the living room, where the others had settled down with a movie. *A Christmas Story.* "Let her do what she wants, Mom," she said.

My mom called in to my dad, "Dave, Charlotte's talking about leaving."

He walked out into the kitchen. He squinted and raised a hand against the room's brightness after the relative dark of the living room. He asked, "What's the fuss? It's a good time to be driving! Hardly a soul on the road!"

"That's what worries me!" my mom said. "And she wasn't feeling well earlier! Besides which, she just got here!"

"Well, dear." He patted her shoulder. "What's she got to talk about to a bunch of uneducated yokels like us?" He winked at me, like it was all in good fun.

I laughed, the way I was supposed to. "But, really, I've been writing stories most of the break. I need to spend some time getting ready to teach my second-semester classes."

My dad looked back toward the living room and the movie on the television. Maybe he knew that I was lying, that I really wanted to get back to Iowa City so I could write. "Those who can, do," he muttered. "Those who can't, teach."

"A bit hostile from a guy who has two daughters who teach," I said. "And I'm trying to *do*, too."

Martie put her arm over my shoulder and whispered, "Let it go. It's not worth it. Drive carefully." Then she walked into the living room and sat down on the couch next to Jessie, who, I was happy to see, snuggled up close.

"That about ruins Christmas for me," my mother said.

"Christmas is for little kids." My dad waved toward the living room. "Look in there. They're enjoying themselves. Don't bother your little head about it, dear."

After I got through the good-byes and the door closed behind me and I started across the frozen lawn to the station wagon, I began to feel better. I felt fortified by the icy air and the sound of the grass crunching under my boots. The sky over the tail end of the town was clear and glittered with stars. I breathed it in and felt glad to know that I headed to my desk.

19

"But, Charlotte"—Esmé was doing a Jane Fonda exercise video in the living room; I stood at the bathroom sink, re-brushing my teeth after a bout of mostly ineffectual heaving over the toilet—"what if it turns out you're pregnant, babe?"

My friend sounded as if the possibility were a happy one! I immediately responded with a shrill, automatic, "I can't be pregnant! I'm on the pill!"

This was early February. Although Esmé now spent her nights with Jeremy Fletcher, she continued to come by the apartment in the morning to do her beauty regimens and workouts; hence, she had been a witness to my continuing nausea.

"Work it! Work it! Work it!" Jane Fonda urged her legions. I grabbed up the bags and books that I'd dropped by the front door before running to the toilet (my students would arrive at my cubicle for office hours in fifteen minutes).

"Just saying"—Esmé's voice was strained by the exercises, but nonetheless full of contented teasing—"accidents do happen, Char!"

Ice coated the windows of the station wagon, but, before I started scraping, I hopped inside and switched on the engine, hoping the heater might generate some warmth for my drive to the university. There was a damp to the cold that morning—so pronounced that it weighed down my clothes, my movements. The opaque, pearly sheen of the sky overhead made me think of the lard in white paper tubs that my mother sometimes brought home, a gift from a co-worker at the hatchery who occasionally butchered a hog.

As I drove along, people on NPR discussed the uproar over novelist Salman Rushdie's *The Satanic Verses*. Iran's leading cleric, the ayatollah Khomeini, had announced that the author must be put to death for blasphemy. Iranian Muslims in England had burned a thousand copies of *The Satanic Verses*. An Iranian businessman was offering a three-million-dollar bounty on Rushdie's head.

Unbelievable! I thought. Throughout the day, I asked the students who came to sit across from me in my cubicle of plastic and burlap if they had heard about Rushdie's troubles. Some of them had. No one seemed to feel nearly as surprised or outraged by the news as I did.

By the time that I finished with office hours, sleet had started to fall. Luckily, not very many people were on the road. As I drove up steep Washington Street, the rear end of Will's station wagon spun out twice, and it did it again when I made the turn into the parking area alongside the apartment house.

All I wanted to do was get inside, take a bath. A bath with Will—that would have been the best.

Before I entered the apartment, I always knocked—just in case Esmé was home and had something private going on in there. "It's

Charlotte," I called. There was no response, but while I rummaged through my bag for my key, I heard a telephone start to ring. Our telephone, I was quite sure, and then I was sure, too, that the caller was Will—Will had felt me yearning for him. Why didn't I always put the key back in the same place?

I dumped my bag upside down and onto the hall floor. *There!*

By the time that I got the door's tricky lock unlocked and reached the telephone, I was breathless.

"Am I speaking to Charlotte Price?" the caller asked. Not Will, but a man with a friendly voice. I had learned from Esmé, however, that I should ask callers to identify themselves before identifying myself, and so I said, "May I ask who is calling, please?"

"This is Mike Curtis. Is this Charlotte Price?"

Mike Curtis, Mike Curtis. Why did I know that name?

"I'm the fiction editor at the *Atlantic Monthly*. Do I have the wrong number?"

C. Michael Curtis, fiction editor of the *Atlantic Monthly*. I had sent C. Michael Curtis my story "The Magic."

In my excitement at learning that Mike Curtis wanted to publish "The Magic," I pulled the telephone plug out of the wall, and then had to endure almost a minute of agony while I reinstalled the plug and waited for him to call back.

"Actually," he said—a very nice man—when I picked up the second time, "you're not the first writer who's done that."

The story was dark, he said, but he thought that it earned the darkness.

"Oh, good," I said and hoped Will would not mind that a bit of the story's dialogue drew on a conversation he'd once had with his little sister (she'd confessed she couldn't stay in a relationship once "the magic wore off").

The amount that I would be paid for the story was inconceivable to me, but, at that moment, even though I needed money, the payment mattered to me strictly because it meant that that the *Atlantic Monthly* would publish the story. As the editor and I said good-bye, I felt a sense of success unlike anything that I had felt in the past, different from receiving high test scores or a scholarship to college or even my graduate assistantship. I felt . . . full. Good. Right with the world. And I was not drunk.

My movements fluid, graceful, I set the receiver in the cradle. I smiled. Then something very curious and sad happened. As if holes had opened in the bottoms of my feet, all of the good things that I was feeling—they rushed right out of me, *whoosh*, head to toe. Like that, they were gone.

I consoled myself with the thought that at least I still had the news to share.

I telephoned Will at the Milan apartment he shared with several other art history people (I reasoned: If I waited until five, when the rates went down, it would be midnight there). Will was not at the apartment, but the young man—an American—who took my message was excited. "The *Atlantic*! That's incredible! And you're Charlotte. Got it! Great! Congratulations, Charlotte!"

I wished that Esmé would come home! Everyone in the Workshop longed to publish in the Big Three (the *Atlantic*, *Harper's*, the *New Yorker*), but I didn't see how I could tell anyone but Esmé about the sale without seeming to brag. They'd just have to see the story in the magazine.

A drink would have been so nice! Maybe it would have brought back that elation I'd felt for one moment. I paced the apartment.

I wanted *not* to want to telephone my parents, but, at five o'clock, there I was, on the line, waiting for someone to pick up at the house in Webster City.

"How much are they going to pay you?" my dad asked. He was impressed by the amount, although he never had heard of the *Atlantic Monthly*.

"It's been around for over a hundred years, Dad."

My mother got on the line to ask—sounding both happy for me and nervous—"Are we going to have to hide our heads when people read it? I haven't come off very well in the stories of yours I've read so far!"

"It's fiction, Mom," I said. "Don't worry about it."

Esmé had given me the number for Jeremy Fletcher's place. Before that day, I had viewed it as something to use strictly in an emergency, but, in the end—wouldn't she chew me out if I didn't tell her?—I telephoned her.

"Brontë," Jeremy Fletcher said before handing me off to Esmé.

After I told her my news, she blurted, "Damn you!" Then laughed. "But—of course, that's fantastic! Hold on." She covered the telephone for a moment. "Jeremy says you should make sure it isn't a prank, though."

I hadn't imagined such a thing. "Who would do that?"

"Call Curtis back!" she said. "You can get the office number from my *LMP*! Top shelf of the bookcase. Right side."

In the background, I could hear Jeremy Fletcher ask Esmé what story I had sent. When Esmé passed along my answer, he chortled and said a loud, *"Really?"*

"Call their office and let us know what you find out," Esmé said.

Well, I couldn't. Which drove Jeremy Fletcher and Esmé almost insane. That night, the two of them actually drove over to the apartment with carryout Chinese and beer to try to cajole me. At one point, Jeremy Fletcher gave me a look that I thought was a bit too familiar—like *Hey, I know you; you want to do this*—but, eventually, he and Esmé gave up. He lay on the futon with his head in Esmé's lap. He began to talk about the weaknesses of the Workshop and his classmates and where he pictured himself, overall, in what he termed *the field*.

"With all due respect, I reckon no one currently writing English prose composes a finer sentence than I," he said, then added with a chuckle, "course, it may be a magazine like the *Atlantic*—a magazine pitching to the mass audience—don't appreciate the level at which I work."

Esmé nodded and stroked the fine strands of hair on top of his head (hair I could not swear that I myself had not stroked during all that falderal after Thanksgiving).

Two days later, FedEx delivered an envelope containing a letter from Mr. Curtis and the *Atlantic* contract. Jeremy Fletcher or Esmé saw it and, apparently, one or both of them told Workshop people about the sale. I went to pick up stories from the copy room, and the director called out to me as I passed by his office (actually, I hadn't heard the man, but his assistant had, and, remembering that I was half-deaf, she kindly came after me). I'd never spoken to the director before—while other students felt free to drop in for a visit, I felt I would have had to invent some dull pretext for doing so—but he congratulated me like we were old friends, and, then, passing out into the hallway, on my way to meet Esmé at the River Room, I found that many more people suddenly knew my name and said hello.

Esmé and I had staked out a River Room table with our coats and backpacks so we'd have a place to sit once we got through the line when—snaking his way through the noisy cafeteria's crowded tables, holding up his coffee cup like a scepter—Jeremy Fletcher called ahead of himself, "So, Brontë, will y'all still say hey to us when you're rich and famous?" I'd looked forward to talking to Esmé without Jeremy Fletcher around, but Esmé was clearly delighted to see him. She kissed his cheek above his fizzy beard. "You two sit," she said. "I have to run to the restroom."

Jeremy Fletcher and I sat. As if he were Dr. Freud and I a case to be solved, he pulled his fingers through his beard and stared out at me from under the brim of his fedora. Whatever he was up to, I didn't want to be part of it, and I turned toward the wall of windows and looked out. The Iowa was moving fast and wide. Their feet blazing orange against the snow-patched riverbank, a pair of mallards—the male glamorous with his emerald-green head and gold necklace, the female less so in her simple tweed—clambered toward a woman and tiny girl in matching red coats and berets who were in the process of opening plastic bags of Wonder bread.

"But, Brontë," Jeremy Fletcher said. Nothing more.

I looked toward the hallway from which Esmé would return to the cafeteria. She was not in sight. "What is it?"

He dropped his eyes. "Brontë," he said, "I swan I'm lookin' at the burgeoning breasts of a pregnant lady."

That fast, his fedora, his beard and heavy shoulders in their burgundy V-neck sweater, the students and professors standing and sitting and raising bites of bag lunches and cafeteria food to their lips, the windows and the riverbanks and the dark river and the Art Building and beyond—all of it unfurled like a rude wire-and-paper New Year's party favor. Then, there was a moment in which I could not see a thing: The screen went gray.

Of course, he was right. Also could not be allowed to know that he was right.

The gray began to clear. Jeremy Fletcher, like everything else in that emergency moment, began to reemerge in staticky bits of color.

"New birth control pills, dude," I said. *Dude.* Not a name that I used, except in jest, playing the part of a slacker or a stoner. "It's a common side effect."

He took another look at my breasts, smiled and shook his head. "Have it your way. Just don't fuck things up for me and Esmé."

I slid my chair back from the table and stood. When Esmé and I had arrived, I had taken off not only my overcoat but also the old Borgesian tweed jacket. The thing had grown so threadbare that as—trembling, dry-mouthed—I went to put it on, I mistakenly stuck my arm not into the actual sleeve but into the space between the sleeve and its lining. When I tried to extricate my arm, I brought along a length of the torn lining, a trail of satiny gray stuff—completely grotesque to my eyes at that moment, and damning, too, a sign of my lack of grace, my ineptitude and general cursedness. I swung my backpack onto my shoulder and bundled the torn jacket and my overcoat against my front. *My burgeoning breasts.* "Tell Esmé I couldn't stick around, okay?" I said in Jeremy Fletcher's general direction. "Tell her I remembered I had some papers I need to grade."

"Sure. Sure. Work, work, work. Brontë's busy like a bee-bee-bee."

I was on the telephone with the appointment scheduler at the women's clinic when the apartment door flew open and hit the wall behind it with a crash.

"Charlotte!" Esmé came running across the living room toward me. Her woolly, pastel pink scarf covered most of her face, but I still could see that she was crying. In a panic, I dropped the receiver into the cradle and flattened myself against the wall at my back.

"You have to swear you'll never tell a soul!" she said while tearing off the scarf—under which was a crumpled, trembling, but joyful smile.

I nodded.

Like two different mothers checking her temperature at once, Esmé set the backs of both of her fine-boned hands against her glowing cheeks. Although she went on crying, she clearly needed to talk—she stopped and bent over and laughed and shook her head—"Remember how I thought I might arrange an accident with my pills?" she asked.

I nodded again.

"Well, it worked! It worked! I'm seven weeks along!" She shivered and laughed. "I told Jer right after you left! I've wanted to tell you, but I had to tell him first, of course. Anyway, he thinks it's great!" She stopped laughing then, her face suddenly serious. "You understand, right? He thinks it was an *accident*." Before I could answer, she put her fingers to her lips—*sh!*—and said, her voice loud, I guessed for the benefit of any neighbor who might have overheard, "It was an accident, but he's really happy! We called my parents! We're going to get married weekend after next!"

She hugged me and I hugged her; then she stepped back and held me at arm's length and peered at my face. "You're not worried about my half of the rent, are you, Charlotte? I'll pay till the lease is up! You're happy for me, right?"

Happy. Jeremy Fletcher was not a person whom I thought my friend should marry, but I was overwhelmed with gratitude that Esmé still viewed me as her friend, and I answered, "Honey"—and I meant it—"if you're happy, I'm happy, too."

20

I'd driven by the women's center (and the anti-choice picketers out front) dozens of times—in Will's car and Esmé's, and, in earlier days, in the van that occasionally ferried English majors from Mount Vernon to Iowa City for the Writers' Workshop's reading series. On the day of my first appointment, I did wish that the center sat on a less well-traveled street, but I was glad to see only one protester present (a man about my parents' age and wearing a fur-ruffed parka, he waved a sonogram in my direction and called out, "Have you seen a picture of your baby, miss?").

The gentle-faced lady with whom I met—puffy multicolored socks, nubby linen pants with elasticized ankles—was all kindness. I appreciated the warm hand that she patted against my icy one.

I brought my package of birth control pills out of my pocket (as a character witness, I suppose).

"Could you have vomited some pills?" she asked.

I nodded. I told her about Thanksgiving. "We all got sick."

"In the future," she said, "if you experience vomiting, keep on with your pills, but use another form of protection for a full month." She patted my hand again and smiled. "You're lucky you came in when you did. At your stage, very few people—one in a hundred— have complications. We like to say that it's safer than having your tonsils out!"

I smiled to make her feel good about her job, but by no means did I feel "lucky." After I'd been handed my appointment card and started walking toward the apartment (hurrying—collar turned up— to get onto a side street), I felt very alone, like a prisoner scheduled for execution who did not dare entrust even a cell mate with the knowledge that he secretly had dug an escape tunnel through the wall alongside their bunk.

Had Will been the only possible father, I would have told him I was pregnant. He would have expected—as I would have, in theory— that I would want an abortion. He would have been sorry that I would have to go through with the procedure (also, possibly irritated and perplexed that it had taken me so long to get the message).

At the library, I found a big book whose shadowy black-and-white photographs informed me that although the fetus was only an inch and a half long, it was already becoming either a boy or a girl. Also, it had webby—and undeniably dear—outlines of actual fingers and toes. In my notebook, I carried the same three-ring ruler that I'd had since grade school. "Charlotte Price" I'd gouged and re-gouged into its pale, varnished wood over the years. An inch and a half looked bigger than I would have liked.

With my Workshop meeting and my seminar in British Autobiographies and Biographies of the Nineteenth Century, along with the two classes that I taught, it was hard to schedule the maximum five hours that the clinic said might be needed (observation time after the procedure varied from client to client), but the place did stay open in the evening, and I managed to set up an appointment for four o'clock. It was a blessing that Esmé no longer came back to the apartment to sleep. There would be no need to lie to anyone about where I'd been if I did not get back to the apartment until nine.

Unlike the day of my first appointment, on the afternoon of the procedure, three scowling picketers walked back and forth in front of the clinic. The man with the fur ruff and the sonogram was there again, and, at a break in the traffic, I darted out into the street to skirt him. All three picketers shouted at me. One was a woman in a pink acrylic version of Esmé's *papakha*, but even she put me in mind of those carloads of boys who shouted obscenities from their rolled-down windows as they sped past female pedestrians.

The clinic clearly meant for the reception area to look homey (floral cushions, a tweedy carpet, table lamps with low-wattage bulbs). Two couples, probably close to my age, were seated on the twin rattan love seats. The male halves of both couples wore heavy metal T-shirts and chains around their necks. One of them was very tall, taller even than Will, and he sat slouched forward, headphones on, listening to a Walkman. He laughed every now and then. "Listen to this!" he said and removed his headset and tried to put it on the woman who I assumed was his girlfriend or wife. She batted the headset away. "You know I hate him!" she said. "You know I think he's sick!" The man laughed.

The other couple sat quietly holding hands, heads leaned one against the other. They looked incredibly sad.

I had come directly from the university and wore "teaching clothes" and, while I filled out forms on the clipboard that the receptionist had given me, it occurred to me that the two couples might imagine that I hoped to pass myself off as a social worker or something, not just another knocked-up young woman. This absolutely was not true. I would have been glad if one of those women had started to talk to me. I was apprehensive. I wouldn't be able to ask for the "twilight sedation." (The clinic required that all clients be driven home after the procedure; for me, that would mean using a taxicab, and, given that I couldn't risk being seen getting out of a cab in front of the apartment building, I would need to be alert enough to walk the last block or two on my own steam.

It's odd what you remember. During the procedure—just five minutes, as several people on the staff told me—over the clinic's antiseptic odors, there rose the good smells of cumin and garlic and onions. A worker heating up leftover Indian food in a microwave, I supposed. I almost commented on it to the very nice African-American woman who was holding my hand and smiling down at me, but then I thought better of it in case she or someone else might imagine I was being a smart aleck. The woman squeezed my hand and said something to me, but I couldn't make it out (she stood on my deaf side and the aspirator was whirring away). It might have been simply *Almost through*.

After the observation period, I dressed. I used the clinic's telephone to call a local taxi service and a cab came and it ferried me—and a bag holding stapled instruction sheets, three pain pills, and a bunch of very fat sanitary pads—to a spot about a block from the apartment.

As expected, Esmé was not at home when I arrived. That made it easier to do everything that the instruction sheets said to do, including, when I started to have severe cramps despite the pain pill, sitting on the toilet every hour or two, massaging my lower abdomen. The abortion took place on Monday. On Tuesday, with the help of the second of my three pain pills, I was able to teach. I even attended my workshop class late Wednesday afternoon, but very early on Thursday morning, the last pain pill gone, I felt so bad that I lay down on the bathroom floor and I stayed there.

You could hear the chimes from some church at the apartment. That morning, while I waited for the chimes to signal eight o'clock—the instruction sheets said that the clinic would open at nine—I rehearsed things. Over and over. Exactly what words I would use when I telephoned. How, once I finished talking to the clinic, I would call for a cab—though not from the company that I had used Monday. Next, I would get dressed. Start down to the first floor immediately so that I could be waiting when the cab arrived. It was imperative that I leave the apartment before Esmé came by to get dressed and do her Jane Fonda. She rarely arrived before nine—

But there had been exceptions. I thought of some of the exceptions. *I should leave now*, I thought. *Call a cab now.* I could take the cab to a diner that I remembered sat not far from the clinic. Then, shortly before nine, I'd start walking to the clinic.

In the living room, a key rattled in the lock. I tried to get up. Knocked over the metal trash can that I used for support.

"Charlotte? Is that you?"

I hesitated. I didn't want Esmé to see me on the bathroom floor; but, then, neither did I want her to imagine there was a robber in the place. The thought of *her* scared made *me* even more scared, and I worked my way onto my hands and knees and called, "In here."

From the doorway, she asked, "What happened? Did you drop something?"

I looked up at her. "What's wrong with you?" she said and crouched down beside me and set her hand on my forehead. "We're going to Student Health!"

I pointed toward the stapled sheets of paper that I'd carried from my room and left lying on the floor. She frowned as she read the top page.

"Thanksgiving," I said. "When we were sick—I guess I threw up my pills."

She sat back on her heels. "But—it's almost March!"

"So I'm stupid. Will you take me there, please? At nine o'clock?"

A portion of the tissue had not been expelled. It was septic.

During that visit, I accepted the twilight sedation. Whether or not someone held my hand while I was reaspirated, I do not know. I have no memory of Esmé driving me back to the apartment or getting me to the third floor, but I do remember waking up in my bed that night. When I rolled over, there was Esmé, sitting in my desk chair, reading. She got right up and brought me pills and water. She took my temperature.

"Almost normal," she said. "That means the antibiotics are working." She showed me a chart she had made up for the pills that I was to take for the next ten days, along with the rule sheet that I needed to follow until I went back to the clinic in two weeks.

I shook my head. "Thank you. For everything."

She settled her hand on her belly, clearly thinking about her own baby. "You're welcome, of course, though I *am* pissed that you didn't trust me enough to tell me! I don't know if Will agreed with you—"

"Will *doesn't* know anything!" I sat up in the bed. Yelped. A large, heavy brick was lodged inside me, its edges in flame. "No one ever can know! You're the only person in the world besides the clinic that knows!"

"All right, sh, sh." She stroked my forehead. She grinned. "You realize, of course, I'd feel a lot more honored, being your special confidante, if you'd *wanted* me to know?"

As it happened, I hardly saw Esmé again after that night. Maybe three or four times. Her parents had asked that she and Jeremy

Fletcher get married by a justice of the peace in Evanston—something to do with allowing Esmé's grandmothers to be present. Very happy, tipsy. A lot of racket in the background—she called me from a pay phone at the noisy restaurant where the family had gone to celebrate after the ceremony. "I had to tell you! We've decided not to come back!"

The two of them were moving to Mobile, Alabama.

A few weeks later, Esmé's little brother and one of his friends drove to Iowa City, and I helped them pack Esmé's things and carry them down from the third floor to a U-Haul exactly like the one that I'd help Esmé unpack a few months before.

I lived in the apartment alone until May. In May, I flew to Milan to meet Will. In July, when we returned to Iowa City, we moved into an apartment that we had picked out together.

PART THREE

21

I left the mess from the WRITERS' WORKSHOP/DRAFTS box where it lay, scattered across the dusty floor of the shed, and I returned to the empty house.

It was Jacqueline C.'s husband, Billy, a retired contractor—also a member of AA—who picked up my call.

"Charlotte Price!" he said, as if my name were a cause for celebration. Then he called, "Jackie! Charlotte Price is on the line!"

After she had listened to me for a couple of minutes, Jacqueline said, "But all this is old news, honey."

"Not somebody's asking me to rig an award or else they'll tell Will about it. *That's* not old news."

The sound of her long inhale let me know that she had gone back to smoking cigarettes since the last time I had seen her, a month or so ago. "Have you been drinking?" she asked.

"No."

"Well, that's good, but you need to get regular with meetings. If you'd kept going to a couple of meetings a week, you'd be a whole lot better equipped to deal with a problem like this. Hold on, hold on." She held a brief muffled conversation with Billy. I undoubtedly was upsetting their plans for the day. "Okay, Charlotte. Look, it's eight. I'll come get you and we'll talk. Then we'll try to go to a nine o'clock."

While I hurried to dress, I thought about the day ahead. I was scheduled to be at my office at noon in case any of my graduate students wanted to talk with me before our workshop started at one thirty. I could not imagine going into school at all, but while canceling office hours wouldn't be too difficult, canceling a workshop class would be. Even if I could find someone who was free from one thirty to four to lead the workshop, I'd first have to deliver the stories to the person, and, then, he or she would have to read them—

I ran to the front hall to see if Jacqueline had arrived. No car in sight, so I ran to my desk. The three fat, green envelopes holding Poulos Prize finalists sat in a stack on one corner. I stuck them in my briefcase. Added the manila folder containing the Melody Murphy material (her CV, one of her articles, and my notes on her demo class, which I'd somehow have to organize before the search committee met on Monday).

Jacqueline was driving a car I didn't know, a sporty thing, tiny for her rather large self. As I came down the walk, she leaned forward and, through the rolled down passenger-side window—smiling and upbeat and sociable—she called to me, "Everything's grown so much since I last was here, Charlotte! It looks lovely!" Once I got into the tiny car, though, she hugged me in a consoling way.

"You're an angel," I said.

"Not hardly."

"I always feel, like, because you lost your son, my problems—"

"Oh, stop." She eased back into her seat and set her hands on the steering wheel. "This is your *life*. You need to take it serious, so . . . none of that." She let out the clutch and we started up the road.

"So, talk to me. I got a meeting list in my purse. We can always find a ten o'clock, if we have to miss the nine."

While I talked and—as my dad would have said—"blubbered away," Jacqueline drove us slowly through the quiet, moneyed neighborhood called El Encanto, where the only other vehicles on the silky, curving streets were the battered pickup trucks that belonged to mostly dark-skinned men at work with blowers and rakes in the expansive yards.

After a while, Jacqueline broke in to suggest that I "let go and let God," which was all well and good except, as I reminded her, "I don't even know if I believe in God."

She stopped her tiny car right in the middle of the street, and, as if to say, *Lord, help me*, looked up at the ceiling, which was located not far from the tip of her cute nose. "That's because you're not willing to be transformed, Charlotte! Man, you're stubborn! Stop being so stubborn!"

I didn't argue with Jacqueline, although, actually, I would have liked very much to be transformed. Against my better judgment, there had been a number of times when I'd gotten down on my knees and prayed for transformation.

Maybe if I'd felt some stirring, I would have been willing to believe what otherwise couldn't be believed—but I hadn't.

Jacqueline drove us into pretty Reid Park—several times, in fact, because its streets were short and meant only to deliver you to the playground or the rose garden or the band shell. On one of those trips, she parked, and we got out of the car and sat on a shaded bench so that Jacqueline could smoke a cigarette. She was wearing a heavy gold charm bracelet that Billy and her kids had been contributing to for years, and she looked up from picking at one of the charms—a little dog with rhinestone eyes—and she said, "I'm always embarrassed for you to see me smoke. I know you used to smoke."

"Please," I said. "Do something a whole lot worse. I'll be consoled."

She laughed at that and I did, too, and then I coughed a little sob. "He'll never forgive me."

Firmly, Jacqueline said, "Now I don't believe that, Charlotte. I've seen you two together. There was that big Fourth of July picnic when we sat together, and a couple of New Year's Eve Alcathons. I could see straightaway that Will recognized what a fine person you are— which told me he was a man of real substance." She seemed satisfied with this for a moment, then blurted, "But that's not the point, darn it! Whether he forgives you or not! Work on forgiving yourself. And everybody else, while you're at it. Forgive your old friend, and if you've got a beef against her creepy husband, forgive him, too. Hell, forgive your mom and dad, too, while you're at it. Everybody. Otherwise, you're just treading the same old dirty bathwater."

I nodded, but it was a nod of defeat rather than agreement.

"And Will," Jacqueline said. "Forgive him, too."

"Will? For what?"

She ground out her cigarette with the tip of one of her pointy-toed shoes. "For not always being exactly the way you want him to be? Not getting on board about having kids?"

"I never told you he wasn't . . . *on board*. Where'd you get that idea?"

Jacqueline opened her mouth. Her face went a flushed pink (I could guess mine was the same color). "Forget I said that, Charlotte. That was presumptuous of me. I apologize." She glanced at her watch. Its delicate gold band looked as if it had grown too tight, as if it might be cutting into the soft flesh of her wrist. "We better get going," she said, "or else we'll miss the ten o'clock meeting, too!"

I think we both felt a bit awkward after that. We didn't talk as Jacqueline drove east on Twenty-Second Street. As she turned north on Columbus Boulevard.

Was what she had said about Will true?

We passed a large, straw-colored building. The words UNCLE BOB'S POPCORN were spelled out in red paint on its south side. I usually passed Uncle Bob's Popcorn when I went to a meeting at the Alano Club. The painted words always looked oddly naïve to me, like a child's writing STORE on a building in his drawing of a little town.

My head—it seemed to be filled with concrete that was starting to set.

"Christ, I make myself sick," I said.

"Well, exactly!" Jacqueline said. "So cut it out!"

I had never been to a ten o'clock meeting in the annex. The group was small, under fifteen people. Most of the world already had gone to work. Five or six of the people present were older and dressed in the type of casual knits that Jacqueline wore and that I associated with retirees. One young man in a suit and tie looked as if he'd be headed to an office when the meeting ended. In the front row, there sat a sexy, rather scruffy young woman in a turquoise halter top and very low-slung jeans. She seemed impatient for the meeting to begin. She kept tossing her long dark hair around her bare shoulders, and her expressions ping-ponged between what appeared to be bitter brooding and astonished delight. She was seated between two of the older people in knits, and, from the fond way that they looked at her, and then back at each other, I surmised that they were her parents. The people who appeared closest to me in age were a biker in a pirate bandanna and a sweatshirt whose cutoff sleeves exposed his slabs of heavily tattooed muscles, and a bald, handicapped woman who rode into the building on a motorized scooter decorated with a silky red, white, and blue Arizona Wildcat pennant flying off its rear end.

My people. Not exactly what I'd had in mind when I started out in life, but, hey, as Jacqueline and I had found seats around the table, I'd seen a lot of hand shaking and hugging. People were laughing. They were doing something right. Most of them knew one another and seemed to be friends. Which was the way it was supposed to be. You weren't supposed to graduate from the meetings or drop in every once in a while. You were supposed to attend regularly and be a member of the group and wise up and stick around and share what you learned with newcomers.

Not just periodically ask to be rescued.

That meeting gave out coins ("chips," in AA parlance) to celebrate milestones in its members' sobriety. There was a one-month chip, a two-month, a three-month, and so on; eventually, the chips marked years of continuous sobriety. There also was a twenty-four-hour chip that you did not have to do a thing to earn, and when a very tanned old gentleman in a banana-yellow golf sweater—"Randolph, alcoholic"—started out the day's chip giving by holding up a silver twenty-four-hour chip and asking, "Anybody here want a twenty-four-hour chip? Good-day, bad-day chip? Going-out-of-town chip? My-dog-has-fleas chip?" I raised my hand.

Randolph smiled and nodded, and I walked around the table to the head of the room. "Charlotte, alcoholic," I said. Old Randolph hugged me, and he set the twenty-four-hour chip into my hand and gently folded my fingers over it. I turned and faced the group. "I need to come to meetings more often," I said. "I'm thankful all of you are here, and . . . I'm here."

"Welcome!" the people around the table said. "Glad you're here!"

I returned to my chair. Randolph—grinning, humming "Camptown Races"—looked through the plastic chip box to see if it held a six-month chip for the pretty young woman in the halter top. She was clowning around, excited, standing on tiptoe, lightly clapping her hands together and smiling and smiling at the couple—they were smiling, too—whom I'd taken for her parents.

"Pass your chip," Jacqueline whispered to me (a ritual; each member would briefly hold the chip before it finally made its way back to the recipient).

Forgive everybody.

I tried to pay attention. The man with the tattooed biceps suggested as a topic "how expectations lead to resentments," and I (along with the woman on the motorized scooter) groaned in appreciation.

When it was my turn to speak, however, I said only, "I'm Charlotte, and I'm an alcoholic, and I'm just going to listen today."

Jacqueline passed, too, but at the very end of the meeting, she said, "I'm so happy my friend Charlotte and I could join you today. Some of you remember Mitzi—lots of sobriety when she died, thirty-some years I think—and Mitzi used to say she kept her memory green by coming to meetings. I've always remembered that. We get civilized here, and if we want to stay civilized, we keep coming back."

After the meeting ended, a couple of people nodded at me and smiled. I didn't get the big, open-armed welcome that I'd always wanted, but, then, I probably couldn't have handled it anyway. Jacqueline introduced me to the parents of the young woman who had received the six-month chip. "You mind if I say where you work?" Jacqueline asked me, and when I said no, she explained that the couple worked at the university, too. "Music Department," the woman said; "Engineering," said her husband. The man with the tattooed biceps patted my shoulder in passing and said, "Keep coming back!"

"Thanks," I called after him.

Jacqueline turned to me and smiled. "Maybe you need to get a tattoo," she whispered as we started out of the building. "A motto, like, 'What other people think of me is none of my business.'"

"Right."

Will's Subaru sat parked in the carport, alongside mine.

"I guess I kind of hoped he wouldn't be home," I said.

Jacqueline squeezed my shoulder. "Do I need to drive around for a while so you can recite 'I'm a good person' a hundred times?"

"No."

"All right, then. Remember: Don't grovel. And have some compassion for yourself! You didn't grow up with the tools you needed, Charlotte. You did the best you knew how at the time."

"*That* is not something he'd want to hear."

"So don't say it to him, for pity's sake! But make sure you remember that it's true!"

I gave her a good-bye hug. "One of these days," she said, "I'd be willing to bet money, you're going to see all this as a gift."

I grimaced.

She laughed. "I know, I know, honey, you don't believe everything happens for a reason, so forget I said that, but think how you're going to be able to go forward, from here! Those secrets have made you kind of a scaredy-cat in your marriage, you know."

I nodded. I knew.

Will was seated at the dining room table, at work on his laptop, but he stood as soon as I slid open the door. His face was pale. "I want to know," he said, "what was going on at your friends' place? Esmé's? Something was going on. Tell me what it was."

The night before, I had pictured myself down on my knees, but Jacqueline had said, "Don't grovel," and I didn't allow myself to drop down into a keening ball. My words, though, when I spoke, came out like sludge, dark, heavy, and so *big* that they hurt not only my throat but my temples, my jaws, as if I were forcing the whole of myself, inside out, through my mouth:

That Thanksgiving. You told me you weren't coming back, and I was so upset. Esmé . . . out in the kitchen, without her clothes.

He growled, "What did *you* do, Charlotte?"

It was infuriating, I understood, for him to have to watch me bawl, shoulders heaving. I covered my face with my hands as I said a choked, "I'd give anything if I could change it."

"Go on."

"Esmé—I know it's no excuse—but after you left for the airport, she said she knew you were attracted to her. I got upset, and then Jeremy told me she'd laughed about me being upset. She left town that day, too, and I got stoned—"

Silence. Then a familiar metallic click that I recognized as Will setting down his glasses. I lowered my hands. He was rubbing the red indentations where the glasses' guards pressed too tightly against his nose. "Tell me you didn't fuck that creep," he said.

I raised a terrible index finger. Once.

"Christ." He kicked the leg of the table hard enough that his glasses scooted off the other side and fell to the floor. "So, all that coy shit! *Eat your green beans, Charlotte.* While I'm sitting there like a chump! And, you—you were the one who worried I'd be unfaithful to you while I was in Italy!"

I lifted the neck of my T-shirt and used it to wipe my face. "I'm so sorry, but there's more, Will."

He opened his mouth. Closed it. His expression of fury shifted to one of utter boredom. He glanced away, up toward the light fixture that hung over the table. He had become an official forced to listen to the most tired and improbable tale from a known reprobate.

Was it all rubble between us now? I went on. "After Thanksgiving, I kept feeling sick and losing weight, and when I didn't get my period, I told myself—"

One gape-mouthed glance. Then he snapped to again and said, "Speak up! I hardly can hear you!"

"My being sick threw off the birth control pills. I was pregnant. I didn't know—"

He smiled a poisonous smile, but there was a metallic alarm in his voice when he asked, "Did you tell *Jeremy*?"

I wanted to take hold of him and remind him that I was Charlotte; but, although he never had hit me, I had a feeling that if I were to put my hands on him, then, he might well shove me across the room. "I didn't tell anyone! There was no way I could tell you—I was terrified you wouldn't love me anymore!"

He thrust his arms upward in a big V. Bent forward from the waist. I recognized this dramatic posture as one his father employed at the pulpit. It was nothing I'd ever seen from Will. "I'm sure you were right!" he boomed.

"*No one* was supposed to know, ever, but I got an infection. It was bad. I needed Esmé's help."

His lip curled. He suspected that I wanted to arouse some sympathy in him, and, understandably, that disgusted him. I was beyond that though. I wanted only to finish the story.

"I told her nobody could know—not even you. She assumed you were the father—"

"Well, of *course*!" he said, very jolly.

But that was too much! I raised my hands in the air and made fists. "Please, Will!"

He looked away. "Just . . . finish."

I was shaking again, but now partly in anger. "Esmé saw I was judging the Poulos Prize, so she submitted Jeremy's novel. Now it's a finalist and she wants me to make it the winner. She didn't come right out and say it, but the threat was clear: either I name it the winner or she'd tell you about my being with Jeremy. And that I aborted a baby that might have been ours."

He glared at me; then clasped his hands to his head. "You can . . . drop that baby bullshit, Charlotte. We wouldn't have had a baby back then."

"I might have, though! If I'd known it was ours! Or that having the abortion meant I'd never have a baby at all!"

He stepped to the sliding door and, with a great *whoosh*, shoved the door open on its track. The thing banged so hard against the far side of the frame that it rebounded, came back to a close, the glass shaking, just after Will had stepped out onto the ramada. Almost as fast, though, he flung the door open again and demanded to know why we had gone to the Fletchers' for dinner.

I tried to explain how surprised I'd been by Esmé's visit. "I told you. She said she hadn't known we lived here."

He shook his head. "And you believed that. Why did you believe that, Charlotte? Seriously. In *eleven* years, how could she *never* have seen an announcement for a reading or book-signing by you, a local author? Never read a newspaper article that said you lived in Tucson? *Why* did you believe it?"

I bowed under the weight of the questions. "I don't know," I moaned. "I thought maybe I could make amends to her, Will. Maybe we'd even put it all behind us and be friends."

"Christ," he hissed, "did you really need a friend that bad?"

"I guess I thought I did. I'm not good at making friends. I get lonely."

"Did you ever think about *me* in all this? You had me go to dinner at the house of a man you fucked? And his wife knows all about it, too! Why would you subject me to that?"

"I wasn't sure what she knew, Will. Obviously, I'm an idiot." I knew that Jacqueline would have disapproved of that, but I didn't correct myself, and Will nodded vigorously.

"You are! You are! I feel like I don't even know you! Christ!" He made a familiar motion of patting his front left pants pocket for his car keys. "Christ! And now we've got to go! Are you ready to go?"

"Ready to go?"

"To *school*. You have office hours and class. Hurry up. I'll be in the car."

22

Neither of us spoke during the drive to the university, but when Will stopped the Subaru in front of Modern Languages to drop me off—just the way that he did every Thursday—I leaned forward, laying my upper body flat on my legs. "I don't see how I can go in there now," I said.

He stared straight ahead, silent.

"So are you going to your office, too?" I asked.

A shrug.

I sat up and rested my cheek against his upper arm. "I love you," I said. His muscles tensed. Antipathy. "There's a bus coming," he said. "You need to get out."

"I don't want to go!"

"It's better. I need to be alone." The way he looked at that moment—he looked old, his features cloudy, as if hurt had dropped a veil of age over his face. It shocked me. He was as far from me as he ever had been, but not at all . . . mysterious. I had hurt him terribly and he stood revealed.

Behind us, the bus driver honked. Sick at heart, I kissed Will's shoulder and climbed out of the car. My legs were rubbery as I made my way up the walk, like I'd just come off a ship or a trampoline. It seemed strange that everything could look exactly the way that it had the Thursday before when Will had dropped me off for office hours. The same scrawny plants of red salvia and purple verbena barely held on beneath the palo verde tree where I always waited for Will to fetch me on days when he drove me to school.

But then it also was true that the palo verde had reached maturity since I'd first walked up the sidewalk to Modern Languages. Also, near the bike racks, three tiny jojobas to which I'd occasionally carried cups of water—tubes of chicken wire had protected them their first years—now were as big as linebackers.

Almost as soon as I started down the central hall, a voice behind me called, "Charlotte, Charlotte!"

It was one of the graduate students. Eric Trelor. An intense, nervous guy. He waved a sheet of paper in his hand as he ran toward me. He had a heavy beard but wore red canvas sneakers that would have gotten him teased in certain quarters. I felt protective of him because he was younger than most of his class-mates, and because it had occurred to me that if I'd had the baby when I was in graduate school, he or she would have been around Eric Trelor's age.

Eric Trelor skidded to a stop beside me. "I got the telephone numbers for DFW's agent and editor, Charlotte!"

"That's cool!" *DFW* meant David Foster Wallace. Our program's most famous alumnus, gifted David Wallace had hanged himself the month before. Eric Trelor had been working ever since to arrange a memorial weekend in the writer's honor.

"The dean's going to fund it!" Eric Trelor jumped up into the air, springy as a little kid. "It's cooler than cool!" He grabbed my arm and gave it a friendly shake. "Listen, though, I gotta tell Dana! See you later!" and off he ran, down the hall.

David Wallace had left the program many years before I arrived, but we'd met, we'd corresponded. The last time I'd seen him, we'd been seated at opposite ends of a long table at the noisy seafood restaurant where Creative Writing usually took visiting authors. We'd had little chance to talk. He was as charming as ever, and his reading was a knockout, but he looked bloated; with a grimy bandanna forming a kind of queer chimney around his mess of hair, he could have been mistaken for one of the homeless winos who begged in supermarket parking lots.

The hanging had not been entirely a shock. Given his depressions, everyone who knew him had worried that it could happen; still, when a mutual friend called with the news, I shouted, "No!" and I cried and cried. Since September, now that the answer was "David can't think of this at all, David is dead," I had come to understand how often, writing, I asked myself, "What would David think of this?"

At the thought of that extraordinary man—Will's own age, forty-six—hanging from a beam in his home garage, my heartbeat ticked upward, and I stepped to the side of the hall and pulled my cell from my bag.

"Please, tell me," I said as soon as Will answered, "should I be worried about you? Hurting yourself? Or anything?"

He hesitated. His voice husky, he said, "I'm not going to hurt myself, Charlotte, but I don't want to talk to you right now."

I appreciated the fact that he'd waited for me to say *Okay* before he said *Good-bye* and hung up.

The office of staffer Pema Barkley was on the fourth floor, in a side hall, off to the left, after you entered the main hallway. From the main hallway, I could see a parallelogram of milky light on the linoleum that indicated her office door stood open, and, before I went toward it—wanting to keep our encounter short—I unzipped the top of my briefcase and removed the green envelopes holding the books of three of the Poulos finalists.

At my knock on the doorjamb, Pema looked away from her monitor and smiled. "Hey, Charlotte! How are things going?"

I nodded. "Good, good. I'm bringing these Poulos finalists back, though." I held up the envelopes. "I'm not going to be able to judge the contest after all."

"Oh!" She looked crestfallen. "But I have three more for you!" She waved toward a large plastic tub decorated with teddy bears—a baby's tub—that she'd recently begun using as a place to stash the great quantities of mail that came to Creative Writing. "I was going to give them to you today, once I put them in envelopes."

"Well," I chirped, "no need now! I'm going to talk to Robert, so you hold on to them—and these three, too—until he tells you where they should go."

She already was looking back at her monitor. Dog accessories. Brightly colored collapsible water bowls. Reflective leashes and collars for nighttime walks. I asked, "Should I put them on your desk, or—"

Absently, she patted the top of her cluttered desk (I supposed it was no worse than my own). "Here's good," she said. "Yeah. Thanks."

I walked on down the hall to the main office. In one corner, a beige plastic cubicle similar to the one I'd had as a TA at Iowa had been installed (to block easy access to the office of the department chair?) Inside the cubicle sat the chair's excellent assistant and gatekeeper.

Who had gotten braces on his teeth since I'd last seen him. Comment or not? Probably not. We were not intimate.

"I'm sorry, Charlotte"—the assistant offered a mild, suitable face of proxy apology—"but Robert's in a meeting right now."

"I'll just leave him a note." On a sheet of paper torn from my notebook, I jotted:

Dear Robert,

I apologize for the inconvenience, but I must recuse myself as judge for the Poulos Prize as I've discovered that I know one of the finalists. If you need suggestions for someone else who might be willing to take on the job, please let me know and I will try to help.

All the best,
Charlotte

After that, I went to my own office. No one had signed up for an appointment on the scheduling sheet taped to my door, but I turned on the lights and nudged the brown rubber stop under the door with my toe, the way that I must have done a couple of thousand times over the previous eleven years. I did not have Gregor Poulos's number in my phone, but I had Jenny Ambrose's, and, luckily, she was at home and able to turn me over to Gregor.

(Who sighed at my news, "Oh, Charlotte! Sweetie! Say it isn't so!")

I looked at my hands after I got off the phone with Gregor. Although my hands did not show it, since my conversation with Will at the house—while talking to Eric Trelor, Pema Barkley, the chairman's assistant, Jenny, and Gregor—I had been trembling. Inside. It was an odd sensation. Like I was a set of dinner dishes in a cabinet during an earthquake.

I didn't know what to do about Esmé. I wanted to be done with her, but she wasn't likely to be satisfied by my simply telling her, "Will knows everything, and I'm not going to be the judge, so goodbye." Would I have to bring Will along to testify that this was so? Would he go?

For distraction, I took out the notes I'd made on my impressions of job candidate Melody Murphy. I decided to type them up so I could hand them around at the meeting, and I rolled my chair over to the office computer. Despite my trembling, I felt uncharacteristically brisk and efficient in my movements, just then. Posture perfect—Joan Crawford—I leaned over and pulled open the drawer of my desk and extracted a package of printer paper. This had something to do with a sense that I was under observation and needed to demonstrate that I could proceed through the day *properly*.

I was trying to be Will, I think. I had the idea that I was acting the way Will would if he were in his office.

At five minutes before the graduate workshop was scheduled to start, I crossed the breezeway and headed to the seminar room.

In the car, on the drive to school, I'd entertained the idea that maybe I'd take a seat in the back of the seminar room that afternoon and say, "I'm tired of hearing myself talk. I'm going to shut up today and let you guys run things." I did that on occasion, but I found that I needed to be the teacher that afternoon, walk back and forth in front of the whiteboard, write down my own and the students' pertinent comments with my red dry-erase marker.

During the critique of the first story, I took a minute to discuss setting. "My favorite definition," I said, "comes from R. V. Cassill."

I wrote on the board: "An arena suitable for the conflict."

"That doesn't mean you need an old house for a ghost story. You can use any space for a ghost story—you could use a *Walgreens* for a ghost story, right? I can see it. As writers, what could you do with a Walgreens to make it feel like a suitable arena for a ghost story?"

The students smiled while they considered the question. I thought of Will kicking the dining room table that morning. Then of myself, on Monday, kicking the table in ML 201, trying to make a point of my own.

A solid sense of the physical world. That would be an important part of my answer to the question. Otherwise, why would it be interesting if ghosts could walk through walls?

I abided by Will's request that I not telephone that afternoon. At four o'clock, though, as soon as the students had circulated the stories for the next week's workshop, I hurried out of the building and down the walk to the street.

Will usually was waiting for me when I came out. If he were late, it was rarely by more than ten minutes.

At four thirty, I called the house and then his cell: "I'm out front, waiting," I told voice mail.

"If it isn't Charlotte Price!"

I turned. A colleague of mine—a spunky woman from Rhet/ Comp—was coming my way, and she called out to me over the whine of her big, wheel-along briefcase, "You look like you need a ride!"

I tagged along with her to the surface lot where she'd parked her car. I did not know her well—Karen Munsen was her name—but I learned that afternoon that she was very keen on the job candidate Melody Murphy. For most of the trip to my house, she worked to convince me that Melody Murphy was the person we ought to hire.

"That's it," I said. "Just ahead. The white stucco."

Karen Munsen pulled her car to a stop at the walk that led to Will's and my front door. "And on top of all that," she said, "she's a great dancer! Did you see her dance with Chris Baber out in the courtyard at El Charro?"

While I gathered up my bags, I said, no, that I'd missed that. "Thank you so much for the ride, Karen!"

She stayed, apparently to make sure that I got into the house. I felt self-conscious, going up the front walk. I also wished I'd told her to pull into the drive. That way, I'd have been able to see if Will's Subaru were in the carport, and I could have gone around to the sliding door. To complicate matters, it turned out that the front screen door—rarely locked—was locked that afternoon, and I had to stop and consider which key on my heavy-laden key ring was the right one. After trying three without luck, I waved to Karen Munsen to signal that she really did not need to wait.

"That's okay!" she shouted. "Can I help?"

"No, no!" I went back to the key that I'd tried first. It turned. I opened the door and waved a final good-bye to Karen Munsen, who tapped a merry *honk-honk* and drove away.

Something felt wrong as soon as I stepped inside.

What was it? I thought of David Wallace again, hanging in his garage, dead.

The house opened in front of me, somehow . . . bald, unfamiliar. I moved in the direction of the kitchen, the direction I would have moved if I'd smelled smoke. There was no smoke. I hurried past the dining room table with its three Mexican tin candlesticks and four chairs, nothing out of place, but the light beyond the dining room was too intense, the effect uncanny, like the time I'd seen a building whose outer wall had been razed by a wrecking ball, the intimate room within (sweet floral wallpaper, a marble fireplace mantel) left exposed to the open sky.

The eerie feeling persisted for several moments after I stepped into the kitchen—a space all blasted with light—and then I felt a shift. I slipped back in time and realized that the kitchen looked precisely the way that it had looked when we moved in, before the oleander hedge had shaded the west side of the house.

I crossed that light-scoured room and looked out the window over the sink. There—long hidden from view—was the east side of Helen and Nick Schaeffer's house, plus a long line of freshly cut stumps, bone-bright inside their dark rims of bark. The clear red, bell-shaped blooms that had made the variety of oleander my favorite still were fresh and vivid in the wild heaps of limbs and branches piled along the drive.

I gripped the counter and howled, "Will!"

23

He was not in the house or the yard. His car was gone.

I called his cell phone again. When he did not answer, I left a new message, "That was so wrong. I didn't need to be punished by you." Then I hung up.

Scaredy-cat. I had been startled when Jacqueline characterized me in that way, but she was right. I'd shaped my life around those secrets. I'd punished myself plenty, trying to make up for them, make myself good enough for Will. Just one spot of green in the yard. Never a fire in the fireplace because it would "suck heat out of the house" and acids from the ashes might damage our books or computers. Forget spontaneous plans and meals out ("We're too busy" or "The prices are outrageous, Charlotte"). Always saving money for travel, though every fucking trip was a trip to Italy or to some archive that Will needed to study.

A child! My god! How could a poor little child even have *fit* into a household like ours?

The doorbell—the door*drill.*

I hurried to answer, my clogs clattering on the tile floors. Who now, who now?

Our dear old neighbors, Nick and Helen Schaeffer. Side by side, with their choppy gray hair, lightweight cardigans, and polo shirts, they looked very much a matched set.

They smiled when I opened the door. "Charlotte!" Nick said. "We don't mean to bother you, but—well, we saw you folks took down your oleanders!" Helen, nodding, said, "We went to the movies, and when we came home—"

She looked in the direction of the missing hedge and opened her mouth wide to demonstrate their initial surprise.

"A mistake," I said as I joined them on the steps.

"A mistake? Well!" Nick laughed. "I guess they'll grow back eventually. Not in my lifetime, but eventually."

Helen gave his arm a light slap. "Don't talk like that, Dad," she said; then she smiled at me. "I guess it'll be easier for us to wave to each other while we do dishes, now, Charlotte."

I coughed up a laugh. "Would you like to come in?" I asked. "I could make coffee." I meant it—why not? I didn't want to be alone with my thoughts!—but they said, no, no, they needed to get supper going. They'd been curious about the hedge, that was all.

"But, oh," Helen said, "I almost forgot: I wanted to tell you we've seen that cat, the one you worried the coyotes had eaten."

I nodded. "I did, too. Bad Cat. It wasn't doing very well, though."

Nick shook his head. "It's a scrapper. Always has an ear chewed up or something."

"Well, anyway, I set out food for it," Helen said.

I laughed. "So did I, Helen. Maybe we'll put some meat on its bones."

Meat on its bones. I sounded like my parents.

The year before, Helen had needed to use a walker for a while. Now, when she and Nick started off across my uneven desert yard, the way that they gripped each other—*hard*—it looked as if they worked at steadying both themselves and each other. I'd seen the pair as gorgeous twentysomethings in a wedding photo on top of their piano (photos like that, whenever I see them in the homes of old people, I get a melancholy sense that everyone must be attractive when they're young, but somehow we're incapable of realizing it at the time). The Schaeffers had raised four children, three of whom I'd come to know well enough over the last eleven years that I'd walk over and say hello if they came to town. "Mom," Nick called Helen, and Helen called Nick "Dad," which didn't sound very romantic. Will and I had heard them raise their voices over there on occasion. Still, they always impressed us as being in love. We liked it that we had a pair of old lovebirds for neighbors, and we'd told them so, and each had given the other a proud smile.

Without incident, now they disappeared from my view, into their own yard, and I returned to the house. I walked to the dining room, and looked out the sliding glass door. The backyard appeared pretty grim minus the oleander hedge, but Nick and Helen's visit had drained some of my anger at Will.

Didn't I want the two of us to be together until the end of time? Yes, I did.

In case Bad Cat should come by again, I carried the can opener and a can of tuna and one of the blue-glass Mexican plates to the ramada and set up a little dinner out there.

When I went back inside, I noticed that Will had left his gym bag on the dining room floor, and I picked it up and carried it to the alcove off the kitchen where we did our laundry. Normally, Will emptied his gym clothes into the washer as soon as he arrived home, so I added the clothes and his towel to a few things already in the washer and started a load. His running shoes I carried to our bedroom. So big and heavy—what was it like to move around with those slabs of leather and cloth and rubber on your feet? Usually, the big shoes impressed me, but just now they made me sad, and when I switched on the light in the closet and stepped inside to put them away, I saw how, over time, the heavy fabric that made up the tops of the shoes had developed particular folds in response to Will's feet, and the leather parts had become crosshatched with both fine and deep wrinkles from his wearing the shoes longer than he should have.

I hugged the shoes awkwardly to my aching chest. I felt almost as if Will were dead and the shoes were relics. Jacqueline probably had been right in thinking that it was for the best that he knew the truth. Still, a hole had been blasted in the dam that held the sweet mill-pond of our life in place. I hated to lose the old sweetness, even if it meant that the river now could run on, the way it should.

A *whisk* sounded in the dining room: the sliding door gliding along its track.

I set down the shoes, but I waited until I heard Will call my name before I left the closet and went out into the hall.

He had on a baseball cap, and it threw a shadow on his face; even so, I could see something skittish in his expression when he looked at me, and so I did not step all the way through the doorway and into the dining room.

He groaned and he pulled a chair out from the table and sat. He folded his arms on top of the table and then he cradled his head on his arms. Something dandled from his baseball cap, moving delicately up and down with the motion of his breaths. Normally, I would have gone to him and plucked off the thing. I would have shown it to him and we would have laughed.

What was it?

Oh. A twig from the oleanders, somehow caught in the band at the back of the cap while he worked.

Without lifting his head from his arms, he said, "I drove up there. To the Fletchers'. He didn't know what I was talking about, or else he was drunk, but I told her . . . what you told me. And to leave you alone."

"You shouldn't have done that!" I cried. "I was taking care of things! I already recused myself from the judging! I'm an *adult*, Will!"

"It didn't have anything to do with you being an adult, Charlotte. I wanted them to know you'd already told me and that I was still loyal to you. Not that I know what that means for us anymore. Everything"—his voice caught—"seems different now."

"Oh, Will." I crossed the room to him. I wanted so much to put my hands on his shoulders, rub his neck. "How can learning about something I did twenty years ago change everything we've had in the twenty years since?"

"I don't know." A hard out-breath dimpled the blue cloth of his shirtsleeve. "It seems that way."

He sounded sleepy—like a sleepy, crabby little boy.

He doesn't really want to be right, though, I thought. *He doesn't really want to leave me.*

I dragged another of the dining room chairs over beside his chair and took a seat carefully. I laid my arm across his back. He didn't pull away. After a bit, dusk started to come on. Because the oleanders were gone, the house stayed filled with light much longer than usual that day. Even so, the two of us went on sitting there, like that, until after dark.

Acknowledgments

Over the years, the support of the esteemed editor Nancy Miller has meant a great deal to me. I thank Nancy and others at Bloomsbury (Lea Beresford, Laura Phillips, Gleni Bartels, and Susan Brown) who shepherded the book along to publication.

Lisa Bankoff of ICM continues to be my trusted agent, and I am indebted to her.

I am grateful to the editors Beth Alvarado and Pamela Uschuk of *Cutthroat, A Journal of the Arts,* for their publication of "As Good As Dead," the short story that proved the spark for the novel.

Thanks to my daughter, Nora Evans-Reitz, who, with her usual thoroughness and care—even as she traveled on trains and buses—helped me ready the manuscript for submission.

A Note on the Author

Elizabeth Evans's five previous books are *Locomotion*, *The Blue Hour*, *Suicide's Girlfriend*, *Rowing in Eden*, and *Carter Clay*. She received the Iowa Author Award in 2010. Among her other awards are a National Endowment for the Arts Fellowship, a James Michener Fellowship, a Lila Wallace Foundation Award, and the Four Corners Award. She lives in Tucson, Arizona.